BLOODY SKIRMISH

Half a dozen troopers went forward as ordered. The bullets whizzing around their heads increased as they closed in on the site of the rifle pits. Up ahead, at least double their number of Mexicans appeared out of the battle smoke heading for the same destination.

The battle-seasoned dragoons advanced another ten yards before their commander gave the order. "Halt! Kneel! Aim! . . . Fire!"

A bellow of smoke roared out from the volley.

On their feet in seconds, they charged. The dead bodies of Mexican soldiers littered the dry earth on their way to rifle pits.

Sporadic firing and two more organized volleys blasted out toward the attackers.

Then all was silent as the thick smoke settled on the bloody battlefield.

PATRICK E. ANDREWS

THE SCALPHUNTERS

ZEBRA BOOKS
KENSINGTON PUBLISHING CORP.

This Book is Dedicated to:
Harold and Mary Moore

ZEBRA BOOKS

are published by

Kensington Publishing Corp.
475 Park Avenue South
New York, NY 10016

First Printing: March, 1993

Printed in the United States of America

Prologue

Roberto Weismann could barely see in the predawn gloom and mist that blanketed the small mountain canyon. Now and then a movement in the shadows caught his attention and he silently cursed the man in the gang who had been so careless. Their business was dangerous and deadly on that chilly morning. Any slackness or lack of attention could lead to a bloody disaster.

A slight noise in the surrounding chaparral now caught his attention, but it caused him no alarm. He knew who it was.

Penrod Donaldson joined Weismann at the edge of the thorny plants. "Everybody is ready," he announced.

Weismann, the leader of the men gathered in the darkness, made no response. He was a large man, a bit over six feet of husky muscularity. Weismann sported several scars across his forehead and one down his left cheek. Swarthy, with dark brown hair and green eyes, the man was of undeterminable race or national origin. He exemplified the mixed human population of that part of northern Mexico. He looked down at the sleeping Apache camp less than twenty yards away.

Donaldson followed his leader's gaze. "We done a good job getting this close," Donaldson said.

"These Indians have no dogs to bark," Weismann pointed out. "They must have ate them because of poor hunting."

"Just the same, they ain't expecting nothing," he said. Then he added, "Easy pickings."

"Seguro," Weismann agreed in Spanish.

As soon as it was light enough, Weismann and Donaldson planned on leading their band of men on a murderous raid into the Apache camp. Not only did they intend to kill every inhabitant of the primitive bivouac, but also to scalp them and take the trophies of hair away.

What was to be done in that lonely Sonoran canyon was perfectly legal under the Mexican law called "Proyecto de Guerra." Tired of Indian raids, the government in Mexico City enacted a statute that authorized a bounty on scalps taken from Apaches. The payment, in silver pesos, was one hundred for each man's scalp and fifty for that of a woman. Even the children were not spared the lawmakers' attention. Their hair was worth twenty-five pesos. Weismann and his men were properly contracted under General Antonio De La Nobleza, the military commander of Northern Sonora, to operate as scalphunters. Cruelly efficient, both Weismann and the general were becoming wealthy under the murderous system.

Donaldson, the group's second-in-command, took a look at the eastern rim of the mountains. "Dawn's coming up," he whispered.

"Still too dark," Weismann said. "Espera."

"Why?" Donaldson asked. "Porque?"

"It is not quite light enough," Weismann said. "You must stop mixing English with the Spanish language, eh?"

"What's wrong with that?" Donaldson asked. "There's American fellers in our group here. That way they can pick up on what's being said too."

"But there are also Mexicans," Weismann said. "They don't like to hear their language butchered, pendejo."

"I don't like being called dumb in any language," Donaldson said. "It ain't polite."

Weismann turned his eyes on the man, saying nothing.

Even in the half-light, Donaldson could read the unspoken threat in the stare. He grinned to show he wasn't really angry, then turned his attention back to the camp.

A quarter of an hour more slipped by before Weismann pulled his pistol from its holster. He took aim at the nearest wickiup and pulled the trigger of the weapon. The resulting report echoed down the canyon, and was immediately followed by more shots and shouts as the band of scalphunters charged into the unsuspecting camp.

The Apaches made a slow, confused response. Those who first stumbled out of their lodges were also the first to go down in the hail of bullets splattering across the encampment. The Indians following them from the shelters into the open lurched across the bloody corpses. Within an instant they had also been shot down. A trio of warriors, better prepared than the others for trouble, appeared with weapons ready. Their brave but futile attempt at a counterattack resulted in their own quick deaths. In spite of the Apaches' brief ferocity, they had not managed to inflict even one casualty on the attackers.

Weismann took a deep breath. "Stop the firing!"

The sound of gunfire immediately died off. His men knew the chief of the scalphunters expected instant obedience and would tolerate no exceptions.

"Don't waste ammunition," Weismann commanded. "We are not here to practice target shooting. There are silver pesos waiting for us, so don't waste any more time."

Donaldson pulled his scalping knife from his belt. "Let's get to work, boys. Each head o' hair here means silver pesos for us!"

Whooping, the men rushed to the cadavers and began the grisly job of slicing around the top of the head, then grabbing the hair and pulling hard until the scalp popped from the skull. Donaldson, in his exalted position as chief lieutenant to Weismann, had the prestigious job of dispatching any wounded that were found. If a badly injured Indian struggled during the painful process of being mutilated, Donaldson did a skillful job of slitting the throat, making sure the jugular vein was sliced. The high-pitched screaming of a badly shot-up woman quickly ended with a deep cut from Donaldson's blade.

After the bloody, hairy trophies were stuffed into leather bags brought for the purpose, Weismann gave another order.

"Fuego!" he yelled.

"Fire!" Donaldson echoed for the benefit of the non-Spanish speaking Americans.

The scalphunters rushed around setting fire to the wickiups, making sure each and every one had been set ablaze. Then, with weapons ready, they stood back and waited.

Sure enough, a young woman, her dress smoldering, suddenly burst forth from the flames, screaming. She danced like a puppet on a string as numerous bullets slammed into her torso, the impacts battering her in several directions at once.

The next, and final victim, was an old man. But this one, knowing what they wanted, was bravely defiant. After letting his hair catch on fire and burn to the scalp, he walked slowly and with dignity out into the open. He laughed in spite of his agony, knowing he had cheated them out of one hundred pesos.

Donaldson emitted a low whistle. "You gotta admire a tough ol' geezer like that."

"I will show you the respect I have for him," Weismann said. The scalphunter chief himself took care of the ancient Apache. He grabbed him and threw him back in the fire. The old man emerged again, badly burned and shouting in defiance. He had to be thrown back twice before he finally failed to reappear from the blaze.

"Ornery old bastard, wasn't he?" Donaldson remarked.

"Apaches are as tenacious in their deaths as they are in their fighting," Weismann said. "How many scalps?"

"I tallied her up," Donaldson said. He had increased his childhood education of ciphering through working at a trading post in the Rocky Mountains. "We got eighteen men, twenty-six women, and thirty-seven young'uns." He knelt down and scribbled some figures in the dirt. "Yeah! That comes to four thousand and twenty-five pesos." He stood up. "Too bad that son of a bitch De La Nobleza gets half."

"Without him, we would earn nothing," Weismann pointed out. "Now you tell me how much for us." His knowledge of mathematics was almost nonexistent.

Donaldson went back to his mathematics in the dirt. "Well now, that gets you a thousand and six pesos with twenty-five-centavos. I'm coming out with five hundred and three with a few centavos."

"Tell me what the men get," Weismann said.

"Well, there's a dozen of 'em," Donaldson said figuring some more. "And that comes to — let's see — a little over forty pesos each." He stood up again. "It ain't much compared to us, but when you can buy a pretty decent hunk o' property around here for a thousand silver pesos, they can make something of theirselves if they save up their money."

Weismann flashed a rare grin and pointed to the men who were already swigging hard liquor from bottles they carried in their saddlebags. "Do you think they will save their earnings?"

Donaldson laughed. "Well, maybe the whores they visit will build up a nice grubstake."

"We'll have nothing until we turn in these scalps," Weismann said. "Vamanos! Let's go!"

Donaldson turned to the men. "Knock off the drinking, you stupid bastards. As soon as you're paid off, you can get some decent liquor. Let's mount up and ride the hell outta here!"

There was still a lot of work to do.

Chapter One

A hawk, using instinctive skills bred for eons into its species, soared on the thermals lifted off the desert floor of Arizona's Vano Basin. This flat, arid, sun-beaten land bordering Mexico, spread out for thousands of square miles before easing into the foothills of the Culebra Mountains whose higher altitudes boasted a cooler more agreeable climate that included plenty of water and a deep, thick carpet of forest.

The bird of prey's keen vision scoured the terrain a thousand feet below in an eager search for food. After a half hour of air-sailing, a slight wiggle in the sand far below caught the sky hunter's alert eye. Folding in his wings and nosing over, the hawk began a rapid, steep dive toward the target. At exactly the right moment, he extended wings and tail feathers to brake the controlled fall. Sharp talons grasped the rattlesnake behind the head and in the middle of its thick body, then a powerful flapping of wings carried both the hunter and victim back into the empty heights of desert air.

The serpent, deaf and dull-witted, darted its tongue about in a futile effort to figure out just what the hell was happening to it. When the bird released the reptile to fall to the rocks below, the prey still was unaware of its predicament. Then it smashed to earth, the shock and pain caused it to roll and slither in alarm and pain.

The hawk struck again, taking the rattlesnake back up into the sun-bleached sky to drop it again. After the fourth time, the bird was satisfied that the poisonous reptile would do no harm to the fledglings in a nest not far away in the cooler region of the mountains. The rattlesnake, close to death and unaware of even its own existence anymore, was carried away to nourish the feathered family.

"In the day, in the night, to all, to each,
Sooner or later, delicate death."

The old man quoting poet Walt Whitman was the only spectator to this natural killing. He was a wiry, hairy codger dressed in a strange combination of a battered Mexican sombrero of straw, calico shirt, leather vest, and buckskin trousers stuffed into Apache moccasins. He squatted in the shade of a barrel cactus with his horse. He was also well-armed with a pair of pistols and a rifled musket.

The ancient's name was Eruditus Fletcher. He was a lifelong inhabitant of the Vano Basin and surrounding territory except for the years of his adolescence when he had been back east to obtain some very advanced education that included a couple of years at Yale University. This accounted for his very cultured New England accent.

Eruditus could boast fluency in English, Spanish, Greek, Latin, French, and at least a half dozen Indian dialects. The old fellow's rustic and near primitive appearance belied his deep intellect and classical education.

He chuckled. "Of course being dropped from on high to crash onto the rocks below cannot exactly be described as a delicate death, what?" he inquired of his horse.

The animal, fondly called Plutarch, always enjoyed the sound of the old man's voice. He snorted affectionately and stomped one hoof.

Eruditus glanced eastward out into the vastness of the desert. A small plume of dust that he noted earlier had grown considerably in the previous two hours. Now he estimated the riders coming toward him were a bit less than five miles away. He turned his attention to the book he had been reading before noting the hawk's strike on the snake. It was entitled *Memoires d'Outretombe* by the French author, the Vicomte de Chateaubriand. Eruditus, of course, was reading it in the original French.

Three-quarters of an hour passed before Eruditus once more stirred. This time he stood up and placed the book into his saddlebags. Then he took Plutarch's reins, leading him out into the sun before swinging up into the saddle.

"Now, good steed, yon approaches a stalwart legion of the American Republic to establish Pax Americanus in this desolate region. So we must turn to our duty and sally forth to greet our new friends," he said. A quick nudge in the flanks was all that was needed to get the horse to move toward the men approaching the questionable comfort of the cactus' shade.

The arrivals numbered two dozen. Eruditus knew they were military men. But a casual observer, gazing at them from afar would not have known they were soldiers. Only a close observation could determine they wore various parts of uniforms with civilian attire while boasting of military accoutrements such as canteens, haversacks, and sabers. Their firearms were the same for every man, consisting of the U.S. Model 1841 percussion rifle and a brace of single-shot Model 1836 flintlock pistols. The one exception was the man who headed the column. He sported a pair of brand new Colt Hartford Dragoon revolvers, prominent in their holsters on each side of his waist. It was to this man that Eruditus rode up and introduced himself.

"Sir, your humble servant Eruditus Fletcher," he said extending his hand. "I believe you are expecting me, are you not?"

"Indeed I am, and how do you do, Mister Fletcher," the man said. "I am Captain Grant Drummond, commander of this dragoon detachment." He was obviously in his late twenties or early thirties. Tall, and slim, he sported a sandy-colored, well-trimmed moustache, and hair of medium length.

"Then you are the tribune of this legion, are you, sir?" Eruditus remarked with a smile.

"It is a very small legion, I am afraid," Drummond replied in good humor. "But with a plethora of duties and responsibilities. That is how we rated a contract scout like yourself to be assigned to us by the departmental command in Santa Fe."

"Useful employment is a Godsend, Captain Drummond," Eruditus said. Then he added in Latin, "Aliquid utilatatis pro communi laborans."

"Working at something useful for all in common," Drummond translated.

"Ah!" Eruditus said. "A Latin scholar."

"I was unwillingly immersed in it during my schooldays prior to attending West Point," Drummond said. "By the way, is that not part of a quote by Thomas a Kempis?"

"It is, sir!" Eruditus exclaimed. "Am I to have intellectual companionship out on this desert?"

The captain chuckled. "I wouldn't promise you that, Mister Fletcher." He stood in his stirrups and surveyed their surroundings. "So we are in the Vano Basin now, are we?"

"Indeed," Eruditus assured him.

"This seems a most barren and unfriendly place, sir," Drummond remarked sitting back down on the leather. "After long service in the outback of Texas and Mexico, I consider myself an authority on inhospitable places."

"This is a beautiful Eden, if you learn to survive here," Eruditus said. "But it can be terribly cruel as well." He took a quick glance at the men in the column, pleased with what he saw. "Your command seems well-suited for hard outdoor life, Captain."

"Indeed," Grant Drummond agreed. "We have just finished a two-year war in Mexico. These men are professional soldiers and veterans."

"I see they are not martinets who love to prance about in fancy uniforms," Eruditus remarked.

"Like any veteran of the frontier, each man knows enough to be practical in his choice of dress," Drummond said. "That lesson also applied to the late conflict in which we served."

The war between the United States and Mexico had come to an end a few scant months before. America was the victor and had acquired vast new territories, among them New Mexico, Arizona, and California. The need for regular contact between the rest of the nation and the Pacific Coast made the establishment of communication lines across that particular area of the Vano Basin of utmost importance. Another consideration was the protection of the many travelers headed for the newly discovered gold fields of California. It had become the job of the United States Army—and the dragoons in particular—to provide that lifesaving service. One of the first units assigned to the job was that very detachment under the command of Captain Grant Drummond. He had the responsibility of the Vano Basin along the Mexican border. Eruditus Fletcher had been contracted by headquarters in Santa Fe, New Mexico Territory to serve the detachment as its scout, guide, and interpreter in whatever demands their duties put upon them.

"Have you found a camp for us, Mister Fletcher?" Captain Drummond inquired.

"Indeed, sir," Eruditus assured him. "Roughly ten miles from here there is a spot at the base of the Culebra Mountains that offers shade, water, and natural fortification."

"I suggest we proceed there at once," Drummond said. "We're weary and are in dire need of settling down to recover. Our horses, too, require rest."

"I am at your service, sir," Eruditus said. "We shall ride in a northwesterly direction."

The column resumed its journey with Eruditus easing them into the correct path across the trackless waste of the Vano Basin. In a bit more than two hours they reached the

15

rocky outcrops of the Culebra Mountain's foothills. The old man took the dragoons through a barely discernible trail across a stone-strewn slope, that finally eased down to a spot where a wall of solid rock rose from the earth. A small column of water cascaded down from the heights above, ending its plunge in a vapory collision with a small pool.

Eruditus gestured at the scene before them. "This, Captain Drummond, is the spot I've chosen for our praesidium, as Julius Caesar might say."

Drummond smiled. "I would think that Caesar would be more inclined to describe this place as a castra—a camp—rather than a garrison, Mister Fletcher."

Eruditus chuckled. "I believe you are correct, Captain."

Drummond gave the area a quick look-around. "I would like to be able to truthfully utter Caesar's words of Veni, vidi, vici—I came, I saw, I conquered. However, at this moment I have no feelings as a conqueror."

"Perhaps you feel as I do at times in this wild and wonderful territory," Eruditus said. "Frequently I perceive myself and other humans as interlopers."

"Those may be the sensations I am experiencing," Drummond admitted.

"At any rate, sir, this is your command," Eruditus pointed out.

"And it has everything we need," Drummond said. "You described it well."

"The water there is cold and sweet," Eruditus said. "It arrives to us from the Culebra Mountains that tower above our new home."

"We'll investigate the quality of that pool as quickly as possible," Drummond said. He turned toward his men and barked, "Sergeant Clooney!"

Sergeant William Clooney rode forward and reported with a salute. "Yes, sir?"

Drummond motioned to Eruditus. "This is our contract scout Mister Eruditus Fletcher. Mister Fletcher, this is Ser-

16

geant William Clooney. If I am the tribune of this legion, then the sergeant is the centurion."

"A pleasure, Sergeant," Eruditus said as the two shook hands.

"Take charge of the detachment and set up camp, Sergeant," Drummond said. "We have arrived."

"Yes, sir," Clooney said. "Where'd you like your tent, Cap'n?"

"Right in the center, Sergeant," Drummond said. "And have the men pitch their own between mine and the water. We'll use the open space up here as our parade ground."

Clooney, an old soldier with fifteen years in the ranks, gave the place a quick, professional inspection. "I think we ought to put up rifle pits and rocks along here, sir. It'd make a dandy defensive line."

"Now I do feel the interloper," Eruditus said.

"So do I, but my centurion is absolutely correct," Drummond said. "Carry on, Sergeant."

"Yes, sir!" Clooney turned to Eruditus. "You'll be bunking with me in our own tent, Mister Fletcher."

"I prefer to sleep out under the stars," Eruditus said.

"Suit yourself," the sergeant said. He went off to tend to his duties.

Drummond and Eruditus dismounted and walked over to the shade cast by the mountain wall. "The drainage here seems adequate," the major remarked.

"I guarantee it is, sir," Eruditus said. "Even in the event of the rare cloudburst, this camp will not have standing water."

"That does not happen often then?" Drummond asked.

"You can thank God for that," Eruditus said seriously. "This terrain cannot soak up water. Instead it remains on top and rushes about in torrential flash flooding that is deadly to man and beast alike."

A soldier quickly appeared with a couple of camp chairs, then scurried back to join the other work details. Drummond sat down on one, while Eruditus, ignoring the other, plopped his skinny buttocks down on the ground.

Drummond lit a pipe and gave the scout a long gaze of unabashed curiosity. He spoke frankly, saying, "So! Just who the hell are you, Mister Fletcher?"

Eruditus grinned as he lit up his own smoke in the form of a Mexican cigar. "I am not surprised by your curiosity, Captain Drummond. My appearance and my conduct are of two different worlds."

"Obviously," Drummond said. "Please enlighten me, Mister Fletcher, if I am not becoming too personal."

"I entered this unhappy world not far from this spot in the year of 1793," Eruditus said. "My father was an English sea captain who was shipwrecked off the coast of east Mexico. He was fortunate enough to be able to lead his intrepid crew ashore to safety. This was near the city of Tampico where a small enclave of English people were established."

Drummond puffed on his pipe. "Please tell me what would attract Englishmen to that dreary spot."

"Commerce, Captain," Eruditus said. "They had set up a trading post, complete with tea in the afternoon, of course, to deal with goods from the interior of Mexico. My father saw some monetary advantage to becoming a part of the establishment, and so took advantage of an invitation to join in their efforts."

Drummond closely studied Eruditus' face. "Now don't tell me he married a local lady, Mister Fletcher. You haven't the slightest cast of Mexico in your features."

Eruditus chuckled. "He wed an English lady — widow, as a matter of fact — who would become my mother. Her husband had died a year earlier and she hadn't the opportunity to return to Mother England by the time my father made his own unplanned and thoroughly wet arrival upon the scene."

"I presume your parents ended up this far west if you were born here," Drummond said.

"Of course," Eruditus said. "Sailor men are natural wan-

18

derers and filled with curiosity about the next port of call, or what is on the other side of the mountain if they are ashore. My father wanted to see Mexico. He brought my mother along on his wanderings and ended up in the cattle business in Sonora south of here. That is where I was born and raised, including much time here on the Vano Basin and in the Culebra Mountains."

Drummond nodded knowingly. "I assume he sent you East for an education as a boy."

"That he did, sir," Eruditus said. "I would have received my degree and gone on for a doctorate of philosophy and letters, but bad luck in the guise of bandits took away my parents, their property, and my schooling. Thus, because of other men's evil, I was forced to return here."

"Too bad," Drummond said.

"Au contraire!" Eruditus exclaimed. "This is the scene of my boyhood. Any misgivings I felt were swept away in the grandeur and beauty of this, mine own land."

"Then you know every nook and cranny of the Vano Basin and these mountains, Mister Fletcher?" Drummond asked.

"I do, Captain," Eruditus assured him. "And the people who live here as well."

"Are they agreeable and friendly?" Drummond asked.

"Alas!" Eruditus exclaimed. "They are human beings."

"You are telling me we will face savagery and murder in this quiet, barren land?" Drummond asked.

As an answer, Eruditus did what he liked to do best — quote poetry. This time he chose words from the English poet William Blake:

"Cruelty has a human heart,
And jealousy a human face;
Terror the human form divine,
And secrecy the human dress."

Drummond knocked the tobacco from his pipe. "You make

the duty of pacifying this country sound like an impossible task, Mister Fletcher."

"I'm not saying it is impossible, sir," Eruditus assured him. "But in order to make peace, often men must die. Both good and bad."

Drummond glanced around. "Yes," he said once again feeling a soldier's excitement at being in a new, unknown area that offered excitement. "This is going to be one hell of a job."

Chapter Two

The two spying Apache warriors, hidden from the view of those they observed, did not have to worry about making noise. Any sounds that resulted from them moving around or rustling vegetation were covered by the waters of the small stream rushing past their position. From their viewing spot the water arched out into empty air to fall a hundred feet down to the pool below where the white men they spied upon were situated. The Indians called the small body of water the Pool-Beneath-the-Cliff.

The name of the Indian leaning the farthest out over the edge was Quintero. He was short, very muscular, and so dark his skin color could be described as mahogany. Quintero was very much admired in his age group of males within his clan. Smart, aggressive, and fearless, he had evolved into a natural leader since his entrance into warriorhood. As was his habit, Quintero carried a flintlock rifle he had taken from a Mexican vaquero killed in a cattle-stealing raid less than a year previously.

Looking down from his concealed observation post, the Apache fighter did not like what he saw. Quintero spat at those he considered interlopers into his people's land.

His best friend, a warrior called Chaparro, glanced across the stream, and studied the scowl on his companion's face.

He was pleased at the hatred he could see. Quintero's anger always meant excitement. Chaparro glanced down, but his eyesight at distances was poor, and he was unable to make out much of what went on below. He turned back from the view and walked to the spot where their horses were tied to some scrub pine trees. Chaparro squatted down on his haunches to wait for Quintero to finish watching the men below.

The sun moved an eighth of a way across the sky before Quintero pulled back from the edge and joined Chaparro. He was so furious he could not speak. He stood there slapping the stock of his rifle with loud smacks of his hand as he considered what he had seen.

"Are they Mexicanos, Quintero?" Chaparro asked.

"They are White-Eyes," Quintero said. "One of them is the old man Erudito." That Spanish word was the closest the Apaches could come to pronouncing Eruditus' name.

"The friend of old Aguila?" Chaparro mused. "What is he doing? Bringing White-Eyes into El Vano to live with him?" The Apaches called the Vano Basin "El Vano" the same as the Mexicans.

"I do not know," Quintero said. "I have always fought to keep the Mexicanos out of El Vano." It was typical of the young man to refer to himself alone and no others when speaking of past events. "Now it looks like I must fight White-Eyes as well."

"Maybe they are not going to stay long," Chaparro suggested. "I cannot see well at that distance, but it seems the wickiups they erect are of cloth, not of adobe or wood."

"It makes no difference. White-Eyes and Mexicanos are the same," Quintero told him. "They like to call land their own and live on it without ever going away. It does not matter what sort of lodges they put up. They will build stronger ones later."

"Perhaps these new people have cattle with them," Chaparro remarked hopefully. "We can use the meat."

"They are not building a rancho down there," Quintero

22

said. "Those men are soldiers. White-Eye soldiers are like Mexicano soldiers. They are paid to fight. We will have to make war against them."

"But if Erudito brought them in, then Aguila will not want us to fight them," Chaparro pointed out. "He will speak against making war at the council."

"Aguila is an old man like Erudito!" Quintero spat. "Instead of meddling in matters concerning younger people, those two should be sitting somewhere getting drunk together on mescal or tequila and stay out of the way."

"True," Chaparro agreed. "It would be a natural thing for them to do. They are good friends, no?"

"Did you not know they were boys together in days even before our own fathers were born?" Quintero said.

"That makes a strong friendship," Chaparro said. "We spent our boyhood as friends. Now we are grown warriors and are like brothers."

"Our friendship is strong," Quintero said. "But I tell you this, Chaparro. If you ever brought in White-Eyes or Mexicanos into El Vano, I would kill you even if I do love you as a brother."

"Then I will not do that," Chaparro said seriously. "You are a stronger warrior than I."

"I am also a stronger warrior than Aguila," Quintero said.

"You would fight him?" Chaparro chided him. "He is not young and does not go to hunt or fight, yet he is listened to on the council."

"The day is coming when they will listen to me!" Quintero said. "Come! Let us return to the village and talk to our friends."

Chaparro, knowing that it wouldn't be long before Quintero stirred up some excitement and bloodletting, happily swung up on the back of his horse.

The two warriors were members of a mountain and desert Apache tribe called the Chirinatos. Fierce warriors and relentless hunters, that particular clan was both respected and

23

feared by other Indians and Mexicans in the area. Although they principally inhabited the Culebra Mountains, the tribe's beginnings were on the great desert of the Vano Basin that stretched out from that forested, craggy range. Because of those early days, they sometimes felt drawn back to the hard-packed sandy terrain of the arid, harsh land their ancestors had roamed. To them, the area held many sacred and deeply spiritual qualities. Because of this, bands of Chirinatos would spend months wandering and living in one of the most merciless lands on earth.

Although prone to break up into small groups, this Indian clan could gather together in a very short time in cases of emergencies. Most of the time the men hunted, fought other Indians, and stole what they could from Mexicans during forays south. The women were homebound with their own duties and pastimes. They gathered food such as cactus fruit and yucca stems on the desert, or nuts and berries when up in the high country. Although the Chirinato females planted small crops of corn and squash from time to time, wandering from mountain to desert and back again did not give much opportunity for any serious agricultural undertaking.

The band to which Quintero and Chaparro belonged were presently residing in a camp in the Culebra Mountains. The pair urged their mounts upward into the higher reaches of the range. In only a half hour of travel, the weather cooled and the vegetation went from scrawny chaparral to stubby trees. In another thirty minutes, the trees had thickened until the Apaches' horses threaded through a veritable forest of pine and evergreen.

They found the village's wickiups strung along a shallow mountain valley with a stream running through it. It was that same ribbon of water that ran down through the mountains to pour off the cliff into the pool on the desert floor. They went directly to a far corner of the area where four of the lodges were pitched close together. Quintero and Chaparro liked to stay near their other two friends, who were a couple of war-

24

riors as fond of fighting as they. Their names were Bistozo and Zalea.

Bistozo, noting his comrades' arrival, looked up from his chore of cleaning the bore of his musket with a brass ramrod. He raised his hand in greeting, then noted Quintero's furious expression. Quickly getting to his feet, he approached them. "What has happened?"

Chaparro answered. "We have seen White-Eyes at the Pool-Beneath-the-Cliff. They were with Erudito."

Bistozo was interested. "What were they doing?"

"The White-Eyes had set up cloth wickiups," Chaparro answered.

"Are you sure they were not Mexicanos?" Bistozo inquired.

Quintero finally spoke. "I saw yellow hair among them and very light skin. These are men of Erudito's race. Of this there is no doubt."

Bistozo was curious. He knew that Quintero could not tolerate outsiders in El Vano. "What do you want to do, Quintero?"

Chaparro laughed. "He wants to kill them."

Bistozo now grinned. "Then let us go do this thing."

Chaparro shook his head. "No! The council has already warned us about making war after we killed the White-Eye family last year."

Bistozo nodded. "Aguila said—"

"I don't care what that old grizzly bear says!" Quintero interrupted. "I will pay him no mind."

"But he speaks wisely," Bistozo argued. "He said the White-Eyes were lost and confused, so nobody knew they were here. If they did, then the family would have been missed. In that case the soldiers would have come to punish us. He said our people were lucky for all that."

"If you think Aguila gives wise counsel, why don't you stay by him?" Quintero asked.

Bistozo grinned. "What fun is that?"

The group's fourth member, a bandy-legged fellow named

Zalea, who had been out doing some informal hunting, came walking into camp from the slopes above. When he spotted his friends, he hurried over to join them. Chaparro wasted no time in appraising him of what he and Quintero had seen at the desert pool.

"How many are there?" Zalea asked. "Can we kill them?"

"We can kill them if we are brave and cunning," Quintero assured him.

"But we must inform the council of what we saw," Chaparro said. "That is what the customs demand."

"I grow weary of the customs," Quintero said. "They tie a warrior down tighter than rawhide ropes drying in the sun." But he knew they had to follow tradition and law. "We will speak at the council tonight."

"Are you going to call for a fight?" Zalea asked.

"I will see what I will do," Quintero said. He had too much respect for the Chirinato council to boast of wanting to defy its authority and advice. "But I will speak my mind."

Bistozo's woman joined them with clay mugs and a jar filled with tiswin, a corn beer of which the Chirinatos were particularly fond. After serving the warriors, she properly made her exit without having said a word.

"Tiswin is good after being busy all day," Quintero said.

"Yes," Chaparro agreed. "But for real drinking, I prefer mescal."

"Or tequila!" Zalea added with a laugh. "I have two bottles. Shall we drink them?"

"No!" Quintero exclaimed angrily. "You know my feelings about this! I will not go to the council or war with anybody who is drunk."

The other three, although thinking how much fun it would be to get drunk and maybe quarrel and scuffle, showed their desire to stick close to Quintero by not defying him. He was their leader through long years of evolvement that had begun in their boyhood.

"We will stay sober, don't worry," Chaparro said.

26

Quintero glanced at the sun above them, then swung his gaze to the large wickiup at the center of the camp. "We will have time to eat a little. Then we go to the council and I will talk to them about the White-Eyes at the Pool-Beneath-the-Cliff."

The entire encampment moved into its late afternoon and early evening routine. Any hunters who had gone out looking for game returned with fresh kills. At that time of year in the Culebras, only a blind-and-deaf man could not find game. Smoke from cooking fires drifted across the small valley and all activity eased down to soft talking as the women tended their cooking chores while hungry men and children waited for the meals to be served.

Later, with full bellies and the first evening fires being lit, the people who desired to hear the council and chat with their friends, moved toward the meeting area in front of their chief's wickiup. The leader of that particular band of Chirinatos was a husky, prematurely gray warrior called Lobo Cano. Craggy-faced and with heavy lids, he seemed like a wolf lying in wait to all who observed him.

Lobo Cano was already seated cross-legged, waiting for the others to make their appearances. The first to arrive was a slim old man who greeted him silently with an upraised hand. This was Aguila, an old warrior who was a close and valued friend of the white man Eruditus Fletcher.

Two other men, all veteran fighters and hunters, showed up and took their places, forming a semi-circle with Lobo Cano and Aguila occupying the center. Interested onlookers murmured among themselves. Then Aguila's brother Nitcho, the tribal medicine man, following Chirinato custom, shook the sacred rattles and called on Spirit-Woman-of-the-Desert and Coyote-Ghost-of-the-Mountain to bless them with wisdom and visions.

At that point, before the chief could bestow proper greetings to the rest of the council, Quintero pushed his way through the crowd and presented himself in front of the

27

group. He stood scowling, arms crossed, as his three friends joined him.

Lobo Cano made no remarks regarding this discourtesy. He waited to see where the breach of etiquette might lead.

Aguila smiled wryly and said, "Buenos noches."

"Speak to me in the White-Eyes' language, old one," Quintero said.

"Then I say to you, good evening," Aguila said. "Why do you wish a greeting in that tongue, Quintero?"

"Because your friend Erudito is at the Pool-Beneath-the-Cliff with many White-Eyes," Quintero announced.

Excited talk broke out among the people at the news. Lobo Cano spoke sharply, "How do you know of this?"

"Earlier today, Chaparro and I hunted on the southern rim and spotted them." He glared at Aguila. "These were not men with women and children. They were soldiers."

Lobo Cano looked at Aguila. "What do you know of this, elder friend?"

"Nothing," Aguila said. "I have not spoken with Erudito since the season of the moon of the cold winds."

Quintero was not a man to waste time. He shouted, "This is bad for our people! We must kill them!"

A shout of approval rose from the young men in the crowd.

Lobo Cano sprang to his feet. "Wait!" He realized the possible serious consequences if the young warriors roared out of camp looking for White-Eye blood. The chief sighed. "The crying of women and children make me sad."

Aguila, also appreciating the seriousness of the situation, looked straight into Quintero's face. "If they are soldiers they will not be easy to kill like the man and his family you attacked last year."

"I do not care if it is one White-Eye or many," Quintero boasted. "I will kill all I see. They are as bad as the Mexicanos."

Aguila knew that serious and logical conversation would not be possible with the younger man. "Since there is no danger, we can be patient. It is important to find out what the White-Eyes are doing at the Pool-Beneath-the-Cliff. Perhaps they are only camping for the night or a few days while journeying someplace else."

"Do they number more than our fighting men?" a member of the council asked. His name was Zorro, and he was a man known for his cunning.

"Our band is enough to kill them all," Quintero said.

"Then they are no threat to us," Aguila said. "We must find out what they are doing there."

"And how long they plan to stay," Terron, the other member of the council, interjected.

"Their bones will stay forever if I have my way," Quintero said.

"You are quick to strike," Aguila said. "Many times that is not an act of wisdom."

Chaparro stepped forward. "My friend Quintero strikes quickly against the Mexicanos! He has killed many. I listen to him when he says to kill the White-Eyes."

"You do not care for wisdom, Chaparro?" Aguila asked.

"Not if wisdom is the prattling of an old man," Chaparro sneered.

"Silence!" Lobo Cano roared at the mouthy young warrior. "Aguila has proven his manhood in battles and his own wisdom at councils before you were born. I followed him as a young warrior and learned much while we killed many of our enemy."

"Show respect!" Zorro added.

"I will show respect, but eventually I will lead warriors to kill the White-Eyes," Quintero boasted.

"You will lead nobody," Lobo Cano threatened. He was a better warrior than Quintero. Though advanced in years, he was still strong, and could make up for any lack of quickness through experience and guile. "Do not issue commands here."

"I respect the council," Quintero said. He turned and left

29

with the same abruptness he had demonstrated at his entrance. His friends followed.

"There is trouble here unless wiser heads take over," Lobo Cano said. He turned to Aguila. "Go find Erudito. Tell him we would speak with him and the White-Eye chief."

"I will waste no time," Aguila said seriously. "If we are not careful, the sands of El Vano will soak up blood like it does the spillover from the Pool-Beneath-the-Cliff."

Chapter Three

His excellency, General Antonio Eduardo San Andres De La Nobleza, commander of the Northern Military District of the State of Sonora for the Republic of Mexico, held his arms out as his valet slipped the heavy uniform tunic on him. It was of a bright green, with a high collar and cuffs made of brilliant scarlet silk, complemented by a large pair of fringed epaulets. The rest of his uniform consisted of dazzling white trousers worn inside a pair of shiny black boots.

Although he was temporarily in the field and living in his tent, De La Nobleza still maintained a luxurious lifestyle. His living quarters, rather than being of canvas, were of a heavy, oiled leather and consisted of three large rooms. Oaken furniture, a thick carpet, hanging drapes, and his servant were part of the accommodations.

The general studied his image in the full-length mirror in front of him. He adjusted the tunic slightly, inspecting the effect. He gazed at himself from different angles, striking poses to appear as if he were at a formal soiree in Mexico City. Then he adopted a stern demeanor to see how he would appear in front of troops.

De La Nobleza liked what he saw.

"The tailor was a credit to his trade, was he not, Luis?"

31

The valet, a short, thin, distinguished-looking man of middle years, nodded nervously. "Yes, Excellency. The uniform fits you well." He stepped back. "Por Dios! And it makes you appear younger! More virile!"

"Really? Does it really?" De La Nobleza asked, pleased.

"I swear by all the saints, Excellency," the valet assured him.

De La Nobleza was also a slim man. His slimness made him appear taller than his five-and-a-half-foot height. With black hair and muttonchop whiskers, his coloring and high cheekbones betrayed the Indian that was mixed into his Spanish bloodline. "Are all preparations made, Luis?"

"Yes, Excellency, all is in order," Luis replied. "Capitan Perez has assured me of this."

De La Nobleza smiled at his servant. "You are not nervous, are you, Luis?"

The servant licked his lips. "I am not used to this sort of thing, Excellency. I would have preferred to remain at the hacienda."

"But we could not do such a thing as we plan back there," De La Nobleza said. "Think of it as no more than a social event, Luis." He raised his arms again to allow his belt and saber to be put around his waist.

"It will not be one of long duration, Excellency," Luis remarked as he fastened the buckle.

De La Nobleza laughed aloud. "Perhaps not for our honored guests."

The tinkling of the bell mounted on the tent flap interrupted them. Luis went to tend to the call while De La Nobleza continued to admire his reflection in the tall mirror. Moments later, Luis reappeared.

"It is Señor Weismann, Excellency," he announced.

"Ah! Bid him join me, Luis."

The servant opened the flap leading to the foyer, allowing Roberto Weismann to enter the dressing chamber portion of the tent. Although bathed and wearing fresh clothing, the leader of the scalphunters was nonetheless attired for the trail.

"Buenas tardes, Excelencia," Weismann said doffing his sombrero.

"And how are you, Don Roberto?"

"At the moment I am rather wealthy," Weismann said. He was always pleased with the way the general addressed him as a caballero — a gentleman. "But I fear as time goes by, I slip back toward poverty rather rapidly, Excellency."

"Do not worry, Don Roberto," the general said. "That situation will be remedied quite soon."

"I hope so," the scalphunter leader remarked. "As do my loyal men."

De La Nobleza pulled out his pocket watch and noted the time. "The festivities will begin shortly."

"How many guests do you expect, Excellency?" Weismann asked.

"Quite a few," De La Nobleza answered. "More than a hundred actually. Particularly after I was so careful to mention in my message the copious amounts of tequila and mescal that would be available."

"My own men will appreciate that," Weismann said.

"Even your American? Do the native drinks of Mexico please him?"

"Any liquor pleases him, Excellency," Weismann answered.

"What is his name again?" De La Nobleza asked.

"Penrod Donaldson," Weismann answered.

"The Gringos seem to favor strange names," De La Nobleza said.

"I don't consider his name, Excellency," Weismann said. "He is a good fighter and leader who serves me well."

"As a military man, I can well appreciate that," De La Nobleza answered. "One loyal lieutenant can be worth a hundred men. Even a thousand under certain circumstances."

"That is why I keep Donaldson in my group," Weismann said.

"Still, I have second thoughts of Gringos," the general said turning to the mirror once again. "Did they not roll into el

33

Tejas in ever-increasing hordes, finally illegally wresting it from Mexico?"

"They did so," Weismann affirmed.

"For that reason, I shall always harbor a deep hatred of them," De La Nobleza said. "Particularly after the ending of this latest war with them."

Weismann didn't give a damn who ruled in the areas he operated since it made no difference to him whose nation's laws he broke. He shrugged without comment.

Luis presented himself once more. "The arrangements are ready for your inspection, Excellency." He retrieved the general's cocked hat, complete with plume, and set it on the officer's head.

"Esta bien!" the general exclaimed after checking his appearance in the headgear. "Come, Don Roberto. Let us make sure our guests will be pleased with the fiesta we have planned for them."

Weismann, unsmiling, followed De La Nobleza through the tent and out the front flap. Penrod Donaldson, standing there, came to attention and saluted the Mexican officer.

De La Nobleza returned the gesture with a look of surprise. "Very soldierly, Señor Donaldson. Am I correct to assume you have served in your country's army?"

"Yeah, Gen'ral," Donaldson said. He chuckled. "Several different times, under several different names."

"Ah, then you are a true adventurer," De La Nobleza said.

"It sort of depended on my circumstances at the time, Gen'ral," Donaldson explained. "A lot of folks don't know it, but being in the ranks is the best hiding place there is."

"I suppose," De La Nobleza said wary of getting into much of a conversation with someone he considered a hooligan.

But Donaldson was in a talkative mood. "I sure do take a fancy to that hat o' yours, Gen'ral. It's plumb elegant."

"Thank you, Señor Donaldson," De La Nobleza said.

"You look like them pitchers I seen of that famous French gen'ral name o' Nappy-olen."

"Yes, thank you," De La Nobleza said. "Luis!" he called out. "Give us a tour of our fiesta."

"This way, please," the servant said. He led them over to a table filled with various bottles. "All mescal and tequila," he said. "Plenty for everyone."

Donaldson glanced at the alcohol. "Any rye whiskey there, Pedro?"

"No, Señor, and my name is not Pedro," Luis said.

"I call most Mezkins I don't know by that moniker," Donaldson said with a wink. "It's kinda like calling us Americans Joe, know what I mean?"

"I do not, Señor," Luis said.

"I'll explain it to you sometime when we can talk," Donaldson said.

Luis merely cleared his throat to show his distaste. He led them over to another table. "And here we have roasted pork, goat, tortillas, chiles, and frijoles."

Weismann noted a couple of large tents set out to each side of what was obviously the official gathering place for the guests. One of the structures was fifteen yards further out than the other. "What is the purpose of placing the tiendas de campanas in that manner, Excellency?"

De La Nobleza smirked. "It is the pièce de resistance of this whole affair, my dear Don Roberto. And I must caution you not to allow any of your men to wander into that area. It is reserved especially for our guests."

Weismann was obedient without questioning. "Of course, Excellency."

But Penrod Donaldson had a Yankee's curiosity. "How come we got to stay outta there, Gen'ral?"

De La Nobleza turned and faced the American. When he spoke, his voice was cold and venomous. "Because I have thus commanded you."

"Yes, sir!" Donaldson said smiling. He fully realized he was speaking against a powerful and ruthless man. It had always been Donaldson's style to see how far he could go. Now he decided it was time to back off. Here was a man who could have just about anyone he wanted killed at the snap of a finger. "I'll sure do what you want quick and cheerful like."

"See that you do," De La Nobleza said.

"Where is it exactly you wish for my brave men and me to place ourselves, Excellency?" Weismann asked.

"We have arranged a place of concealment for you on the other side of the food and liquor," De La Nobleza said. "Luis will show you the correct place to situate yourselves. It is important that you remain out of sight."

"As you wish, Excellency." Weismann glanced around. "I do not see many soldiers, Excellency. Will they also be concealed nearby?"

"Not at all," De La Nobleza said. "As you will find out, Don Roberto, I have as many troops as I need."

Weismann glanced around again, a worried expression on his face. "You said you would have at least a hundred guests."

"Perhaps closer to a hundred and fifty," De La Nobleza said. "But, fear not, Don Roberto. Even if they number more than two hundred, I am well prepared."

Weismann indicated his acceptance with a nod of his head. "Tengo confianza en usted, Excelencia."

"Your confidence warms my heart, Don Roberto," De La Nobleza said sincerely. He admired Weismann in spite of himself. The man was cunning, intelligent, and absolutely dependable. His loyalty might be bought by silver pesos, but Weismann could be trusted to give his all until bribed away by an enemy. De La Nobleza actually considered the scalphunter chief handsome with his dark brown hair and green eyes. Only the scars on his face marred his appearance. The general wondered what blood mixture of races coursed through Weismann's veins.

Further conversation was interrupted by the arrival of a Mexican soldier on horseback. He rode up to the general and quickly dismounted. "The Indians approach, Excellency," he reported with a salute. "They are even now crossing Arena Creek."

"Your report is accepted," De La Nobleza said. "Now join your comrades and wait for my command."

"Yes, Excellency!" The soldier handed the reins of his mount to Luis, then trotted down to one of the tents and slipped inside the front flap.

"Follow Luis," De La Nobleza ordered Weismann and Donaldson. "He will take you and your men to your positions. When the work is done, the fiesta will begin."

The general went to a point in front of his tent which offered him a grand view of the desert panorama spread out to the front. He could see a cloud of dust as his guests approached, their images dancing in the shimmer of heat rising from the sandy ground of the desert. After a half hour they were easy to make out. The Apache men, all on horseback, rode to the front, with their women and children bringing up the rear on foot. A spot of green in the crowd would be his adjutant and escort of two soldiers who had gone to guide the Indians to the fiesta.

When the group arrived at the site, the adjutant and soldiers took their charges into the area between the two tents. De La Nobleza could hear some instructions shouted and the mounted Indians swung off their horses' backs. Then the group of Indians, with the exception of one, squatted down. All looked hungrily at the table where the liquor and food was so conspicuously displayed.

The adjutant and soldiers marched up to De La Nobleza with a lone Indian. The adjutant, a young captain named Perez, halted and saluted. Then he announced in a loud voice, "I present Topalez, chief of the Disierto Apaches." He turned to the Indian. "And I present—"

"I know De La Nobleza," the chief said coldly.

The general said, "And I know you, Topalez. Therefore, I say to you, greetings to you and your people in the name of the Republica Mexicana."

"My greetings to you, De La Nobleza," the chief replied. "It is good what we do today."

"Yes," De La Nobleza said. "We will feast and drink together, then talk about a lasting peace between the Mexicans and the Disierto Apaches."

"We have fought long and there is much hatred everywhere," Topalez said in a pessimistic tone. "Although everyone wants peace, there will be bitter talk. Anger will flare from both sides."

"Yet the fighting must end somewhere, sometime, no?" De La Nobleza said. "Why not here and now?"

Topalez shrugged. "Porque no? But we will all have to work hard to make any peace last."

"But if it is done, the lives of everyone will be better," De La Nobleza pointed out. "Is there not an Apache saying which states that the animals that require the most hunting skill to catch always make the better food? The peace will be like a wily antelope trying to evade us. But if we are skillful, we will bring it to ground and feed from its carcass."

"I prefer Mexican cattle," Topalez said in a boastful tone.

"Thus, we shall discuss such arrangements, my friend," De La Nobleza said cheerfully. "I know how much such meat pleases Apaches."

"You know much about us, De La Nobleza," Topalez said. "Sometimes, I think too much."

"Let us drink and fill our bellies," De La Nobleza said with a big smile. "Then we will turn serious and have our talk."

"So it will be," Topalez said.

"When my man Luis calls to you, all the Apaches may come up and take liquor and food," De La Nobleza said.

Topalez's tribe had experienced a hard winter. The smell of the cooked pork and goat, along with the sight of the bottles of liquor caused him to lick his lips. "We will do that." He turned and walked back to join his people.

De La Nobleza and Captain Perez stood by the tent looking at the gathered Apaches. Perez asked, "Are the men ready in the tents, Excèllency?"

"Of course, Capitan," De La Nobleza said. "And I will prove it to you now." The general removed his cocked hat and waved it back and forth as if to acknowledge the throng of Indians.

The heavy, dark barrels of cannon slid out the flaps of the two tents flanking the scene. Slight hissing sounds of burning fuses could be heard that caused the alert Apaches to look around.

Too late.

The cannon belched fire and triple canisters, each containing dozens of iron balls an inch-and-a-half in diameter. The ammunition ripped into the crowd of Indians, the small, cruel spheres battering and rending flesh and bone of the unsuspecting victims.

Topalez was able to stand up and bellow at his people to run for their lives. The few survivors not maimed or killed by the cannonade, leaped to their feet as the warriors formed a living shield around the women and children. Instinctively, they began a disorganized, frantic rush for the open desert. When they came abreast of the second tent, the cannon positioned there was fired by its hidden crew.

The remainder of the Apaches were swept down as if a gigantic, invisible broom had slammed into their midst, knocking them helter-skelter among the skimpy desert vegetation.

General De La Nobleza turned to the rear, shouting, "Don Roberto! Al ataque!"

Roberto Weismann, with Penrod Donaldson close behind with his other men, came into view. Running as fast as possible with the excitement of scalping and earning money egging them on, the scalphunters swept past the tables of food and charged into the Apaches. All they found were the dead and moaning. Not one Indian had gone unscathed through the two quick barrages.

Donaldson laughed as he pulled his scalping knife from its

scabbard. "There ain't nothing left to do but collect hair for loot, is there?"

The eager scalphunters went to work with a vengeance. Now and then, when one of the victims' skulls had been ruined too much for a good scalp, an angry curse would be heard. Some of the wounded died more quickly than they normally would have after the tops of their craniums were sliced and ripped off.

De La Nobleza, grinning and thinking of silver pesos, stood sipping from a wine glass as the pile of grisly trophies was tossed at his feet.

Captain Perez, not quite as enthusiastic, but still an Apache hater, did not drink from his glass. But Weismann beside the Mexican officers, pointed to the three groupings. "You see, we are being orderly about this. My men place the male trophies there." He pointed to another spot. "The females there and the children over there." Now and then he shouted angry encouragement at the mutilators as they brought the objects of their scalping knives in for the count.

When the work was done and the bloody corpses of the Disierto Clan of Apaches lay sprawled and violated in the red light of the sinking sun, De La Nobleza announced the count.

"Eighty men, one hundred and four women, and one hundred and sixteen children," he said.

The scalphunters cheered knowing that several of the larger children had been counted as women.

"Now that your work is done, feed yourselves!" De La Nobleza shouted. "And drink. This is now a true fiesta!"

More shouts of joy sounded as the men rushed to the tables of refreshments. Penrod Donaldson ignored the party and joined the general, Captain Perez, and Weismann.

Donaldson didn't seem particularly happy, but he conceded it had been a good count. "We'll pull in some good coin on today's work."

De La Nobleza looked at him. "Why are you so glum then,

Señor Donaldson? Soon you will have silver pesos with which to purchase women's favors and good drink and food."

"I'm just looking to the future, Gen'ral," Donaldson said.

"Yes, Excellency," Weismann said. "I fear this depletes the population of Apaches in this part of Sonora."

"They speak the truth," Captain Perez said. "In my duties, I have noticed a great shrinking of the Apache population in the district."

De La Nobleza smiled and shrugged. "Y que importa? I know where more Apaches can be easily found."

Weismann was interested. "That is good news, Excellency. But where?"

"To the north, in El Vano of Arizona," De La Nobleza said.

"But, Excellency!" Perez protested. "That is now part of the United States."

"Yes," Weismann interjected. "That could mean big trouble, Excellency."

"Believe me, Don Roberto, the authorities in Mexico City will have no way of knowing from which side of the border Apache scalps come," De La Nobleza assured him.

Donaldson nodded his agreement. "That's true, Gen'ral. But while we're doing our work, any surviving Apaches is gonna take out their hate on the folks living in Arizona."

"For the most part, that would be your fellow Americanos, would it not?" Perez asked.

"I reckon," Donaldson said.

De La Nobleza displayed a cold smile. "Do you really care, Señor Donaldson?"

Donaldson shrugged. "Not a damn bit, Gen'ral."

De La Nobleza raised his glass. "Then here is a toast to El Vano of Arizona—and the Chirinato Apaches who live there."

Weismann showed a rare grin. "I will drink to their scalps, Excellency."

"Then let us do just that!" De La Nobleza exclaimed leading them over to the table with the liquor.

The general's servant Luis looked out the front of the large leather tent. He could see the mutilated corpses in the last light of the day's sun. He had heard the three speaking of going into El Vano of Arizona, and Luis knew well such an action was soon going to bring a veritable hell-on-earth to that area.

The servant crossed himself, then withdrew to the interior of the tent away from the horror.

Chapter Four

The bugle's clear, crisp notes sounded reveille. The traditional martial tune, calling the dragoons to a new duty day, echoed off the cliff wall and reverberated far out into the desert country of the Vano Basin.

Captain Grant Drummond, already awake on his cot, listened to the trumpeter sound the call twice; each time to separate sides of the bivouac. Within moments, a bustle of activity could easily be discerned throughout the camp as shouting noncommissioned officers rousted the dragoons from their blankets and tents. Equipment rattled and the bantering between mess mates built up as the men formed up under the less-than-gentle supervision of their squad leaders. It was the usual, boisterous beginning of a new day of soldiering in the field.

The early morning routine always reminded Captain Grant Drummond of West Point and his cadet days. Neither the passing of years nor distance from the academy dulled that memory of the ancient call to the day's duties. At the academy the cadets were rudely taken away from their peaceful slumber by a battery of fifers and drummers, called the Hell Cats. This small, but loud organization of field music whistled and thundered its way back and forth across the quadrangle until the Corps of Cadets was awake, dressed,

43

and standing tall in formation. This recollection was not the fondest in the captain's remembrance of his education to become an officer.

Grant Drummond had graduated from West Point in the spring of 1835, fourteen years previously, as an enthusiastic young officer seeking military adventure. During those years of varied duties and responsibilities, Grant had experienced the complete spectrum of soldiering in the United States Army. His service varied from months of tedious boredom and inactivity to the heights of horror and rage in brief spasms of excitement brought on by war against Indians, Mexicans, bandits, and other enemies of the fresh American republic that had been stretching its muscles for a bit more than half a century.

Grant's first half-year was dictated by certain family connections his wealthy father, a New England lawyer, had in Washington City. The well-meaning sire caused Grant's initial entry into the army to be one of idle staff routine in the War Department. But that quickly came to an end in January of 1836 during the Second Seminole War. A band of the tribe's warriors ambushed and wiped out a company of troops in Florida. When units were ordered to the field, Grant immediately volunteered for campaign service and found a billet in an understaffed dragoon regiment.

At that time, Grant had been engaged to be married to a local belle in the nation's capital. She was a strong-willed young woman who insisted that he stay in Washington to avoid both a separation from her and the perils of war. But Grant was not going to pass up this opportunity for real soldiering. The young officer's enthusiastic desire to ride with his new regiment to whatever adventures and fate awaited him, led to the dissolution of his engagement to the beautiful socialite. This would not be the last time his desire for action would prove detrimental to his love life.

When Grant's unit arrived in Florida they were immediately sent overland to Fort King. On the way to the post, they reached the spot where the bones of the dead soldiers whose ambush had caused the war, lay scattered among the tropical growth. After taking time to bury the remains, the column moved on to the Withlacoochee River to join a besieged garrison at a place called Camp Izard. Here young Second Lieutenant Grant Drummond received his baptism of fire during repeated attacks from hostile Seminoles. At one point, during the long weeks of being surrounded and cut off, rations ran so low that the beleaguered garrison was forced to eat their horses. But they held on, defending their position against a determined and skillful enemy.

The troops finally broke out and, joining up with later arrivals, began fighting a war of hit-and-run that carried both sides through the wild Florida wilderness. It was during these bloody encounters that Grant Drummond developed an appreciation of and much skill in irregular warfare of patrols, ambushes, raids, sneak attacks, and melting away into the wilderness when the advantage was the enemy's.

The battling finally came to an end in March of 1837 with a treaty that brought about the cessation of hostilities. Grant returned to Washington City with his regiment, bloodied, wiser, and an eligible bachelor once again on the social scene. Being a handsome and dashing officer, it wasn't long until he was once again involved with a young lady. This one was the beautiful daughter of the French ambassador. Plenty of young swains' hearts were broken when her engagement to First Lieutenant Grant Drummond was announced in the local newspapers.

Unfortunately for both the country and the young couple's future, the Seminole fighting was in full swing again by the summer of 1840. Once more, faced with the choice offered by an angry young woman, Grant's engagement to be married went to hell as he spurned romance for war.

But breaking up with the girl that time proved physically dangerous. Her brother, a hot-blooded chevalier, decided his family's honor had been insulted by this refusal to give in to his sister's demand to continue the engagement on her terms. That led to a challenge to a duel that took place on a particularly dreary and gray dawn beside the Potomac River.

The fight was done with pistols as carefully selected friends acted as seconds for both parties. All the traditional rituals were religiously followed as Grant fretted about the possibility of being late for his regiment's departure. It never dawned on the self-confident officer that it might be he who received a pistol ball in his carcass rather than his impetuous and temperamental opponent. Inwardly irritated, Grant went through the exchange of words, the carefully orchestrated pacing to the correct position, and, finally, the order to turn and fire.

The challenger's pistol ball went high and wide, but the combat-veteran officer found his mark by hitting his opponent in the upper arm. Surprisingly, the Frenchman seemed happy about the whole thing. His family's honor had been defended, he had nobly shed his blood, and would be able to walk around Washington society with his arm in a sling attracting welcome attention from impressed young ladies. He even wished Grant good luck as the officer galloped away to join his regiment.

This time Grant's sojourn into war was to be two years of difficult, almost impossible campaigning under the aggressive leadership of Colonel William Jenkins Worth. Worth took his troops hell-for-leather after the Indians in a relentless manner in spite of high casualties, sickness, and an unforgiving steamy climate. The end result was another army victory in which the Seminole chief and his followers finally gave in to the soldiers, allowing themselves to be removed to Arkansas Territory. That left less than three hundred Seminoles in the whole of Florida. Thus, with no more threat to the local population, the war was declared over and done with in August 1842.

This time, Grant did not return to peaceful garrison duty and the opportunities for more spoiled romances. He went with his regiment to Louisiana to guard the Texas frontier against encroaching squatters, Indians, and other people bent on hell-raising in the beleaguered area. The U.S. Army fought warriors, American desperados, Mexican bandidos, and other less identifiable foes during that turbulent time. By the time outright war with Mexico broke out, Grant was a captain leading his own company of dragoons.

Grant spent two years of active fighting, leading his men in near-suicidal cavalry charges against artillery barrages and infantry volleys. He scouted and raided in the enemy's rear areas, destroying lines of communications and supply depots as the American forces pressed onward toward Mexico City and ultimate victory. When the shooting ended, the United States ended up with hundreds of thousands of square miles that had belonged to Mexico, including California, New Mexico, and Arizona.

When Captain Grant Drummond received the chance to lead a detachment of dragoons into Arizona to open up a line of communication between Texas and the Pacific Coast, he jumped at the chance with the same enthusiasm he had demonstrated as a subaltern. Grant happily chose to accept the responsibility that offered danger and hardship rather than make a belated return to the soft garrison duty available in the East.

It was that choice that led him to the Vano Basin where he now made ready to begin a most important day. As the sound of troops outside showed a marked increase in the camp activity, Grant quickly pulled on his trousers. After picking up his toiletries bag, he went outside the tent to tend to his shaving.

Eruditus Fletcher squatted by the officer's campfire, sipping fresh, hot coffee. He raised his cup in greeting. "Novus dies, novus initium," he said with a smile.

"Yes," Grant replied. "A new day is a new beginning. And how are you this morning, Mister Fletcher?"

"I am in excellent spirits, my young friend," Eruditus said.

He took a sip of coffee. "Why is it this brew of caffeine tastes so delectable in the great outdoors?"

"It's the sharpened appetite brought about by fresh air," Grant said. He put his shaving mug into the hot water on the fire, tipping it just enough to get the soap heavily moistened. After whirling his brush around on it, he began his shaving routine.

Eruditus, with a full beard, watched his companion's efforts. "This will be an important day."

"So it will," Grant agreed as he skillfully guided the sharp straight razor down his cheek. "By the way, I do thank you for lending me that fine novel. Charles Dickens is an excellent author."

"David Copperfield is his latest," Eruditus said. "I am fortunate to have friends back East who see to it that I am kept up to date on the best of contemporary writers." He sighed. "Even if the mail is irregular at best."

"No matter the two or three months it takes a packet to arrive out here, it appears as if I, too, shall reap much literary enjoyment from that arrangement," Grant remarked working on the sensitive skin beneath his chin. "Provided, of course, that your generosity continues."

"And it shall, my intelligent friend!" Eruditus exclaimed. "Fiden daro!"

"I shall hold you to that promise then," Grant said. He finished shaving and wiped the remaining lather from his face. He glanced over at the other area of the camp, glad to see that Sergeant Clooney and his corporals had the men well into the early morning routine. "I'll be attending to assembly presently," Grant said. "What time is it that we'll have our meeting with the chief of the Apaches?"

"Actually, he is chief of a certain clan of that race called the Chirinato Apaches," Eruditus said. "The gentleman's name is Lobo Cano."

"Lobo Cano," Grant repeated. "I must remember that."

"You must also eventually meet another leader of the tribe,"

Eruditus said. "He is the medicine man called Nitcho. He prefers to spend most of his time out on the desert."

"What is his exact role in all this?" Grant asked.

"As spiritual leader of the Chirinatos, Nitcho has much influence," Eruditus explained. "The Apaches put great stock in their religious beliefs. Therefore, the tribe will make no serious moves without consulting him."

"Do you know him well?" Grant asked.

"He is the older brother of my Chirinato friend Aguila," Eruditus answered. "However, on this occasion, it will be enough to impress Aguila. That old warrior's wisdom and experience is well appreciated and respected among the Chirinatos almost as much as Nitcho's. Chief Lobo Cano relies much on Aguila's counsel and advice."

"Is Aguila the fellow you practically grew up with?" Grant asked. He went back to his tent with Eruditus following.

"Yes. We are like brothers," Eruditus said. The older man stopped at the tent flap as if his return to the wilds of the Vano Basin had made him find even the inside of a tent as repugnant as a smelly sulphur mine. He watched as Grant slipped into his tunic. "But my influence with him is as limited as his own with the young Turks of his tribe. This parley is not going to be all that easy."

"Nothing worth gaining is," Grant said setting his cap on his head.

Eruditus said, "I trust you have brought gifts with you for such an undertaking."

"I have much experience in dealing with Indians," Grant replied. "I believe they will find what we have most appealing and useful." He glanced toward the dragoon detachment that was drawn up in three ranks with Sergeant Clooney at the front. He smiled. "The legion calls to its tribune," he said. "My centurion awaits with the cohorts at the ready."

"Gere, Tribunus!" Eruditus said. "Carry on!"

Grant walked from his tent to a position in front of the dragoon formation. He came to a sharp halt directly in front of Sergeant William Clooney.

Clooney saluted, announcing in crisp tones, "Sir! The detachment is all present and accounted for!"

"Very well, Sergeant," Grant said. "I shall take charge of the formation."

They exchanged salutes again before Clooney marched around the dragoons to a position in the rear. The men, knowing that today was to be taken up by a very significant mission, waited expectantly for Grant's announcement.

"Stand at ease, men!" Grant ordered. "At mid-morning we are going to have an important meeting with the elders of the Chirinato Apache Indian tribe at a place on the cliff just above this bivouac."

The men, all veterans of both the Mexican War and miscellaneous Indian-fighting campaigns, appreciated of the gravity of what their commander had to accomplish.

"I will take Mister Eruditus Fletcher as scout and interpreter, and Corporal Rush and his squad as escorts," Grant said.

If any of the men had not been properly impressed with the danger involved, they were at that moment. Rather than having his second-in-command Sergeant Clooney along, the commander would take the more expendable Corporal Charlie Rush and his half-dozen dragoons to accompany the mission. Any murderous treachery by the Apaches would leave the experienced Clooney in charge of the majority of the detachment back at the camp.

Grant returned the command of the detachment to Sergeant Clooney. Corporal Rush, flattered that his small squad had been chosen to go to the parley, quickly marched them out of the formation and over to the picket line to saddle their horses. The commander's mount would also be readied for the short journey up into the Culebra Mountains.

In less than twenty minutes the small column rode from the bivouac and, following Eruditus's lead, went to the narrow trail leading to the summit of the cliff. As the column was forced into a single file, Grant nervously glanced around knowing that at that particular moment they were terribly exposed to any sort of ambush. Unable to turn, the dragoons would be forced to charge forward into a hail of incoming bullets.

But no treachery met them during their ascent. Actually, the men enjoyed the very noticeable drop in temperature as they moved slowly upward into increasing greenery. Finally, after a half hour's slow climb, they topped the rise and hit softer ground, noticing sparse trees.

Eruditus, a few yards ahead of Grant, looked back and called out, "We'll be there shortly, Tribunus. See where the vegetation thickens? That is the creek that flows over the cliff and falls to the pool where the bivouac is located."

The dragoons went deeper into the increasing numbers of trees. The veteran soldiers instinctively reached out and put hands on their carbines as the visibility lessened to a great degree.

Suddenly a trio of Indians stepped into view. They exchanged greetings with Eruditus who reined in his faithful Plutarch. He turned and motioned Grant to join him.

Grant rode up and took note of the first Apaches he had ever seen. They were short, wiry, and very dark in skin color. Their shiny, black hair was worn shoulder-length and held in place by bandannas of various colors. They wore cotton shirts, breech cloths, and high-topped moccasins that reached past their mid-calves. Their weaponry was old flintlocks and they carried powder horns and leather bags of shot.

Eruditus looked at the officer to judge his impression. "These are your escorts to the conference, Captain Drummond."

"Tell them I am honored to have such brave warriors show me the way," Grant said.

Eruditus translated the words. None of the Apaches showed any emotion other than to slightly raise their eyebrows. Eruditus chuckled. "They are very flattered and pleased, believe me. You were not exaggerating when you said you have dealt with Indians before."

"In Florida and Texas," Grant said. "We were successful in all cases."

Eruditus's smile lessened. "You'll find the Apaches altogether different, Captain Drummond. Para ipse!"

"Thank you for the advice, Mister Fletcher," Grant said. "I am, indeed, prepared."

"Then let us go to our fate," Eruditus said. He motioned to the Apaches. The warriors turned and led the column deeper into the woods.

Chapter Five

Roberto Weismann and Penrod Donaldson rode slowly, almost lethargically, across the Sonoran desert on the second and final day of their short journey.

Out of habit, Weismann was in no hurry. Having survived many dangerous situations by keeping his head while making well-thought out judgments and choices, he preferred a deliberate, paced approach to everything he did. He sat in the saddle in what appeared to be a state of absent-mindedness, but in actuality he surveyed the landscape around them in an alert manner, missing nothing that went on in the vicinity, be it a lizard scurrying for cover or a bit of dust kicked up by the desert gusts. Now and then the scalphunter chief glanced over at his American companion, noting the nodding head and drooping eyelids.

Donaldson, though just as quiet as Weismann, was neither as comfortable nor as alert. His slowness was more due to his physical condition than any ingrained habits of deliberate action. The scalphunter's head ached and his stomach burned from many consecutive nights of heavy drinking. During the time he and Weismann spent in the small city of Cananea in Northern Sonora, he had squandered the silver pesos he earned scalping Apaches. He partook of all the delights the fleshpots and cantinas the tiny metropolis offered. The whores who had taken on his seemingly limitless sexual strength had finally drained him of energy, leaving the American exhausted and as impotent as an old man.

Weismann, who preferred gambling to whoring and drinking, was in fine fettle. He had been able to increase his personal wealth through several long evenings of shrewd card playing. There was the one incident when he had killed a man who displayed enough audacity to accuse him of cheating, but the scalphunter chief's sojourn into recreation had been restful. He felt rejuvenated and relaxed.

Their destination on that particular day was approximately five miles south of the ill-defined border between the Mexican state of Sonora and the new American territory of Arizona. At that spot lay the sun-baked village of Juntera. It could have been described as a crossroads, except there were no roads in the area. It was a junction where certain routes known to smugglers, bandits, scurrilous travelers, and other refugees from decent society came together to find a handy spot to meet, rest up, or avoid the law.

Roberto Weismann had given his men some time off to spend their money after the scalphunters had cashed in on the merciless skill of General De La Nobleza's artillerymen. Weismann's gang had two whole weeks to spend their blood money on saloon wenches, mescal, and celebration. On that same day Weismann and Donaldson rode across the desert, the band was to report to their chief at Juntera. This was to get organized and ready before crossing into Arizona to lift the scalps of the unsuspecting Chirinato Apaches.

"Donaldson!" Weismann barked.

Donaldson's head snapped up as he was startled out of his reverie. "What the hell?"

"There ahead, is Juntera," Weismann said.

Donaldson forced his bloodshot eyes to peer into the distance. He could barely make out the smudge of the village on the horizon. "It's about time," he said in a husky voice. "I need a drink."

"I would think you had drunk enough," Weismann said. "I think the liquor has a hold on you."

"Only when I'm celebrating," Donaldson said. "You ain't never seen me drunk on the job, have you?"

"No," Weismann said. "And I had better not." He disliked any sort of craving weakness in the men he chose to be his chief lieutenants. It mattered not to the scalphunter chief whether the vice be sex or liquor. As far as he was concerned, men were in the world to fight and struggle for survival and dominance over others in pursuits that should gain them money and power. The only other alternative, in Weismann's mind, was failure, which meant a sure death. Anyone not following this philosophy was a lackey, not suitable for leadership.

By the time they turned from the desert and rode into Juntera, the afternoon sun was beginning its westward drop. The two scalphunters went straight to the cantina where their men were supposed to be waiting. When they dismounted and tied up at the hitching rack, a small boy scurried forward with a friendly smile on his face.

"I will watch your horses, Señores," he offered. "And only for five centavos, eh?"

Weismann reached down and grabbed the youngster by the front of his shirt, pulling him up to face level. "You listen to me, you urchin turd shit by a street whore! If these horses or the equipment on them is disturbed in the slightest, I will come looking for you and all little bastards your age in this village."

The boy gasped in fear. "Si, Señor!"

"Stay away from them horses, Pedro," Donaldson said. Then he added in an open threat, "You do not touch them horses or we'll kick your butt. Comprendes?"

Weismann snorted a laugh and dropped the boy. The kid

scrambled to his feet and made a panicky retreat from the scene. "I think our animals will remain unmolested in this village, Donaldson."

"Yeah," the American agreed. The excitement of bullying the boy brought him out of his hangover. "I wonder what his ma looks like?"

"She's probably employed hereabouts in one of the cribs or cantinas," Weismann remarked. "But forget it. We have work to do." He pulled his long gun from its saddle boot and walked into the saloon and paused a few steps inside to survey the scene.

"Jefe mio!" a voice called out. "My chief!"

Weismann recognized one of the Mexicans of the scalphunter gang. He went over to the table with Donaldson following. Both carefully glanced around the room. The American also toted his own long gun.

Weismann said, "Hello, Guerrero. Where is everybody?"

"They are with Ambroso," Guerrero answered. "Will you buy me a drink, Chief? My money is gone."

"Stupid bastard," Weismann said.

"Yes, Chief," the scalphunter said humbly.

Weismann signaled to the bartender. "Bring a bottle and some mugs over here." He and Donaldson sat down. Weismann eyed Guerrero. "Why are the others not here?"

Guerrero lowered his eyes. "I told you, Chief. They are with Ambroso."

Donaldson didn't like the sound of the situation. "So why are they with him and not here like they was told to be?"

Guerrero shrugged. "Quien sabe? Who knows?" He watched hungrily as the bartender set a bottle of tequila and some mugs in front of them. He smiled at Weismann. "You are generous, Chief."

"Pour us all a drink," Weismann said. "But not too much in mine, eh?"

"As you wish, Chief," Guerrero said.

"Give me a lot," Donaldson said.

Guerrero complied, then took a deep swallow of the fiery, clear liquor. He wiped his mouth and spoke in a whisper. "I think there will be trouble, Chief."

"Tell me about it, Guerrero," Weismann said. He had known Guerrero for many years. The man's method of imparting news was as roundabout as the way he lived. He had never been the type to give out information in a quick, efficient manner. Guerrero always played around as if he wasn't quite sure where the advantage to himself might lie.

Donaldson was impatient. "Tell us what you know is going on, Guerrero, damn your eyes!"

"Ambroso is talking big," Guerrero whispered. "He says he is no longer content to share the wealth from the scalps with you and Donaldson or even His Excellency De La Nobleza. But he admits the business of bounty payments must come from the general."

Weismann appeared amused. "De veras? Is that true? Has our friend Ambroso grown stingy over these last couple of years?"

"He wants to be the chief," Guerrero said, putting the whole situation out in the open.

Donaldson quit drinking, even going so far as to push the mug away from him as he realized he would soon be in a situation that called for a clear head. "Just how many of the boys is with him?"

"It is hard to tell, Donaldson," Guerrero said. He looked at Weismann. "Most will wait to see who wins—you or Ambroso." He smiled. "But not me, Chief! I am on your side right now. From the very beginning."

"I appreciate that, Guerrero," Weismann said.

"Good, Chief," Guerrero said. "I respect you much more than Ambroso."

"I think I know who is with him," Weismann mused. "He would have Platas, no?"

"Yes, Chief," Guerrero said. "And Avila and Montez and Lopez."

"That's five of 'em altogether," Donaldson said. "God only knows what the other six is gonna do."

"The bastards of donkeys will wait to see who comes out ahead," Weismann said. "But maybe two or three might jump in on one side or the other during any confrontations, I think."

"Yeah," Donaldson agreed. He looked around the cantina, then went to the door and peered out at the street. He came back and sat down. "I wonder where they're at?"

"The challenge to my leadership will be here, where we are," Weismann said. "We do not have to go out to look for trouble."

"Maybe not," Donaldson said. "But we better damn well be ready for it."

Weismann just started to nod a silent agreement to the statement when the shot from the door blasted into the interior of the saloon. A hot whip of wind brushed the scalphunter chief's ear before the bullet slammed into the faithful Guerrero's chest, knocking him tumbling from his chair.

Donaldson, with every bit of his hangover now whisked away in that one instant of angry fear, had hit the floor and come up pumping hot lead with his Colt. One slug flew into the cantina wall, but two splintered the batwing door at the entrance, driving metal and wood into the chest of the would-be assassin. The man sat down in full view of Donaldson who peered through the bottom of the door. The American almost fired again, but the pistolero slumped to the dirt street, blood streaming out to form rusty-colored mud beside him.

The other patrons in the cantina were on the floor. The bartender, out of sight behind the bar, called out in a shrill voice, "Por favor, Señores! Please, gentlemen! Take you

58

fight outside!"

"Shut your turd-eating mouth," Weismann warned him. "Or I'll put a bullet in you."

One of the cowering drinkers, glancing wildly about, made a dash for the door. He just hit the flimsy, damaged portal when a fusillade of shots twisted and crumpled him like a rag doll.

Donaldson checked his other Colt, glad to see it ready to fire. Two spare loaded cylinders were nestled in the pockets of his leather vest. He winked at Weismann. "Say, there, Roberto. How d'you say 'surrounded' in Spanish."

"Rodeado," Weismann answered.

"Then that's what we are," Donaldson said. "We're damn sure rodeadoed, ain't we?"

Weismann, ignoring the remark, crawled over to where Guerrero lay sprawled next to his overturned chair. The scalphunter took note of the wide-eyed, vacant stare of death the loyal man displayed. He called out to Donaldson. "Guerrero is dead. You watch the front and the right windows. I will take the rear and the left ones."

"You bet, Don Roberto," Donaldson said cheerfully.

Another patron, desperate to get out of the death trap, tried a rush to the door. He made it through, the disappearing sound of his footprints quickly fading away.

"They have calmed down now," Weismann said. "They are being careful when they shoot, no?"

"Yeah," Donaldson said. "And who!"

The bartender and the two remaining customers made a spontaneous run out the back door, knocking it off its leather hinges in their fearful haste.

Weismann shrugged. "Ahorra tu y yo."

"Yep, just you and me," Donaldson said.

Weismann checked his weaponry. He had one Colt along with a Wilkinson over-and-under double barrel pistol and a six-shot Pepperbox pistol. Both men would save their muzzle-loading long guns for the last. The fight in and around the cantina would call for short-range shooting. Hand guns served better in such a situation.

A shadow flitted across one window then disappeared. One of the men was obviously trying to draw fire. But neither Weismann nor Donaldson was tempted by the daring self-made target. Caught in the open room, with the situation going into a period of inactivity, they glanced desperately around for cover. The only possibility was the bar. Although constructed of thin slats, it at least offered some concealment. The thick adobe walls of the building would protect their rear. In silent agreement, both men eased toward the protection, leaving the dead Guerrero where he lay.

A few moments passed. Donaldson noted a clay jar under the bar. He checked it out and found it full of fresh water. "The bastard was watering down his liquor back here," he said. He treated himself to a sip. "But it'll keep us going. Want a drink?"

Weismann took the earthen container and gulped a couple of swallows. "I suppose we can treat ourselves to this liquor if the situation turns completely against us."

"Yeah," Donaldson said. "We can die drunk and mean."

"Without giving a damn," Weismann added.

Donaldson looked at him. "I don't think you give a damn now."

"This is all part of the game," Weismann said casually. "Win or lose, live or die, it is decreed." He handed back the water. "So you might as well die with dignity and courage."

"I ain't that happy about it," Donaldson said.

"Believe me, I do not accept any situation without a willingness to fight for my own survival," Weismann said. "Remember those words: dignidad y valor—dignity and courage."

"How about these words?" Donaldson said. "Put hot lead in their butts!"

Further conversation was interrupted at the front door when the battered batwings were sent flying by the sudden intrusion of two men.

Weismann and Donaldson cut loose with a couple of shots apiece. Three of the bullets found their marks, knocking one man sideways to fall in instant death while his companion, unable to spot where the scalphunter chief and his American companion had located themselves, staggered backward. Snarling in pain and surprise, he fired wildly around the room.

Another attacker came through the back door. He stopped short at the sight of Guerrero, the dead customer, and the other man on the floor. A stray bullet from the wounded gunman hit him in the abdomen, doubling him over and dropping him to his knees.

"Stupid bastard!" Donaldson snapped. He turned to put a final, killing bullet into the man on his feet.

Weismann fired at the gut-shot attacker, hitting him in the head and sending a pinkish spray of blood and brains onto the far wall. The victim rolled over on his side and twitched in his death throes.

Once again, all was silence.

"What's the score?" Donaldson wondered aloud.

"We have Platas lying in the street, Avila and Montez dead from their rush through the front door, and Lopez over there," Weismann said.

"Unless Ambroso talked them others into joining up with him, he's alone," Donaldson mused.

"We will just have to bide our time," Weismann said. "Give me another drink of water."

"You bet," Donaldson said complying.

Weismann took a couple of sips, enjoying the coolness of the drink.

"Hey!" a voice outside called. "Don Roberto! It is me—Dabido!"

Weismann took a breath. "Y que quieres?"

"I want to tell you that we have Ambroso for you," the scalphunter named Dabido said. "You have killed everyone on his side. Me and Kravek, and Saline, Cotera, and Valverde did not betray you."

Donaldson was furious. "And you didn't help out none, did you?"

"Alas, no!" Dabido admitted.

"You push Ambroso through the door," Weismann commanded.

Several long moments passed, then several struggling, snarling, cursing men could be heard approaching. Once more, Dabido spoke, saying, "Hold your fire, Don Roberto. Me and Kravek are going to push him into the cantina. He is tied up."

Three men briefly appeared in the door, then one stumbled forward. He was Ambroso with his hands tied behind his back. He affected an embarrassed grin. "Buenas, Chief."

"Buenas," Weismann said returning the greeting. "You became greedy, did you, Ambroso?"

"Yes, Chief," Ambroso said. "I am sorry. Will you forgive me?"

"No," Weismann said. "Not for an instant."

"I didn't think so." Ambroso swung his glance at Donaldson. "Hey, Gringo! Watch how a brave Mexican can die."

Donaldson grinned. "I'm real interested."

Weismann's bullet struck Ambroso in the throat, making him stagger only a little. Ambroso gamely fought to keep to his feet, but the shock and bleeding fast took its toll. Finally he sank to his knees, staring vacantly at the cantina floor. He lasted almost a minute more before falling face-down.

The rest of the scalphunters came into the cantina. They

stood sheepishly looking at their chief and Donaldson. "We are happy you are well, Chief," Dabido said.

"We'll have to gather up five more men to replace these dogs," Weismann said.

"There are plenty of pistoleros here who will ride with us," Dabido assured the scalphunter leader. "Some probably have experience in taking Indian hair."

Weismann glanced over at Donaldson. "It appears as if our trip up to the Vano Basin will not be delayed after all."

"Then we'd best get cracking," Donaldson said reholstering his weaponry.

"Yes!" Dabido said. "Let's see how much blood we can spill up there."

"I do it for money," Donaldson interjected.

Weismann shrugged. "For blood or for money, the results to the Chirinato Apaches will still be the same."

Chapter Six

The air was balmy and pleasant in the heavy shade of the trees. The intertwined boughs of the tall pines kept the sun from the clearing, while gentle wisps of a mountain breeze both cooled and refreshed the atmosphere. It seemed the ideal setting for a meeting brought about for peaceful intentions. Even the horses of both the soldiers and Indians displayed a restful, relaxed state as they grazed on the forest flora.

On one side of the open area, the Apache contingent—consisting of Chief Lobo Cano and his council of Zorro, Terron, and Aguila—sat cross-legged in the thick grass. Standing behind them, blank-faced and silent, was a group of warriors that included Quintero and his close followers Bistozo, Chaparro, and Zalea. That quartet situated themselves close together, near the center of the group, their arms folded and backs straight, the stern postures showing their stubborn opposition to the object of the meeting.

On the other side also situated comfortably on the grass, sat Captain Grant Drummond and Eruditus Fletcher. A red-and-white dragoon guidon planted in the ground had caught the Apaches' attention. The unit flag seemed a sort of totem to the Indians and many wondered if the object was some strange and strong medicine of the White-Eyes.

The squad of dragoons, forming a semi-circle, with their

leader Corporal Charlie Rush standing prominently in front kept a close eye on the warriors across from them. While avoiding any open, challenging glares, the veteran cavalry troopers showed they were obviously experienced and confident fighting men. The blue uniform jackets with high collars, worn especially for the occasion rather than the plainer and more practical buckskins, were resplendent with yellow facings. The bright colors impressed most of the Apaches as much as the soldiers' weaponry.

The army horses, properly picketed and under watch, were twenty yards away. The animals, enjoying the difference in the climate as much as the humans, continued to contentedly munch on the sweet mountain grass.

Eruditus Fletcher got to his feet and held up his hand in greeting. He walked to a point between the Indians and the soldiers. When he spoke, he alternated between English and the Chirinato dialect to benefit all present as he opened the proceedings.

"You all know me," he said.

Chief Lobo Cano acknowledged this by lifting up his hand in greeting. "You have friends among the Chirinatos."

"I would like to give special greetings to my old friend Aguila," Eruditus said.

"I greet you, querido amigo," Aguila said warmly.

Eruditus glanced around. "I do not see your brother Nitcho," he said.

"As our medicine man, he has gone out on the desert to strengthen his spirit on the land where our ancestors roamed," Aguila said.

"I suspect he will go where your forefathers came out of the earth," Eruditus said.

"I think he wishes to teach things to his grandson," Aguila said. "It is that time in the boy's life."

"Give Nitcho my greetings when next you see him," Eruditus requested. Then he pointed to Grant Drummond.

"This man's name is Drummond. He is a war chief of the Americans." Following that, he introduced the Apache council to Grant, pointing to each man—Lobo Cano, Aguila, Zorro, and Terron—in turn.

Lobo Cano could not contain his curiosity. "Why are we here to talk together, Erudito?"

"There has been a big fight between the Americans and the Mexicans," Eruditus said.

"We know of this fight," Aguila interjected.

"Did you know the Americans defeated the Mexicans and made them give up large areas of their land?" Eruditus said.

"We have heard so," Lobo Cano said.

The Apaches, who had fought and hated Mexicans for years, grinned and nodded among themselves. Although there didn't seem to be any particular advantage to them in how the war ended, they enjoyed hearing of an enemy's misfortune.

Eruditus continued. "Part of that land is called Arizona in which the Vano Basin—El Vano—is located."

Now Quintero interrupted. "El Vano belongs to the Chirinatos! The Mexicanos cannot give it away to anybody no matter how many times they are beaten!"

"The Americans recognize the Chirinatos live here," Eruditus said diplomatically. "They know the land is truly yours. That is why the Big Chief of the Americans has sent Grant Drummond to speak with you."

Lobo Cano looked over at Quintero with a furious frown. "Keep your voice still until it is time to speak!"

"But first," Eruditus said wanting to take away any tension no matter if it be between Grant and the Apaches or among the Indians themselves. "The Big Chief of the Americans has sent gifts to the Chirinatos to show he has much affection and respect for them." He turned to Grant. "Time to bring the gifts out, Captain."

Grant nodded and motioned to a couple of dragoons. The two soldiers lugged a heavy wooden crate out between the speakers. Using hammers, they quickly pried off the top.

Captain Grant Drummond stood up and walked over to the opened container. He reached in and withdrew a particularly large and well-decorated Bowie knife. "This is a special present from the Big Chief of the Americans to the Big Chief of the Chirinatos," Grant said. He carried it over to Lobo Cano and handed it to him. "He wants his friend Lobo Cano to remember him when he uses this."

As Grant returned to his seat, Eruditus quickly interpreted the words for the Indians using gestures to emphasize the affectionate generosity of the American leader.

Grinning with pleasure, Lobo Cano pulled the knife from its sheath. He and the others gasped at the well-honed shininess of the implement.

"The Big Chief of the Americans is a good friend. What is his name?" the Apache leader asked.

"His name is Polk," Eruditus said. "He sends the rest of his gifts to be divided among the Chirinatos. There are knives and hatchets for the men, and mirrors, necklaces, and bracelets for the women."

"We will take the gifts back to our village," Lobo Cano said. "Tell us more what my friend the Big Chief of the Americans wants of us." He continued to admire the brand new knife.

"I will let his War Chief Grant Drummond tell of what the Big Chief desires," Eruditus said. He nodded to Grant.

Once again the army officer stood up and walked forward. He sat down directly in front of Lobo Cano. As he spoke, Eruditus translated.

"When we won our war, the Mexicans had to let us use vast areas of land they once claimed as their own," Grant

67

said. He had not failed to appreciate the warrior Quintero's objection to having the Vano Basin described as part of Mexico. Instead of saying the Americans had taken the Vano Basin from the Mexican Republic, he indicated they had forced the Mexicans to let them use it. "We wish for our people to be able to travel across the Vano Basin to reach our other brothers who live by the great waters that lie to the west across the desert and mountains. We ask the Chirinatos to allow our travelers to pass through unmolested. Eruditus, who knows you well, feels this will cause no harm to the Chirinatos."

Aguila, very mindful of the hotblooded Quintero and his friends, spoke. "My old friend Erudito has been among us a long time. But there remains things to discuss and to learn from you, War Chief, even though we trust Erudito."

"Not all of us!" Quintero shouted. Once more he received angry glares for his impertinent disregard of protocol. He stared back defiantly.

Aguila went on as if nothing had happened although he had expected a loud reaction from the young warrior. "But we cannot trust other White-Eyes. We have seen them before and, like the Mexicanos, they want to stay on land and call it their own and not let other people hunt or fish or camp there."

"Our people do not wish to settle on the Vano Basin," Grant said. "It is of no use except to travel across to reach the West where we have villages and our own hunting grounds."

Quintero shouted, "Did you take those hunting grounds away from other Indians?"

"We took them away from the Mexicans," Grant said.

"They took them away from Indians," Quintero said. "I know Mexicanos."

"Perhaps they did," Grant conceded.

"Then why does not the Great Chief of the Americans

return the land to those Indians?" Quintero wanted to know.

Eruditus, who fully understood the way a Chirinato warrior thought, knew how to handle that situation. "We cannot give the land back to those Indians because the Mexicanos killed them all."

That made sense to Quintero. He quieted down to see what else would be said.

"I am worried," Aguila said. "What if the Americans crossing El Vano look up at these mountains? They will want to come up here to hunt and fish. Then some will want to stay. We had to drive the Mexicanos away. We do not want to have to drive the Americans away."

"The Big Chief of the Americans knows these mountains belong to the Chirinatos," Grant said. "He will not let his people come up here. If they do, he will punish them."

Quintero laughed aloud. "No! The Chirinatos will punish them."

"That will make the Big Chief both sad and angry," Grant said in a stern voice after Eruditus translated the harsh boasting. "If his people do wrong, he must punish them. He is very powerful."

Quintero sneered. "What will he do? Come up here and make war against us?"

"Yes!" Grant said in a loud voice. He repeated, "He is very powerful."

Aguila nodded his agreement. "I think so. Has he not defeated all of the Mexicanos?"

"Every one of them," Grant said looking straight into Quintero's eyes. He sensed an antagonist and troublemaker in the young Apache warrior.

Quintero glanced at his friends Chaparro, Bistozo, and Zalea. They, like him, had to admit to themselves that the Big Chief of the Americans seemed a strong man with many warriors. A mutual, silent exchange of thoughts passed among the four Indians. It seemed better to wait out the situation and see what would develop.

The other two members of the council, Zorro and Terron, had remained silent. Now Zorro entered the talks. "Why has the Big Chief of the Americans sent his blue-coat warriors if he wants to be friends with us?"

"Yes," Terron said. "We know that not all White-Eyes are warriors. Some farm like Hopis or live in towns like the Zunis. Why did he not send them to speak with us instead of fighting men?"

"We came to keep the Mexicans from trying to take back land we won from them," Drummond explained. "We are not here because the Big Chief wishes for us to fight the Chirinatos."

Eruditus showed his approval of the reply with a secret smile and wink at Drummond. He turned to the Apaches and added, "The Big Chief of the Americans does not take Chirinato land. He is not like the Mexicans. He will leave it alone except to have his people travel across it."

Aguila asked, "But will not these blue-coat warriors live on El Vano?"

"Yes," Eruditus admitted. "But they will camp in only one place. That is at the Pool-Beneath-the-Cliff. It is as the war chief said, he and his blue-coat warriors only want to keep an eye on the Mexicans."

"But what if we want to use the water at the Pool-Beneath-the-Cliff?" Aguila asked. "Many of our people spend time on El Vano's desert. They will need to fill their goat-skins with water from time to time."

Grant said, "We will welcome visits from our Chirinato brothers." Then he added, "We recognize you own the Pool-Beneath-the-Cliff."

Once more Quintero entered the exchange. "Then why did you make your camp there?"

"We are not stupid," Grant said. "Would you think we

would make camp out in the sun of the desert away from water? We are men, not lizards!"

The other Chirinatos laughed at the absurdity of purposely setting up hogans away from a known water source.

Quintero sought to save face. "Then why do you not seek permission to stay there now?"

"That is part of which I wish to speak," Grant said. "That is what the Big Chief of the Americans asks of his friend Lobo Cano. He sends the gifts so that you will permit us to camp there at the Pool-Beneath-the-Cliff."

"My friend the Big Chief is considerate if he exchanges gifts for our tribe to allow you to continue to camp at the Pool-Beneath-the-Cliff," Lobo Cano said. He took another admiring look at the knife he had received. "His present to me is a very good one."

"Yes," Grant answered. "If you agree to remain his friends, he promises that he will give the Chirinatos more presents from time to time."

A sudden eruption of approval came from the assembled Apaches. Quintero scowled and fell back into silence.

Lobo Cano looked at Aguila, Zorro, and Terron. All three showed their acceptance of the terms by saying nothing else. The Apache chief turned back to Grant. "We agree to this. We will not molest travelers across El Vano if they are the people of the Big Chief of the Americans. But travelers must not come up into our mountains. If they do we will catch them and turn them over to you for the Big Chief of the Americans to punish."

"That does not include Mexicanos," Aguila added. "They are our enemies for many generations. They have their own chief who will *not* punish them."

"I will try to keep the Mexicans away," Grant said. He signaled to Corporal Rush. "Bring me the papers, quill, and ink."

The corporal quickly complied, setting the items on the crate that contained the gifts.

Eruditus pointed to the two copies of the document. "This agreement is shown by the marks on these skins. When you make crosses on them where we show you, it is proper for them to be seen by the Big Chief of the Americans. Then it will be proof to him that his friends the Chirinatos agree to what he has proposed. Then he will send more presents. You will keep one of the skins for yourself to show others of the treaty you have made with this powerful chief."

Eruditus unrolled the treaties, arranging the quill and ink for use. Grant dipped the writing instrument in the ink and signed both copies. He handed it to Eruditus who passed it on to Lobo Cano. The Apache made awkward crosses above where his name was written in English.

"So be it," Eruditus said. Then, unable to resist the urge, he commented in Latin, "Consensus est facitus! The treaty is made!" He rolled them up again, handing one to Lobo Cano and one to Grant. "The parley is over," he announced.

Under the Apache chief's direction, the crate was picked up and carried away. After final farewells and remarks about other possible meetings, the two groups broke up. By the time the dragoons returned to their horses and mounted up, the Apaches had disappeared into the trees.

The troops, with Eruditus in the lead, returned in single file as they had come. This time, with a signed treaty in their possession, the dragoons felt much less uneasy about any possible ambushes, although there were a couple remarks about the rebellious young warrior who had spoken so rudely during the proceedings. The veteran soldiers recognized a possible troublemaker in the surly Apache.

Even Captain Grant Drummond had the Indian on his mind. When the column reached the bottom of the mountains and rode out onto the desert, he drew up alongside Eruditus. "Mister Fletcher," he said. "Are you familiar with that rather impertinent fellow who kept interrupting the negotiations?"

"I've known him since he was a pup," Eruditus said. "His name is Quintero and you'll not find a fiercer fighter among that clan of natural-born warriors."

"The instincts I've developed over the years lead me to sense an enemy in this Quintero," Grant said. "Those other Apaches standing close to him are his followers, are they not?"

"Yes, Captain," Eruditus said. "Chaparro, Bistozo, and Zalea have been Quintero's constant companions since all were boys. Many a Mexican has lost his life due to the efforts of that quartet."

"So, they are good fighters, are they?" Grant asked.

"Those four display the finest and the worst of their race," Eruditus said. "The Apache is raised in an atmosphere of harshness almost unknown in any other part of the world. Only the strongest children survive into adulthood, and the strongest adults into old age."

Grant pointed to the mountains. "That does not seem a harsh environment to me, Mister Fletcher."

"Not at this time of the year, Captain. The winters there can be deadly with an ever-present threat of hunger when the game animals flee the snows. For that reason, the Chirinatos cannot spend all their time there in those mountains of plenty," Eruditus explained. "They return to the desert both because of necessity and some sort of spiritual bonding they have with that unforgiving land."

"Then as the months roll by we can expect the Apaches to be in our proximity," Grant said. "Most interesting to contemplate. Now I am doubly appreciative of the treaty."

"I hate to point this out, Captain," Eruditus said. "But if something — or someone — stirs up the Chirinatos, that treaty might as well have been written in burning blood by Satan's own hand. It will be more of a curse than a blessing."

The column pressed on, heading for the comforts and food offered by the camp at the Pool-Beneath-the-Cliff.

Chapter Seven

The old Indian held his grandson's small hand as they stood on the edge of the desert arroyo. The pair looked down its length to the spot where it curved out of sight into the harsh landscape.

The boy was only seven summers of age, but he was particularly bright as was befitting a male relative of a Chirinato Apache medicine man. The Grandfather was the elder brother of Eruditus's Apache friend Aguila. He enjoyed a particularly respected position among the tribe's clans.

Nitcho was the ancient one's name. Still straight and dignified in spite of his advanced age, he had served the spiritual needs of his people through countless seasons and changings of the moon. In the Apache world, dominated by supernatural powers and evil spirits lurking either invisibly or in certain animals, the shaman was absolutely necessary to ensure good hunting, warmaking, and health for the Chirinatos. After years of being the tribe's medicine man, Nitcho had begun looking for someone to carry on his important post. It had been very difficult to find a suitable candidate. He'd almost lost hope of finding the right replacement to administer and supervise the religious side of the tribe's life. Even his own son could not measure up to the high standards and keen perceptions necessary for the office. Nitcho's younger brother Aguila, though a wise and experienced member of the tribe's counsel, did not have the makings of a spirit doctor. Besides, he also was fast advancing in age making him a second choice at best even if he were able to absorb the spirits into his soul needed for the deep meditation and ministering necessary.

But the boy, now called Nitchito after the grandfather, suddenly blossomed forth as the one to take over as medicine man. The youngster had already shown more than the quick wit and high-intelligence needed by a successful and accomplished shaman. The boy told of dreams in which he spoke to animals or saw visions of things to happen in the future. When Nitchito's announcement of a dream about a large herd of deer appearing at the foot of the mountains came true, everyone was convinced he was destined to be the Chirinatos' next medicine man. He had demonstrated the power to get information from the spirits that would feed the people of the tribe. By the time Nitcho died in a few years, the boy would be mature enough to take on the awesome responsibility of communication with the world of ghosts for the Chirinatos.

Little Nitchito, through long, deep conversations and exchanges of ideas, shared the views and philosophies of his grandfather. Like the old man, he also preferred to live on the desert. The milder climate and living conditions of the Culebra Mountains held no special favor in the boy's eyes. He realized the challenges and hardships of the desert increased one's spiritual strength and awareness.

Nitcho was pleased. The lad would learn that while the high country provided certain herbs, roots, and barks needed in his profession, the mountains in reality, were foreign to real Apaches. Even if the Culebra range was the home to Puma-Ghost-of-the-Mountain who bestowed wisdom on the Chirinatos, the desert was the true native soil of the Chirinato clans. For it was on that baked land where

76

the invisible female deity called Spirit-Woman-of-the-Desert lived. The dry earth was her belly and many lifetimes before, after Life-Giver had impregnated her, the female spirit's belly had come open and given birth to the Chirinato Apaches.

"What do you think of this ravine, Nitchito?" the old man asked the grandson.

The boy studied it for a few moments. "It is long and narrow, Grandfather. It goes for a long way, I think."

"How do you think it got here?" Nitcho asked.

Again the boy settled into thought before speaking. "I think Spirit-Woman-of-the-Desert cut it in the earth."

"That is true, Grandson," the spirit doctor said.

"Is this the same ravine from which our people emerged into the world?" the boy asked.

"No, my grandson, that one was so deep that it went straight to the bowels of the earth. Then it was closed up," Nitcho said. "Spirit-Woman-of-the-Desert put this one here, like all she has made to serve us, for two reasons. First, so the Apache could have a hiding place that cannot be seen unless one is very close to it."

"What other reason did Spirit-Woman-of-the-Desert have for cutting the earth?" Nitchito asked.

"To give the sudden waters some place to go," Nitcho said.

"Why is that, Grandfather?"

"When it rains without warning and the clouds open up to throw rivers down on the earth, the waters that come must have some place to run rather that on top of the earth," the Grandfather explained. "The flood can go down into the ravine. That way, the Apache will not be knocked down and swept away and die from trying to breathe the swirling torrent."

"Unless he is in the arroyo when the flood comes, Grandfather," the boy duly noted.

The old man cracked a toothless grin. "Ayee! Then you know to stay away from gullies and other low places when it rains in the desert."

"This I learned long ago, Grandfather," the boy assured him. "At least two summers ago."

The old man laughed again, this time amused by what the boy must perceive as a long time past. "It is good to know the real-life things as well as the spirit things, Nitchito. Now let us return to the wickiups, Grandson," Nitcho said. "There is roasted rabbit and I can sip some tiswin."

Nitchito laughed as he thought of his grandfather drinking the corn beer. "Then you will start to sing, Grandfather."

"Yes," he admitted thinking of the effect of the drink. "But tiswin is gentle to an Indian instead of making him crazy like mescal and tequila. That is something else for you to remember."

"Yes, Grandfather."

The two walked up the gentle slope leading to the spot where their group of Chirinatos had camped since coming down from the Culebras more than a moon before. They walked in silence, each lost in his own thoughts, until a sudden noise broke their reveries.

A dozen riders, all wearing the garb of Mexicans and Americans, swept into instant view at the far end of the camp and charged toward it, firing pistols into the surprised and unsuspecting Apaches.

Nitchito, his dark eyes wide open, gasped, "What is this, Grandfather? Is it a raid against us?"

"Yes, Nitchito," the medicine man replied. He quickly surveyed the scene, appraising the situation as an old warrior would. "Quick, Grandson!" he said making an immediate decision. "Jump into the arroyo and hide there."

All Apache children learn early that instant obedience is the key to survival in a dangerous adult situation. Nitchito was no exception. He practically dived into the depths of the ravine.

Nitchito crawled up to a point where he could see over the rim into the village. He could see his grandfather run on spindly legs toward the wickiups. By the time the oldster reached the camp, several dead people lay scattered among the lodges. The few Chirinato men, mounting the best defense possible, fired arrows at the attackers. The horsemen charged through the wickiups, appearing to be coming straight at the arroyo. Nitchito ducked down. When he looked up again, he could see the enemy had turned and made another run at the camp.

That second attack ended with all the Chirinatos down, their blood running along the top of the hardpacked soil like flood water from a cloudburst. Nitchito looked frantically about, finally spotting his grandfather Nitcho's corpse lying beside the wickiup the boy had shared with his grandparents. Nitchito fought the desire to leap from the natural ditch and run to the scene of the murders.

Now the attackers dismounted and, to the boy's horror, began cutting and hacking at the dead and dying Chirinatos. He could see both Mexicans and White-Eyes among the group. They seemed to be working on the heads of the dead Indians, although the boy wasn't sure what they were doing.

Finally, knowing his duty, the boy slid to the arroyo floor. Taking a deep breath, he began running down its length, away from the carnage, heading for the first opportunity to get out into the open desert.

Running is something drilled early into Apache boys. Many times, because of the harshness of their environment and the need for concealment, all Apache tribes went to war on foot rather than riding horses. Their natural skill at using even the skimpiest of terrain for the ultimate in cover and concealment, sometimes made clumping about on

79

horseback a distinct disadvantage in warmaking. Therefore, in order to be an excellent fighting man for the tribe, a warrior had to be able to run far and fast.

Now Nitchito ran as he had been taught, in easy loping strides that carried him rapidly down the cover of the long ravine. He leaped over rocks and twisted through the turns and sharp angles in the arroyo's uneven route. After a bit, he stopped to scramble to the edge and look back toward the camp. Since he could perceive no followers, the boy judged it safe to head overland. He climbed to the desert floor to orient himself and make preparation for what would be a trying ordeal. After picking a spot in the distant Culebra Mountains, he began running toward it.

The men of the Chirinatos made boys take mouthfuls of water, then run for long distances. At the end of the exercise, the youths were expected to spit the water out to show they could resist the temptation of the physical comfort of soothing their parched throats by swallowing, and also as evidence that they had breathed properly through their noses without opening their mouths.

Nitchito ran with his thin lips clamped shut, his moccasined feet slapping an even staccato on the earth. Fatigue was something his mind would not accept. No burning sensations of aching muscles or cramps of exhaustion were evident to him. All the boy could think about was reaching those mountains in the earliest amount of time.

Spirit-Woman-of-the-Desert pushed the burning sun across the sky under which Nitchito's unbroken gait continued. Nitchito was unaware of the amount of passing time as the deity eased the burning torch toward the western horizon, reddening the sun and finally easing its flames down until it was an orange disk that lengthened the shadows.

By the time the deepening darkness had turned to dusk, Nitchito reached the bottom slopes of the Culebras. He forced himself into extra effort as the terrain steepened, demanding more of his courage and strength. He pushed his way through the ever-thickening vegetation and into the trees as he continued in his self-imposed quest.

When the unexpected hand grasped his arm and turned him around, Nitchito gasped aloud in startled fright. He felt himself lifted up, then turned and dumped to the seat of his breech cloth. The arm still held him and he scratched it with his fingernails and bit into the flesh.

"Ayee, Nitchito!" Quintero's voice said. "Do you think of me as cooked venison?"

The voice of Chaparro came from nearby. "He is like a little puma, that one, eh?"

The warrior called Zalea said, "Let's give the little puma a few kicks."

"Yes," joined in the fourth warrior named Bistozo. "That will teach him to run with more care and not be taken by surprise by any enemy waiting for him."

The boy did not take an instant to reflect on the unexpected meeting with Quintero and the other warriors. "They are all dead!" he blurted out.

"What are you talking about, Nitchito?" Quintero asked.

The boy gasped out, "Mexicanos and White-Eyes have killed the people at the camp at the gully. My grandfather too!"

"Nitcho? Our shaman!" Quintero exclaimed. Without wasting any time in useless questioning, he ordered his friends to fetch their horses. "You will take us back there, Nitcho. Are the bad men still at the camp?"

"I do not know," Nitcho said. "Grandfather told me to hide in the arroyo. When I saw he was dead, I made a run for the mountains."

The horses were brought up. As soon as Chaparro mounted, Quintero put Nitchito up behind him. "The moon is bright," he said. "We can travel fast until we find a good place to stop and hide the horses."

"I know where there is an easy place for them to walk down into the ravine," Nitchito said. "Let us hurry, big brothers."

It took the horses barely an hour to easily cover the same distance that had taken young Nitchito nearly all afternoon to travel. Following the boy's direction, the warriors turned down the arroyo, following it until they reached a gentle depression that eased down into the depths. They allowed the horses to descend into the natural ditch, then dismounted.

"We will hobble the horses here," Quintero said. "Bistozo, you go ahead as scout."

After securing their mounts, the warriors and the boy eased down the arroyo, stopping from time to time as they listened for movements of any unfriendly people who might be lurking or moving about nearby. It took them a long time to travel the entire length of the ravine. At various times, they even chanced looks above at the open desert to see if anyone stirred, but the night and the land were quiet and peaceful. Not even a coyote broke the silence with a howl.

Finally they reached the point in the arroyo's travels where it curved at the site of the camp. A dull glow of dying embers threw a weak light over the scene.

"Where does that light come from?" Zalea asked.

Quintero chanced a glance. "The wickiups were set on fire by the raiders. The flames are still dying in some of the lodges."

"It will make it easier to see if the enemy has stayed," Chaparro pointed out.

A longer, but very cautious look by Quintero showed no movement in the area. Still, wary from lessons learned in past war experiences, the warriors took no unnecessary chances. They would not jump out and rush over to the camp. This time Quintero ordered Nitchito to stay back.

He took the lead now, and the others followed him as he crawled out of the gully and eased his way through the sparse barrel cacti toward the glowing coals.

It wasn't long before he reached the first corpse. Quintero recognized the dead woman from the various times he had wintered on the desert when the snows in the Culebras made life impossible in the heights. He looked around and saw more slain people.

"There is no one here but those who have passed over to the spirit world," Quintero said. He stood up.

Chaparro, Bistozo, and Zalea did the same. Chaparro turned toward the arroyo. "Nitchito! You can come up here now."

There was a scrambling sound as the boy scurried from the ravine. He ran through the camp and went to the spot where he had seen his grandfather lying in death. He knelt down beside the body and clenched his small fists in anger.

Zalea looked around. "They are scalped! Everyone!"

"Even the women and children," Chaparro said.

Quintero spat in anger. "Mexicanos! They cut the tops off heads and pull the hair away."

Nitchito controlled his desire to weep. "I saw them cutting at our people, but I did not know what for."

Bistozo walked over to Nitchito. "Did you say you saw White-Eyes here too?"

Nitchito, his eyes dry but his lip trembling, nodded. "Yes. They were light-skinned and shouted in words that sounded different from the language of the Mexicanos."

"Why take the top of heads?" Zalea asked. "Do they do it while their enemies live so they can gain strength from the suffering?"

"They do it whether their victims are dead or alive," Quintero said. "I think the scalps of dead enemies give them strength whether the deed causes pain or not."

Chaparro glanced around at the scene visible in the combined light of the moon and the dying fires. "Many of our people have died here this day."

Quintero was silent for a few moments. "Do you remember the wagon with the two White-Eyes we saw earlier today?"

"Yes," Bistozo said. "They traveled across El Vano as the agreement with the soldiers allows them to do."

Quintero snarled. "I will no longer honor that agreement!"

"Nor I!" Chaparro shouted.

The other two also voiced their opposition to the treaty made with Captain Grant Drummond.

"We will go find those White-Eyes with the wagon and kill them," Quintero announced.

The four warriors went back to the arroyo toward their horses. Sad little Nitchito took one more look at the dead, noting the melancholy sight of his slain grandfather, the top of his head nothing but a bare, blood-stained skull. Anger boiled up inside his little body.

"Death to all Mexicanos and White-Eyes!" he shouted as he turned to follow after Quintero and his warrior friends.

Chapter Eight

The dragoon, a grizzled veteran named Donegan, stepped away from the other soldiers, to bend over and vomit in the sand. When he'd finished, he spat, saying in an embarrassed tone to his mess mates; "Damn my eyes! I'll never get used to this even if I see it a thousand times."

"Well, I'm doing ever-thing I can to keep my own chow down," another soldier remarked somberly.

The sick soldier's other companions made no joshing remarks at him either. They stood in a semi-circle around the charred corpses of two individuals who could barely be discerned as having once walked the earth as human beings.

Captain Grant Drummond looked closely at the cadavers. "It's hard to tell if those are the same men that came through camp the other day."

"It's them alright, sir," a dragoon said.

Eruditus Fletcher glanced over the wagon. "I must agree. I vividly recall their vehicle. Although this one is a burned hulk, there is enough left to identify it as theirs."

Grant clenched his fists in anger. "During their stopover at the camp, I personally told them it was safe to cross the Vano Basin."

Sergeant William Clooney grimaced. "There ain't nothing left of 'em. It's for sure that the buzzards ain't gonna have no use for these two."

The gruesome scene had been discovered earlier by a patrol led by Corporal Charlie Rush. The young noncommissioned officer, with plenty of battle experience in Mexico, made sure his men did not destroy any tracks in the area. Since it was obvious the victims were beyond help, he went directly back to camp and reported the terrible find. Captain Grant Drummond, alarmed by the incident, immediately put the bivouac on full alert. Then, with Eruditus and Sergeant Clooney in tow, he led a detachment out to investigate the incident. Upon arrival, he immediately had the sergeant form the bulk of the men into a defensive perimeter with weaponry ready for any trouble should the killers come back still thirsting for blood.

Grant turned to Eruditus. "You are sure this was done by Apaches?"

"Indeed, Captain," the old man confirmed. "I fear I must add they were Chirinato Apaches." He slowly shook his head. "It appears these unhappy chaps died slowly in great agony over a long period of hours."

Sergeant Clooney turned away. "How's come they torment pris'ners, Mister Fletcher? Are the bastards just natural mean like that?"

"The Apache lives in an unforgiving world," Eruditus said. "That severe environment puts a streak of hard cruelty in their makeup. But there is a bit more to it than that. When it comes to torturing captives these desert Indians feel they draw strength from an enemy's suffering. The longer the agony, the greater the vigor gained."

Grant was angry. "Well, sir, they'll have gained more than vigor from this disgraceful episode. That tribe is going to know the wrath of the United States Army. They broke their word and, by God, I'll personally see to it that they're punished."

"I suggest we look into this before any action is taken, Captain," Eruditus said.

But Grant was not convinced that prudence applied in

the situation. "They promised they would not harm travelers going across the Vano Basin. In return, we assured them we would keep any interlopers out of the Culebra Mountains. I also said—my personal word, Mister Fletcher, spoken in an official capacity as a representative of the president of the United States—that if they harmed anyone, they would be punished. I told them President Polk would be angry if they broke the treaty. Therefore, I intend to mete out swift and terrible justice, sir!"

"I do sympathize with your position and attitude, Captain," Eruditus said. He well appreciated the anger and contempt the officer felt, but he had no desire to see a full-scale Indian war start in the Vano Basin. "Let us consider all the facts or we could end up taking action to punish many because of what only a few may have done."

"Then that chief had better start controlling his people," Grant said. "That goes for any medicine men too. If they don't, the few will bring a great deal of grief on the many."

"Rash action could start a war in which blood would flow on both sides of the border," Eruditus said. "You're holding a flame over a powder keg, Captain. I wouldn't be properly doing my duties if I didn't point this out to you."

Grant calmed down a bit. He had a tremendous amount of respect for Eruditus's intellect and experience in the area. "Then what do you suggest, Mister Fletcher? Please keep in mind that I must make a full report of this atrocity to headquarters in Santa Fe. My reaction to this crime must be immediate and effective."

"I believe another meeting with the Chirinato council is in order, Captain," Eruditus said. "I would beg of you to refrain from filing any communications on this incident until you've spoken with the Chirinato council. After all, they may be as appalled by this action as we are."

"How soon can this be set up?" Grant asked.

"Immediately," Eruditus informed him. "In fact, I can

ride out now and arrange for the principals to be there. You could follow with an escort of troops."

"A *large* escort," Grant insisted.

"Perhaps you are correct, Captain," Eruditus said. "I am in no way saying the whole tribe is not involved. But I sincerely doubt if they are." He walked over to his horse Plutarch and pulled himself up into the saddle. "I will meet you at the same spot we held the other meeting. I should have the Chirinato council there by the time you can complete your duties here and get up into the Culebras."

Without a further word, the old man pulled on the reins of his horse and galloped off toward the mountains.

"Let's get these poor wretches buried, Sergeant," Grant said. "I'll say a few words over the graves, then we'll go to the bivouac first. I want an escort of a dozen, heavily armed men with plenty of ball and powder. Have another dozen, similarly armed, follow and situate themselves at the top of the trail. They can provide cover in case we must make a hasty retreat from those goddamned Indians."

"Yes, sir!" Clooney turned to the troops and quickly organized a burial detail.

Grant left the scene to walk along the defensive line of dragoons who peered intently out into the desert from where they had been posted to keep watch. He pulled his field glasses from their case and scanned the horizon in slow, careful sweeps.

A dragoon kneeling with his carbine ready glanced up. "Anything out there a'tall, sir?"

"Nothing," Grant said. "I fear the culprits are long gone by this time." Nevertheless, he gave the surrounding area a careful scrutiny. Finally he replaced the binoculars, glancing back to see that Sergeant Clooney and the burial detail were waiting for him. He returned to the scene of the killings and noted the fresh, neatly packed graves. He sighed aloud. "Let us bow our heads."

The dragoons removed their hats and reverently lowered

their eyes to the ground that now held the two dead men.

"God above, we commit these poor men to your care. I don't know if they were sinners or not, but if they lived errant wicked lives, they've paid for any transgressions through the terrible deaths inflicted on them by merciless devils. We pray you take them into your kingdom. Amen." He gestured to Sergeant Clooney. "Let's move out!"

"Yes, sir!"

The troopers mounted up and, with flankers properly posted for security and look-out, made the return ride to the bivouac. Once there, Grant waited as Sergeant Clooney organized a detachment of well-armed and equipped men. It took only a short time for the professional soldiers to form up and swing into their saddles, properly equipped for the job ahead.

With the scarlet and white guidon flapping, the detachment galloped across the sandy terrain to the trail leading upward to the meeting place. Once more, in single file and every man alert and ready for trouble, the horse soldiers ascended into the cooler regions of the Culebra Mountains. When they reached the end of the climb, Sergeant Clooney detailed Corporal Rush to pick out and position a few men. In case of attack at the parley, they were to cover any retreat while those withdrawing would pass through them, then turn to lend increased firepower to the defensive position. After that, a slow but organized withdrawal to camp would be made.

"We hope," a veteran added under his breath after receiving the instructions.

"Quiet in the ranks!" Sergeant Clooney roared. "Keep yer mouths shut and yer eyes open or yez'll end up like them poor wretches we put in this cruel sod earlier on today."

When the men were properly deployed, Grant led the remainder of the detachment forward through the trees to the meeting that Eruditus was supposed to have arranged. But before they got there, they met the old scout on the trail.

Grant signaled a halt. "What is happening, Mister Fletcher?"

"I'm afraid blood has been shed on both sides, Captain," Eruditus reported. "A group of Chirinatos were killed on the desert yesterday."

"How the hell could that have happened?" Grant demanded to know. "And where and by whom?"

"I've yet to learn the details myself, Captain Drummond," Eruditus said. "But Lobo Cano and the council wait at this moment to inform us of the incident." He shook his head. "I fear a most serious and distressing situation has arisen in our midst."

Captain Grant Drummond had dealt with plenty of serious and distressing situations in his thirteen years of soldiering. He took a deep breath and nodded. "Let's get to the parley then, Mister Fletcher."

Eruditus led them deeper into the trees. Just before they reached the spot, however, Grant called a halt. He ordered the small detachment of dragoons to prepare for a quick withdrawal.

"Sergeant Clooney," Grant instructed. "If you note that Mister Fletcher and I are in a perilous situation in which the lives of several men would be lost in a rescue attempt, you are to abandon us here and see to it that the men are pulled back per my plan for a quick withdrawal."

One of the men, the old private named Donegan who had gotten sick, quickly spoke up. "I'll stick with you, Cap'n. I been doing it for the past five years."

"I appreciate that Donegan," Grant said. "But those are my orders."

"Yes, sir," Donegan said. "But more'n one of us would—

"At ease!" Clooney barked. "Yez'll do as ordered or it'll be the back of my hands and the heel of my boots for the bunch of yez!" He turned to the officer. "I'll see to it proper, sir."

"Carry on, Sergeant."

Grant left the troopers under the sergeant's care, then followed Eruditus the rest of the way to the parley. When they arrived, they quickly dismounted then walked up to a spot in front of the assembled Apaches and sat down. The warrior Quintero, openly scowling, stood with his close friends. They watched the approach of the two white men with glares of hatred. Grant looked back boldly, taking great care to show anger and determination.

The chief Lobo Cano along with Aguila, Zorro, and Terron waited for the two white men to make themselves comfortable in the thick grass. "We greet you," Lobo Cano said. "We have something to tell you."

"The soldier chief awaits your words," Eruditus assured him.

"Yesterday, a group of our tribe who had gone to stay awhile on our ancestral desert were all killed," Lobo Cano said. "Men, women, and children. Only one boy escaped."

Aguila was stony faced, but his voice trembled slightly as he said, "Among the dead was the Chirinato medicine man."

Eruditus's eyes opened wide. "Not Nitcho!"

Aguila answered, "Yes. My brother."

Eruditus controlled his facial expressions as he translated, but he leaned toward Grant and added in a desperate whisper, "This is terrible news. The loss of a spiritual leader has all sorts of possible and unpleasant repercussions."

"We have no replacement for him except for his grandson Nitchito," Lobo Cano said. "But the boy is far from ready to be our shaman. Now we cannot communicate with the spirit world or fight sickness or ill-fortune for many, many years."

"Tell me how they were killed," Grant requested.

Lobo Cano called out and the boy Nitchito stepped from the crowd. He walked fearlessly forward and spoke in a loud, clear voice telling of how he had witnessed all the people, including his own grandfather, shot down. Then he

91

ended the narration, stating, "The bad men cut off the skin and hair from the tops of their heads and carried them away."

"Scalped!" Grant exclaimed in surprise when Eruditus told him of what the boy said. "Ask the youngster to describe the killers for us."

"They were White-Eyes and Mexicanos," Nitchito answered.

Eruditus slammed his fist into an open palm. "Scalphunters! By all that's terror and horror in this whole world! Scalphunters!"

Grant glanced about at the Apaches, studying their faces. He realized he would have to speak carefully or he and Eruditus would be filled with arrows within the blink of an eye. "I am saddened and my heart weeps for your dead people."

Eruditus, very much relieved to see the attitude the young captain had adopted, translated carefully, putting much emotion in his words as he described the grief expressed.

"I am also saddened by the death of the two white men with the wagon," he added. "They were only travelers across the Vano Basin and totally innocent of any bad acts against the Chirinato Apaches."

Quintero stepped forward, frowning ferociously. "Do you want to punish the Apaches who killed them?"

Grant spoke quickly, but carefully. "The Big Chief of the Americans will be saddened when he learns of the cruel deaths of his Apache friends. His grief will be so great that I do not believe he will even think of anything but the pain in his heart."

Several of the Apaches, with the notable exception of Quintero and his crowd, nodded in approval at this expression of deep feelings for their losses.

"When the Big Chief of the Americans learns of the death of a medicine man for the Chirinatos, he will then become angry with the bad ones who killed him and the others," Grant went on. "He will tell me to find them and punish *them*—not Chirinatos. You have suffered greatly enough."

Eruditus let loose a long sigh after translating. "Thank the Lord for your astute intelligence, my young captain!" He added, "I can tell you now who is responsible for the deaths of the Apaches."

Grant snapped his eyes around to the older man. "Are you sure? Can we get our hands on the miserable sons of bitches?"

"I shall give you all the necessary information when we return to our camp," Eruditus said. "But now, it is time for a dignified withdrawal and leave our Chirinato friends to their grieving. Sometimes the Apache way of mourning can become dangerous for any outsiders in the vicinity."

Both white men stood up. "We go now and must mourn the dead," Grant stated. "I will send word to the Big Chief of the Americans."

Eruditus translated, then added, "The grief of the Big Chief will be terrible to behold. He will cry out and shout in anger and hit his wife. His children will flee from his wickiup and stay away until his spirit is again at rest. Only this can be accomplished when the bad ones who killed his Apache friends have been punished."

Quintero shouted out, "Take Chirinato warriors with you. We want to draw blood to match the blood of our dead!"

Eruditus turned to Grant and translated, then he added, "I can tell he has the backing of the tribe with him."

Grant went through the motions of showing regret. "It is the custom of the Big Chief to do things for his friends. He will want to punish the bad men for you."

But Quintero wasn't satisfied. "How will we know when this is done?"

"Do not worry," Eruditus assured him. "Every living man

and animal in El Vano will know when vengeance is struck." He turned, taking Grant by the arm. "Let us go now without hesitation," he urged.

Grant allowed himself to be led away into the trees. He and Eruditus wasted no time in mounting and riding back to the spot where Sergeant Clooney and the dragoons waited. They also quickly swung into their saddles, the whole group riding back to where Corporal Rush waited with the rear guard.

Grant and Eruditus led the column down the narrow trail toward the desert floor. "I am anxious to hear of these men you refer to as scalphunters, Mister Fletcher. Almost as anxious as I am to drag those sons of bitches kicking and screaming to the gallows!"

"Fundere sanguis hostilis, aliquando necessarius vester sanguis fundere," Eruditus said.

"That's quite a mouthful of Latin," Grant said with a wry smile. "I believe that comes out to something like, 'In order to spill enemy blood, sometimes one must spill one's own.' "

"Close enough, my young captain," Eruditus said seriously. "And whether the aphorism be in Latin, English, Spanish, or an Apache dialect it is the truth." He paused. "But in this instance, I fear it is an accurate look into our very near future."

"Are you telling me these scalphunters are more formidable than I imagine them to be?" Grant asked.

"I am telling you that they are ruthless killers without mercy or souls," Eruditus said. "You may rest assured fighting them can be as horrendous as fighting Apaches."

Chapter Nine

Captain Grant Drummond put his signature on the routine administrative report he had just finished. It was another one of those maddening chores forced on field commanders by the paper-crazy denizens of the Adjutant General's Department.

"More waste of my valuable time," Grant said to himself. He carefully folded the document before stuffing it into a large, official envelope addressed to the commanding officer of the Ninth Military District at Santa Fe, New Mexico Territory.

"Sergeant Clooney!" he called out.

"Yes, sir?" the sergeant said stepping into the detachment commander's tent.

"Put this in the dispatch pouch," Grant said. "Is the rider ready to leave for Santa Fe?"

"He'll be able to leave camp within an hour, sir. He's drawing extry ammunition and rations right now," the sergeant reported, taking the envelope. "If he manages to stay on schedule, he'll reach Santa Fe in about three days."

"Make sure he doesn't tarry," Grant said. He was isolated by three intense days of hard riding from his nearest headquarters. That was one of the reasons he hated to send a man on a mandatory, but useless errand. Not only was the distance a great disadvantage, but the dearth of soldiers stationed in the area kept critical dispatch riding to a minimum. That meant any exchange of news and communiques could only be done every sixty to ninety days. Requesting immediate aid in the event of an emergency was completely out of the question.

"Let's hope the paymaster from Santa Fe finds us pretty soon, sir," Sergeant Clooney said.

Grant only shrugged. "What would the men spend their money on out here?"

"A soldier likes his pay, no matter what," Clooney pointed out.

"So he does," Grant said.

"Besides they'll gamble, no matter what we do to stop it," the sergeant remarked. "Cards and dice jump outta ever' haversack even before the notes of Pay Call has faded away."

"Yes," Grant said. "The only reason I try to keep that activity down is because of the fights it causes."

"They get to spend money when travelers show up now and then," Clooney said. "A lot of them folks start out with too much. By the time they get this far they're willing to part with some of their extra belongings for hard cash. Even stuff that was dear to their hearts only a month before."

"I suppose," Grant said. "Let's not forget the occasional visit from an itinerant whiskey peddler who also has a few slatterns available."

Clooney fought down a grin. "The men have to relax now and then, sir."

"Another reason for an understanding commander to look the other way when the situation demands it," Grant said.

"Yes, sir," Clooney agreed.

Grant asked, "By the way, is there any sign of Mister Fletcher yet?"

"No, sir," Clooney said. "It's been a coupla days now. If we're gonna ever see him again, it should be soon."

Grant smiled. "I don't know whether to call that optimism or not, Sergeant."

"Yes, sir," Clooney said. "It's just that—" He hesitated. "We're in a hell of a situation, ain't we, sir?"

"Yes, Sergeant," Grant answered truthfully. "We certainly are."

"It ain't like open warfare," Clooney said. "When it comes to these goddamned Chirinatos, a feller don't know whether to load, aim, and fire or to wave, grin and say 'Howdy.' "

Grant smiled at the sergeant's comment. "We'll have to do our best in a difficult situation. Right now, we've nothing to gain and plenty to lose if we rouse those Apaches."

"We'd never get reinforcements in time, sir," Clooney said. "There sure as hell ain't enough of us fight off all them Indians if they decide we've been here long enough."

"We're also short of ammunition not to mention medical aid for any potential wounded," Grant said. "But we'll handle this situation like we've handled others just as difficult."

"I reckon we will, sir." The sergeant saluted and departed to tend to the dispatch.

Grant walked to the front tent pole and leaned against it. He pulled his pipe from his inside jacket pocket and began to stuff the bowl with tobacco. As he touched a match to it and puffed, his mind turned over the rather shocking information that Eruditus Fletcher had given him after their return from the latest parley with the grief-stricken and very angry Chirinatos.

The two men had settled down at a table in front of Grant's tent for a meal of coffee, beans, hardtack, and salt pork while they discussed the latest developments.

The two had barely begun to eat when Grant asked, "You said you knew who had committed the murders of those unfortunate Apaches." He took a slurp of coffee. "You referred to them by the rather ominous name of scalp-hunters."

"That is exactly what and who they are, Captain Drummond," Eruditus said. "Tell me, have you heard of the Mexican law entitled Proyecto de Guerra?"

"Can't say that I have," Grant answered.

"It is a legally and properly constituted statute established by the Mexican government which allows for the payment of scalps taken from Apache men, women, and children," Eruditus said. "Of course, it doesn't matter if the victims are alive or not when the mutilation occurs. Kindness was not built into that particular piece of legislation."

Grant, surprised and a bit shocked that such a law would be put into effect by a civilized nation, paused with his mouth open holding onto a spoonful of beans. He said nothing, waiting for the old man to continue with his dissertation.

"The Mexican government, through various commanders of military districts, pays one hundred silver pesos for the scalp of a full-grown Apache male. The payment for women and children is fifty and twenty-five respectively," Eruditus explained.

"Women and children?" Grant asked.

"That includes infants," Eruditus said. "Though there would be more of a tiny scalp and not much hair in that case."

Grant set his spoon down. "That is damnably barbaric, sir!" he exclaimed.

"I agree," Eruditus said. "But we must look into the background of the situation before we condemn the Mexicans to the ultimate degree, although I ask you not even to think that I am defending the Proyecto de Guerra law."

"I should hope not," Grant said.

Eruditus motioned to the desert terrain around them.

"This is a cruel terrain. Unforgiving, harsh, and it yields little in the way of comfort or sustenance."

"So we've discussed before," Grant said.

"The Apache has lived in this area for eons," Eruditus said. "Only recently has he wandered this far east to find the bounty offered by the Culebras Mountains. Before that he wrested what he could to survive from the desert." He paused and banged his hand on the table. "No! By God, to be perfectly accurate, I must say he *stole* his livelihood from the desert. He pulled and wrenched the continuance of his race from these scalding sands and blazing hills. This land does not willingly or easily give survival of any sort."

"So, even under the best of conditions, the Apaches were in want," Grant commented.

"They assuredly were, Captain," Eruditus said. "And after the Mexicans moved closer, they provided the Apaches with a source of plentiful, nourishing meat in the form of their herds of cattle. Quite unwillingly, of course."

"I understand," Grant said. "When the Apache wished to satisfy his carnivorous yearnings, he turned to raiding Mexican cattle."

"Yes, and the Mexicans quite naturally resented it," Eruditus said. "Particularly when the Apaches added a bit of killing and raping in the raids. The Mexicans retaliated with the same amount of cruelty until both sides were literally at each other's throats."

"I understand," Grant said. "Eventually, the Mexican ranchers petitioned their federal government for aid, and thus the Proyecto de Guerra was born."

"Those are the facts, Captain," Eruditus said. "And that is what happened to the Chirinatos murdered a couple of days ago." He took the time to wrestle a bite out of a brick-like hardtack cracker. "What has happened, I have decided after some long thought, is that some scalphunters wandered north looking for victims since the Apache population in their usual area of operations more than likely has either dwindled or fled." He chewed laboriously.

"Who would these particular cutthroats be reporting to?" Grant asked.

"His excellency, General Antonio De La Nobleza," Eruditus answered. "That gentleman is the commander of the military district of Northern Sonora. That is the region a few miles south of here. I am sure the general is unaware that the men to whom he pays the silver pesos have wandered into territory now owned by the United States of America. Only a madman in his position would risk another war."

"Perhaps he is a madman," Grant suggested.

"I don't know him, but I prefer to give him the benefit of the doubt," Eruditus said.

"Then we must inform the general of these crimes so he can put a stop to them," Grant said.

"An excellent suggestion, Captain," Eruditus agreed. "As I stated I do not know the general personally. But I am well acquainted with the area where his headquarters is located."

"I would appreciate it, if you would visit him and invite him to visit us here," Grant said. "Or, if he prefers, I would be happy to make a call on him."

"I shall visit him at his headquarters and put forth both offers to him," Eruditus said. He smiled. "After I manage to eat this piece of rock the U.S. Army claims is a cracker, that is."

Grant smiled at the picture of the old man struggling to chew the cracker. "You must learn to soak it in your coffee until it is soft and spongy, Mister Fletcher."

"A capital suggestion, sir!" Eruditus said. He dropped the hunk of hardtack into his coffee. "Meanwhile I shall attack the salt pork."

They finished their meal with small talk, mostly with the older man carrying on a lively and entertaining monologue regarding the anthropological history of southern Arizona.

The following morning, after a good night's rest, Eruditus Fletcher left the camp, heading south toward Mexico and the state of Sonora. Bearing an official letter penned by Grant, the old man was well on his way by the time the day's sun had managed to clear the horizon.

Now, waiting for his return, Grant went back inside his tent and sat down to tend to his other administrative duties. Being the commander of a separate, under-strength detachment meant he had to act as his own staff. In addition to commanding the small dragoon force, he was also its adjutant, quartermaster, and, if at all necessary, its chaplain. He went to work on his supply projections for the future, making sure he listed ample amounts of ball and powder in case of big trouble in the Vano Basin. As usual, he became lost in the paperwork, the time flitting by unnoticed by the hard-working officer.

"Corporal of the Guard! Post Number Two!"

Grant looked up when he heard the call of the sentry.

"Rider approaching!" the soldier called out. "Corporal of the Guard! Post Number Two!"

Grant forgot the administrative chore. He grabbed his hat and rushed out to the Post Two. The guard position was the farthest forward, looking out onto the desert. He arrived at the spot at the same time the corporal of the guard appeared.

The sentry was nonplussed at both the appearance of the commander and the noncommissioned officer in charge of his relief. He decided to let protocol slip as he presented arms, saying, "Rider coming in, sir and corporal."

Grant looked out into the desert. He could see the rider, easily identifiable as Eruditus Fletcher, coming toward them in his now familiar slouching posture on the back of his faithful horse Plutarch.

Grant turned to the corporal saying, "You're dismissed

back to the guard tent. I'll greet Mister Fletcher." He nodded to the sentry. "You're staying sharp and awake, soldier. You had to be alert to spot Mister Fletcher so far out."

"Thank you, sir," the dragoon said. "After seeing them two poor fellers the other day, I ain't dozing much even when I'm rolled in my blankets at night."

A few minutes later, Eruditus rode up and dismounted. "What is it you soldiers say? Mission accomplished?"

"That's it," Grant said. "Come on over to my tent. I've some hot coffee there."

"I'll take advantage of that invitation, Captain," Eruditus said. "But I must warn you. I've been spoiled by General De La Nobleza. A most gracious and generous host. My God! Fresh vegetables, excellent liquor, first rate cigars from all over Latin America, a wonderful—" He shook his head. "Never mind. Let's get to your tent so I can tell you of my visit."

The two walked across the camp to the captain's tent. A dragoon appeared to lead Eruditus's horse to the picket line. The soldiers said, "We'll treat him to a feed of oats, Mister Fletcher."

"Don't bother," Eruditus said. "That old glutton has been living like a king's pampered stallion in a fine stable. He's been feeding on the very best."

Grant smiled as they sat down around the campfire. "It would seem that both you and Plutarch have been basking in the lap of luxury."

"That we have, Captain." Eruditus helped himself to coffee, then pulled an envelope from his shirt. "De La Nobleza, because of pressing duties, is not able to visit us here. However, this is a personal invitation to you from the general to make an official call on him at his headquarters."

Grant opened the missive, noting it was in Spanish. His rudimentary knowledge of the language picked up in Texas along with what he'd learned of Latin, aided him in understanding the words that had been written down in a fancy, pompous style. "Well, I most certainly will visit the general."

"I've managed to pick up quite a bit of information on our scalphunters," Eruditus said. "Though I must confess the information came from conversations I had with border ruffians in a cantina in the town of Juntera."

"I take it that the general was not exactly candid in regards to the bounty payments he had been making," Grant said. "But that's understandable. If I were dealing with a foreign power, I would be close-mouthed about my operations as well." He got himself a cup of coffee. "But tell me about our scalphunter, Mister Fletcher."

"His name is Roberto Weismann," Eruditus said. Then he added, "I know him."

"Strange name," Grant commented.

"Strange man," Eruditus said. "His father was German and his mother Spanish. In fact, the elder Weismann and my own sire were acquaintances. Not friends. Acquaintances. Roberto gets his arrogant cruelty from his father, who literally enslaved Indians to run a gigantic rancho in Sierra Madre."

"How did he come to know your father?" Grant asked.

"They were both in the cattle business," Eruditus explained. "Mister Weismann had decided to branch out and open a cattle ranch in Sonora. He and my father cooperated on a few undertakings. Of course when the Apaches stole Weismann cattle, he reacted violently."

"What about your own father?" Grant asked. "How did he deal with the Indians?"

"He gave them so many head of beef animals a year in exchange for them not raiding him," Eruditus explained. "You may consider that the payment of tribute, but it established a relationship of sorts with the Apaches, and they honored the agreement. It was a cruel attack of bandidos who wiped away our ranching enterprise, not any treachery on the part of the Indians."

"Very interesting," Grant said. "But tell me about Weismann. How did he handle the situation of having his cattle stolen?"

"He fought back savagely," Eruditus said. "The Indians soon learned to fear and loathe him. They, too, battled ferociously. The result was that Weismann and his wife were killed in an Apache raid. I'm afraid they did not die pleasantly. Young Roberto Weismann, only ten years of age at the time, witnessed their final degradation and agony. In fact, he was made a captive and lived with the Indians for several years."

"So he knows the Apaches well, does he?"

"He was adopted by an old medicine man who treated him quite well," Eruditus said. "But there was no affection from the boy toward his benefactor. He never forgave the Apaches for killing his parents. When he was near manhood, he deserted the tribe and returned to civilization."

"You say he *deserted* the tribe?" Grant asked.

"He had gone through the initialization and rites of becoming a warrior," Eruditus said. "He had, to be realistic, become one of them."

Grant took a bite of salt pork. "What did he do when he was once again among whites?"

"A man does what he is best at," Eruditus said. "If he happens to have been trained as an Apache fighting man, he turns to fighting for hire. Anybody, anywhere, anytime—that was Roberto Weismann. When the Proyecto de Guerra law went into effect, he became a professional scalphunter."

"He must be an excellent fighting man," Grant said.

"When I was in Juntera, they told me he had been there a week or so previously," Eruditus said. "Some of his men became ambitious. They attempted a coup d'etat, as it were, and Weismann killed them."

"Well!" Grant said. "I'll certainly be glad when Roberto Weismann is out of Arizona Territory."

"So you should be, Captain," Eruditus said. "He has absorbed both the best fighting qualities and worst cruelty of whites and Apaches. In addition, he has learned some lessons along those lines from the Mexicans."

Grant finished his coffee. "Then may God protect us all from Roberto Weismann."

Eruditus nodded in agreement. "Amen!"

Chapter Ten

The hacienda, its yellow adobe walls bright in the afternoon sun, was situated on a low hill that barely rose from the flat desert terrain that surrounded it.

Two hundred yards away, closely observing the fortified edifice, a pair of travel-dusted horsemen had reined up. One of them, Eruditus Fletcher, astride Plutarch, pointed to the large structure. He spoke to his companion, Captain Grant Drummond, saying, "That, my young Captain, is the home and headquarters of General De La Nobleza."

Grant, wearing civilian clothing, but sporting a military belt, holster, saber, and canteen, scrutinized the impressive layout. "The Mexican army evidently pays handsome salaries to its general officers, or furnishes them excellent quarters."

"I can give you a negative answer on both points," Eruditus said. "That extravagant abode is not the property of Mexico. The entire complex is owned outright by De La Nobleza."

"Do all Mexican generals own their own headquarters?" Grant inquired. "I find that hard to believe if they are not afforded lavish salaries."

Eruditus laughed. "While it is true they are not paid well by their government, they have the extraordinary privilege of making extra money when opportunities present themselves. That is not a legally established right, but this country's government looks the other way when its public servants seek to garner extra income and property."

"I do not consider that a good system," Grant said.

"Perhaps it isn't," Eruditus replied. "But through the secret and subtle benefits of his office, De La Nobleza is able to provide himself with luxurious accommodations and, I am quite certain, is also filling his coffers to provide himself a comfortable old age."

"Not to mention his present living conditions," Grant said. "He certainly isn't depriving himself of anything in the life he now enjoys."

"That is evident in what we now see with our own eyes," Eruditus said. "Once we are within yon walls, you will think yourself the guest of a European prince."

"General De La Nobleza must be the champion of champions when it comes to military entrepreneurs," Grant said. "I suggest we continue on our way."

"As you wish, Captain Drummond," Eruditus said.

It took but a few minutes before they came to a second halt. This time they had reached the entry of the hacienda. A sharply attired Mexican soldier, standing beside a sentry box, snappily presented arms.

Eruditus announced, "Aqui esta el Capitan Drummond del Ejercito de los Estados Unidos de America."

The guard went to a small opening in the gate and exchanged a few words. Within moments the heavy portals swung open. A well-uniformed man, wearing heavy epaulets and a plumed shako, marched out. He rendered a salute, saying in excellent English, "I am Captain Perez, adjutant to his Excellency General Antonio Eduardo San Andres de la Nobleza, the military commander of Northern Sonora."

Since the officer spoke in their language, Eruditus switched to that tongue. "I am pleased to present Captain

Grant Drummond, the American military commander of southwestern Arizona."

Grant saluted the other officer. "Forgive me for not being in uniform," he said. "But I thought it prudent to travel in civilian garb."

"Of course, Captain," Perez said. "That was a wise decision on your part. I assure you that your sensitivity will be well appreciated by His Excellency. I will have you escorted to your quarters. Please feel free to avail yourself of the household staff until I see you again."

"Thank you, Captain," Grant said.

A corporal and four privates suddenly appeared, marching up in correct military formation. Two of the soldiers helped Grant and Eruditus dismount while their companions removed the saddlebags from their horses. The two men with the horses led them away toward a stabling area.

"Favor de seguirme, Señores," the corporal said.

The two Americans, trailed by the soldiers holding their saddlebags, followed the man into a door. They went down a hall, finally turning into an area containing several rooms. Grant was taken to one well-furnished bedroom, while Eruditus went to the other.

Left alone, Grant pulled his clothing from the saddlebags. He found a closet with hangers, and he unrolled the uniform he'd brought, hanging it up. As he turned to tend to his other belongings, a middle-aged woman, obviously a maid, suddenly came into the room. Without a word, she took the uniform and went out of the room, passing by Eruditus who stood in the doorway.

Eruditus nodded politely to the woman. "Muchas gracias, Señora."

Grant looked at his friend. "I hope she plans on returning that to me."

"The maid will press your martial attire, Captain," Eruditus said. "And make it more presentable."

"Excellent," Grant said. "After being rolled up and crammed into the saddlebag, that uniform could use some attention."

"I've been informed there are refreshments awaiting us on the veranda," Eruditus said. "Shall we partake of them?"

"Without a moment's hesitation," Grant said. "That was a long, dusty ride from the Vano Basin."

They went outside to a roofed veranda where a table had been set for them. Fruits, pastry, and cooled wine — the bottle set in a dampened clay container — awaited them. A servant, standing by, did not hesitate to serve them as they situated themselves in the wicker chairs.

Grant took the offered wine and sniffed it. After putting a drop on his tongue, his eyes opened wide. "This is an excellent vintage!" His exposure to good wine during his courtship of the French ambassador's daughter had taught him a great deal about the product of the grape.

"The general lives a life of luxury within the confines of this near-palatial fort that would rival anything to be found in the world's greatest cities," Eruditus said. He winked at the officer. "Wait until you sup this evening."

"I feel fortunate that you bothered to return to our crude bivouac," Grant said with a smile.

"As you should!" Eruditus said chuckling. "My devotion to duty knows no bounds." He treated himself to the wine. "I was told on my previous visit that this nectar of the gods is a French import."

"It most certainly is," Grant said. He sipped the drink in a controlled, calculated manner in order to enjoy its bouquet. He took a pear from the bowl on the table and ate slowly and thoughtfully. "It is difficult to imagine that we are in the middle of a desert far from the best examples of civilization. How does the general maintain this establishment in such a barren place? It would seem impossible even with unlimited funds."

"Quite simply, because of the availability of a natural source of water," Eruditus said. "A series of copious springs are located within the confines of the hacienda. In fact, this is one of several oases scattered throughout Sonora. Most have towns grown up around them. This particular one was chosen as his own private property by our host."

"Ah, yes," Grant said. "As you mentioned before, it is the benefit of being a general in the Mexican army."

Captain Perez joined them. He clicked his heels and made a slight bow. "I trust you are comfortable, gentlemen."

"We certainly are," Grant said.

"I am pleased," Perez said. "His excellency has authorized me to tender invitations to you both to join him at supper this evening at ten o'clock."

"Thank you," Grant said.

"If you require anything more, you will find Corporal Gomez at your service," Perez said. "Good day, gentlemen."

Grant watched the officer leave. He turned to Eruditus. "So we dine at ten o'clock? Why so late?"

"It is the common hour of the last meal in all parts of Latin America," Eruditus explained, "The afternoons are hot and dreary, so all work comes to a halt and everyone takes a long siesta. When the air cools down, they return to their tasks for a few more hours. After that, the final meal of the day is enjoyed in the pleasantness of the late evening." He took a sip of the wine. "Most civilized, is it not?"

Grant shrugged, "I'm afraid it would take a bit of getting used to."

"I am already used to it, my young captain," Eruditus said with a smile. "In fact, when I have had my fill of this wine and pastry, I intend to sleep the afternoon away." He bit into a sugar roll. "By the way, if you feel the need of feminine companionship, simply ask the corporal. Your host will gladly see that an attractive wench is supplied for

110

your enjoyment," He chuckled and raised the wine goblet, "At my age, I treat myself to other pleasures."

"I don't believe such conduct to be prudent at the moment," Grant said. "Particularly because of the seriousness of our visit. But I will take advantage of the siesta. A good sleep after a long journey and a delightful snack will make this a very enjoyable day."

For the most part, the hacienda was silent with little activity. The only sound came from marching men when the guards on duty were changed. After that, the stillness and quiet settled down once again over the scene. After spending an hour enjoying the fruit and pastry, Grant and Eruditus decided to retire to their respective rooms for naps.

"One more thing, Captain," Eruditus said stopping at his door. "Leave your boots out in the hallway. You'll find them shined after you wake up."

Grant removed his boots and left them by the door. Then he went inside to divest himself of jacket and vest. He stretched out on the bed pleased to find it boasted a firmly stuffed feather mattress. He turned his mind to the reasons of the visit to the Mexican general until he drifted off to sleep.

Grant wasn't sure how long he'd slept, but when he awoke, he sat up startled. The feel of the bed, the lack of the odor of campfire smoke, and the closeness of the room brought him to abrupt wakefulness until he remembered where he was. He glanced around the room, then swung his legs over the side of the bed and stood up. An inadvertent glance toward the closet showed his uniform hanging there. He went to it to find the garment pressed and brushed, ready to be put on. A rapping at the door interrupted his inspection of the clothing.

Eruditus's voice sounded on the other side. "Captain Drummond?"

"Yes, Mister Fletcher," Grant said. "Please come in."

Eruditus entered the room carrying a pair of well-shined boots. "I believe these are yours."

"Indeed they are," Grant said. "They've not looked this good in years."

"I've ordered us hot baths," he said. "We'll have enough time for a leisurely soak then a change of clothing and a beer or two on the veranda before supper with the general."

Two soldiers carrying a tub of hot water walked up to the door. Without a word, they entered and set the container down. They left soap and towels before making a silent withdrawal.

"My own bath awaits me," Eruditus said. "Shall we meet outside in about a half hour?"

"Fine," Grant said. "See you then."

He looked longingly at the hot water as he began to undress. Within moments he had stepped into the tub and squatted down to submerge himself in the wet comfort. He grabbed the bar of soap, noting its sweet smell as he began to lather up. Being able to give himself a full wash was a welcome change after weeks of bathing out of a basin at the camp. He stayed in the water until it became tepid, then he stepped out and rubbed himself dry with the oversize, thick flannel towel.

Afterward, Grant dressed carefully in the full-dress uniform he'd brought with him. An official meeting with a general officer of a foreign power called for nothing less in the way of attire. The outfit consisted of a double-breasted frock coat of blue, trimmed in gold, with a metallic, fringeless epaulet on each side of the high standing collar. A red sash was worn under the belt and its gold buckle. His trousers were light blue with a gold stripe down each side. Because of the formality of the supper he was to attend, Grant wore the pants outside, rather than inside, his now highly shined boots.

After a careful inspection of himself in the mirror, Grant

strolled out to the veranda. When he saw Eruditus sitting at the table sipping a beer, he stopped short.

"My God!" Grant exclaimed. "You're an elegant sight, Mister Fletcher."

Smiling, Eruditus stood up to display the formal tuxedo, complete with long tail, that he wore. "This is left over from my days back East. Like your uniform, it was crammed in my saddlebags awaiting the proper attention necessary to make it presentable."

"Well, sir, you are a most impressive sight," Grant said. He helped himself to one of the bottles of beer sitting in water in a large pot. He wrested the cork out and took a swallow of the cool liquid.

"And you've wrapped yourself in martial glory," Eruditus said. "I don't think I've seen you in any but a field uniform, Captain. That always consisted of a military item or two along with practical civilian clothing such as buckskins to meet the rigors of the frontier."

"It's strange when two men meet and live in a single type of environment," Grant mused. "When they go to another situation, the change in their appearance can be most surprising for each of them. You are proper enough to step into a New York opera house, sir."

"Thank you very much for the complimentary words," Eruditus said.

Grant glanced around at the hacienda. "At this moment I am trying to figure out why I gave up a lifestyle similar to this to leave Washington City and become a field soldier."

"Any regrets now, Captain?" Eruditus asked.

He was thoughtful for a couple of moments. "I suppose not," the officer said. "I'm following the life I've chosen for myself."

"I thought as much," Eruditus said. "To speak the plain truth I do not miss my own soft existence back East. I am, sir, like you, in my element."

113

They had time for another beer before a soldier showed up to escort them to the dining room. They followed the man through the house and down a series of halls to the other side before arriving at a large room containing a gigantic dining table set with china service and elaborate silverware.

Captain Perez was waiting for them. He showed them to their seats. "His Excellency will be here presently," he said. "Please excuse him, pressing duties occupy his time."

Grant leaned toward Eruditus and whispered, "Especially since he slept the afternoon away."

Captain Perez suddenly snapped to attention, the loud clicking of his heels echoing in the large chamber. "Caballeros! Su excelencia, el General Antonio Eduardo San Andres de la Nobleza, comandante militar del distrito de Sonora Norteno!" He indicated Grant. "Presento el Capitan Drummond del Ejercito Americano."

Grant and Eruditus stood up as General De La Nobleza walked into the room. He smiled broadly, offering his hand as he walked up to Grant. "Bienvenida a mi cuartel-general. Mi casa es su casa."

"The general welcomes you to his headquarters," Captain Perez translated. "He also says his house is your house."

"It is also his headquarters," Grant said softly to Eruditus. He turned his attention back to the general, extending his hand. "Thank you very much for seeing me on such short notice, General. Your polite reply to my request to discuss an important and serious matter is most appreciated."

This time it was Eruditus who acted as the translator. He changed the words over to Spanish. De La Nobleza made another comment which the older American translated as, "Let us enjoy our meal. Then we shall discuss business."

As soon as the four men settled down, a small squad of servants quickly appeared bearing trays of food. The meal consisted of thick steaks, tortillas, beans, and vegetables along with more excellent wine.

General De La Nobleza pointed to a platter of sliced tomatoes. He spoke in halting English, "The Americanos think the jitomates be the poison, no?"

Grant smiled. "In some parts they are called love apples, General, and some people do consider them deadly. But I have enjoyed their taste during my duties in Texas. I assure you, I have developed a fondness for tomatoes." He took several slices and immediately began eating them. "Delicious!"

De La Nobleza laughed. "Si! Delicioso!"

The meal continued with light conversation. Everyone diplomatically omitted any comments about the late war between the United States and Mexico. Instead, the two officers exchanged bits of information regarding their own armies and the units they commanded. The adventure yarns they told involved fights with Indians rather than each other's armies.

Finally, after a desert of delicate pastries, coffee was served. Almost immediately, De La Nobleza became serious. He spoke rapidly, holding the message which Eruditus had delivered to him from Grant.

Eruditus translated, "The general says he has perused the message and is very upset at the possibility that scalphunters under contract to the Mexican government have violated American territory."

"I fear I brought no hard evidence with me at this time, General," Grant said.

The general made a reply which Eruditus interpreted as, "In dealings between gentlemen, the proof of veracity is in their words. No further communication or reports of these crimes is necessary between us."

"Thank you for your trust and concern, General," Grant said. "I sincerely hope there is some way that these crimes can be halted and the culprits kept on this side of the border."

De La Nobleza, after the translation, spoke carefully and slowly. This time it was Captain Perez who acted as interpreter. He took each phrase and changed it to English:

"I will give my personal guarantee that such illegal behavior will cease immediately. I have dispatched several detachments of my brave soldiers to search for evidence of this. At my first contact with the chief contractor of bounty scalps, I will conduct a thorough and vigorous investigation. If he has crossed into the United States of America, I will have him punished severely and void his contract straight away."

"Could the culprit be turned over to us for punishment?" Grant asked.

When he was given the meaning of the question, De La Nobleza smiled apologetically. "I am sorry," he said. "But my government does not allow our criminals to be turned over to foreign governments for punishment. But, dear Captain, you may find that our method of justice is quicker and harsher than your own." He laughed. "I will simply have the head scalphunter put up against a wall and shot."

Grant weighed the words in his mind. "Very well, General De La Nobleza. I will forward a report of what you have told me to my headquarters in Santa Fe. I am certain the American government will find great assurance in your words."

"Excellent," De La Nobleza said through Perez. "Since we are now neighbors, I hope our next meeting will more social and less business."

"My sentiments exactly, General," Grant said.

De La Nobleza nodded with a smile. He stood up and spoke a few words to Captain Perez, then said to Grant and Eruditus, "Buenas noches, caballeros. Me llaman otros obligaciones."

Perez stood up and saluted as the general withdrew from the room. He sat back down, saying, "His Excellency is called by other duties."

"I see," Grant said. "At least I think we've managed to accomplish something here even after only a brief exchange of words."

"If we haven't," Eruditus mused. "Then you can change the name of Arizona to Hell." He turned to a servant, holding up his empty glass. "Mas vino, por favor."

The man poured him another glassful of wine.

Chapter Eleven

The coolness of the desert during the early morning was almost as pleasant as that of the higher reaches of the Culebra Mountains. The day's sun, although now above the horizon, had yet to turn on the full fury of its fiery blast as Grant Drummond and Eruditus Fletcher, accompanied by Captain Perez, stood by the front gate of General De La Nobleza's hacienda. The two guests waited for their horses to be delivered to them. Both Americans were dressed for the return ride to the dragoon bivouac north in Arizona.

"I wish you would take my advice and travel during night hours," Captain Perez said. "It would be much more comfortable."

"Normally we would," Grant said. "But duties press heavily on me at the moment."

"At any rate, I sincerely hope you enjoyed your stay with us," Perez said.

"We certainly did," Grant answered. "We don't get much of a chance to enjoy the better things of life at our primitive bivouac."

"Knowing that will double the general's pleasure of being your host," Perez said. "However, it is unfortunate that the visit had to be so short. His Excellency sincerely regrets that his obligations as a host were interfered with by unexpected complications arising within his jurisdiction as a military commander."

"Perfectly understandable," Grant said. "Tell the general I only know too well the pressures of administering to a governmental district."

"I suppose the important thing is that you were able to voice your concerns to His Excellency regarding the scalphunters," Perez said.

"I have every confidence that General De La Nobleza will take the appropriate actions required by the situation," Grant said. "I'm returning to my command with a great sense of relief. Because of General De La Nobleza's help, the scalphunters will soon be gone and we won't have to worry about any Indian troubles on the Vano Basin."

Perez smiled, saying, "I give you my personal assurance that he will. After all, peace rather than war is especially better for soldiers."

Two soldiers came around the stables leading old Plutarch and Grant's mount. One of the Mexicans stepped forward and took the Americans' saddlebags, securing the containers for the return trip. The task was followed by snappy salutes, then the troopers returned to their duties.

Grant offered his hand to Perez. "Tanto gusto de conocerle, Capitan!"

Perez raised his eyebrows. "So, you speak Spanish after all, Captain?"

Laughing, Grant shook his head. "Mister Fletcher taught me the phrase. I fear that is my full knowledge of your language although I have picked up various words and phrases in Texas."

"I recommend you acquire fluency in it," Perez said. Then he added, "Since it has been spoken in Arizona for quite some time now."

Grant didn't miss the point. "English will be edging in

119

now, I believe." Then he added, "Of course the Spanish-speaking inhabitants will continue to add the benefits of their cultural influence to the region."

Eruditus interjected, remarking, "As a linguist I find that one cannot acquire enough skill in various languages. Each one is like a separate life one is allowed to live. Also, more friends are gained when it is possible to communicate with a wider circle of people."

"Well expressed, Señor Fletcher," Perez said. "I wish to communicate with you gentlemen just how pleased I am to have made both your acquaintances." He shook hands with Eruditus in turn. "Vayan con Dios. Go with God."

"Gracias!" Eruditus called out as he swung up into the saddle. "Hasta la proxima!"

"Adios!" Perez said bidding them farewell.

The sentries opened the gate to allow the visitors to canter from the hacienda out onto the open desert country. Grant and Eruditus immediately turned north, heading directly toward the Vano Basin.

As they rode out of sight of the hacienda, neither traveler spoke for a long time. They settled into the journey, slowing down a bit as the sun continued its climb into the sky and rapidly heated the countryside under its growing strength. The distant horizon, which had been sharp and distinctive, dulled into a muddled vision of dancing heat waves. The baking desert day was now upon them.

The horses' hooves made a sharp staccato on the sandy terrain during the steady ride. Barrel cactus, standing as mute tributes of defiance of the unforgiving climate, seemed a scattered, leafless forest of dull green thrown down haphazardly on a moonscape. Now and then one of the desert's small creatures created a scurrying sound as it scampered about in the sparse underbrush of agave and yucca plants.

It was Grant who broke their self-imposed silence as he spoke what had been on his mind since leaving De La Nobleza's hacienda. "Do you think we accomplished our mission, Mister Fletcher?"

"Do I detect a hint of pessimism or even mistrust in your tone?" Eruditus asked.

"I cannot bring myself to completely trust a man who has risen to the top in De La Nobleza's world of bribery and corruption," Grant said. "But I must hope the general is a sincere and honorable man."

"Only time will tell, Captain," Eruditus replied. He glanced over at his companion. "Well now, we've traveled across the desert together, shared a campfire, and drunk a Mexican general's wine as his guests, have we not?"

Grant, puzzled by the question, acknowledged the remark with a nod of his head.

"Then, why do we remain so formal with each other?" Eruditus said. "I have absolutely no objection if you address me by my Christian name. It is Eruditus."

Grant laughed. "Then, Eruditus, my friend, my name is Grant."

"Grant it is!" Eruditus exclaimed. "Amacitia usus feret," he added in Latin.

"Friendship brings familiarity," Grant translated. "But to get back to the conversation, Eruditus. Please give me your opinion of General De La Nobleza and his intentions toward our problem."

"As far as I can determine, he has been sincere and truthful with us," Eruditus said. "Would it be that your lack of confidence is no more than perhaps what could be called a concursus humanior — a clash of cultures?"

"To tell you the absolute truth — I don't know," Grant admitted. "Being an American officer, I am not used to dealing with a military in which the acquisition of wealth seems to run hand-in-hand with serving the nation. I've yet to know any man entering the United States Army thinking that he'll be gaining money and property in the performance of his duties."

"Let us not be too harsh on our Mexican neighbors," Eruditus said. "We must remember they inherited much of their governmental philosophies from Spain. Those early Spanish administrators were originally conquistadors who came to the New World looking for wealth and power. The fact that many were impoverished noblemen or adventurers drove them here. They fought and conquered not only to serve their King, but to also acquire as much material gain as possible."

"The cause behind the situation matters nothing to me. I shall never completely trust General De La Nobleza," Grant Drummond said. "I would be as much at ease dealing with an Arabian potentate."

"Let us hope any misgivings you feel are unfounded," Eruditus said.

Once again the two travelers lapsed into thoughtful silence as they traversed the harsh, lunarlike plain of the desert. Pushing on through the growing heat, Grant and Eruditus continued northward toward the dragoon camp. A few hours later, the sun topped its journey across the sky and beat down on the barren terrain from straight above with a boiling persistence that sapped the strength of even the well-nourished horses who carried the officer and scout.

Eruditus took a breath of the hot air. "I suggest it is time we take a brief siesta and let the worst heat of the day wear itself out on this sandy soil rather than us and our faithful mounts."

"An excellent suggestion, Eruditus," Grant said. He took a sip of lukewarm water from his canteen. "God never meant for men to live in this hell."

"The Creator evidently never passed that information to the Apaches and Mexicans," Eruditus replied with a chuckle. "Perhaps. He put so much bravado and stubbornness in both those races simply to have one of his deserts inhabited."

The pair halted to shelter in the small comfort offered by the shade of a close-packed group of barrel cacti. They moved slowly, making absolutely no haste as they prepared to wait out the worst part of the day. They would have preferred to be kinder to their animals by removing saddles and blankets, but the territory held too much danger in the way of bandidos, Apaches, and other human predators who roamed the desolate wilderness far away from civilization.

Two hours passed in which the men sweated heavily, drinking sparingly from their canteens while their horses endured the heat in the dumb acceptance of the discomfort they neither understood nor questioned. Grant and Eruditus spoke little, napping in turns as each stood short stints of guard duty. It was difficult to see through the haze of heat, but the clear air made any sounds sharp and distinct.

Eventually, a slight lessening of the smothering inferno indicated it was time to resume the route back to Arizona and the waiting waters of the Pool-Beneath-the-Cliff.

Grant got to his feet and stretched. He looked over at Eruditus who knelt beside a large cactus, peering out into the desert during his stint as sentry.

"Shall we resume our journey?" Grant asked.

The older man stood up. "As good a time as any if we must do so in daylight in order to save a few hours," he acknowledged.

"I only wish we had the luxury of no pressing duties that would allow night travel," Grant said.

They led their horses from the cactus grove and swung into the saddle. It took little to get their mounts moving again despite the heat. The animals instinctively knew they were on their way home. Within moments, the routine of the trip had been fully resumed by both men and beasts.

The sound of distant hoof beats rapidly approaching was picked up simultaneously by Grant and Eruditus. Both men took quick looks to the east to see numerous horsemen bounding over the horizon heading straight for them. The group definitely did not seem a friendly one. This appearance of hostility was confirmed within moments by the sound of shots that sent bullets whipping through the air.

"Son of a bitch!" Grant instinctively yelled.

"My sentiments exactly!" Eruditus echoed.

Not having the luxury of time to consider the strange event, they kicked their mounts into a gallop, moving slightly westward to increase the distance between themselves and the unexpected company. The incoming fire decreased, showing the pursuers had given up wild shooting in order to close in to bring the encounter to a quick finish.

Grant and Eruditus rode hard, glad they had given their horses a chance to rest in the heat. Only luck had allowed them time to leave the grove of cacti. If they'd been caught inside the prickly cover, their pursuers would have been able to pick them off at leisure.

Eruditus glanced back and noted the pursuers had gained on them a few yards. He knew of a hardpacked plateau less than a mile ahead. If he and Grant reached it first, they might be able to pick up a bit more speed. He shouted at his friend, then turned in the direction he wanted to go. Grant, immediately understanding, galloped alongside, trusting in the older man's knowledge of the countryside.

Within a few minutes they reached the area. The sound of the horses' hooves changed on the parched, hard earth and their speed increased. But suddenly more riders appeared from the west, firing at the two men who rode for their lives. This more recent threat forced them back to the east, into the path of the original pursuers.

Grant glanced at both groups numerous times, trying to estimate their numbers. It was hard to do, but he figured the original group was the larger with approximately ten men. The latest band seemed to have no more than a half dozen members. But one thing was for certain—all those giving chase rode fresh horses. That meant this was no accidental meeting between prey and hunter. The men chasing Grant and Eruditus had planned the event many hours before putting it into effect.

Grant knew that simply making a run for it only put off their deaths. Being a professional soldier, he lived by the motto of instant, aggressive action when in a dangerous position. Many times an unexpected reaction to attackers threw them off balance.

Grant drew his Colt revolver and yelled over at Eruditus to get his attention. "Hey!"

Eruditus waved back with an answering, "Hey!"

Grant pointed to the smaller group, and pulled his horse directly in their direction. Eruditus, whose only handguns were a pair of single-shot .54 caliber percussion pistols, drew one of them and followed closely behind the army officer.

The western group of attackers seemed surprised by the move, but they pressed on. Three scattered shots could be heard popping out over the pounding of hooves. The bullets went wide of their mark as Grant and Eruditus pushed on.

Grant leaned forward in the saddle, gripping the Colt as he closed in. He picked out one man in front of the others and headed straight for him. When the pursuers fanned out a bit as they drew closer, Grant stuck to his target. A couple of minutes later, they closed in and he raised the pistol. Aiming as best he could at the bandido's chest, he pulled the trigger. The fellow flipped over the back of his saddle.

Eruditus, close behind, swung up his pistol and blasted at another horseman close by. Yelling in angry pain, the rider swayed in his saddle as he turned away from the fight.

Grant's impromptu attack gained them the advantage of putting more distance between themselves and the attackers. He took a quick look to the rear to see the riders coming to a stop to turn around.

Eruditus stuck the fired, useless single-shot pistol back in its holster as he rode on after Grant. They swept down a draw and back up onto level ground. Nothing lay ahead of them but open country, studded by cacti and other desert plants. Even reaching the international border at Arizona gave no guarantee of escape in what was really a no man's land.

Grant let Eruditus draw up beside him as they continued on their way. Another rearward glance showed that both groups of pursuers had now joined together and once again drew closer in that wild ride across the barren terrain.

Another few minutes of galloping brought a shadowy view of the Culebra Mountains on the horizon. They were an unreachable sanctuary, hours away at a distance their horses could never reach before being overtaken.

As they continued their flight, Grant fell back a ways to allow Eruditus to use his superior knowledge of the countryside to lead them on. The officer gave the pursuers as much attention as he dared. Even quick sightings made him aware that the bandidos seemed well-organized as they kept to their formation in a tightly controlled group. Their disciplined and coordinated conduct stuck in his mind as the chase went on. But at that particular time, all he could concentrate on was escape rather than mulling over any impressions given by their antagonists.

Another quarter of an hour showed that Grant's horse and faithful old Plutarch were slowing. Both animals, valiant and strong, gasped in the dry heat, long strings of thick saliva now running from their mouths.

Eruditus pulled closer to Grant shouting, "Another mile or two and we shall be run to ground like cornered foxes!"

"Any good defense positions in the area?" Grant yelled back.

"Nothing!" Eruditus bellowed.

Grant stood in the stirrups and looked in vain for even a slight depression. But the desert was like a table top — flat, open, and terribly empty.

Then his horse stumbled and went down.

Grant went over the animal's neck and hit the ground hard, rolling with the momentum of the fall. Aching and bruised, he scrambled rapidly to his feet and rushed back to the fallen horse. As he pulled his long gun — a Hall breechloading carbine — from the saddle boot he was aware that Eruditus had come to a stop, wheeled around and galloped back to him.

"Don't be foolish!" he shouted. "I can delay them here."

Now holding his rifled musket, Eruditus dismounted and joined him. "I thought we declared we were friends, Grant Drummond."

"So we did," Grant said. "But for the love of God! That doesn't mean we both must die!"

Eruditus laughed without humor. "Now why don't I have an appropriate, dramatic quote in Latin for this situation?"

"Probably because no one has ever survived a circumstance similar to this one in order to utter some brilliant aphorism," Grant said.

"I believe you are right," Eruditus said. The noise of their pursuers galloping and shooting quickly drew closer. "We shall have to discuss this later."

"There will be no 'later' for us, my friend Eruditus," Grant said. "Get the horses down!"

They pulled on the reins of their well-trained mounts, getting the animals to lie down on the hot ground. As they took refuge behind the living cover, bullets kicked up small geysers of sand.

Chapter Twelve

Captain Grant Drummond, as an officer who shunned staff duties, had acquired plenty of fighting experience during thirteen years of army service. His exposure to combat had run the gamut from carefully planned and orchestrated battles to the free-for-all hell of spontaneous ambushes and clashes. The harsh lessons learned in those life-and-death situations came to the fore as the attackers closed in on him and Eruditus Fletcher.

Reacting to the danger with a combination of knowledge and instinct, the officer issued terse orders as if he were taking a squadron of dragoons into battle rather than facing overwhelming odds with but one companion. As he spoke to Eruditus, Grant kept an eye on the foe, "Take my carbine, if you please."

Eruditus, holding onto his own musket, followed the instructions. "You have a defense worked out, my friend?" he asked as he also watched the horsemen drawing rapidly nearer. "Or perhaps some tactical plan has leaped into your mind." Then he added, "I most sincerely hope."

"It has," Grant said. "Fire the long guns at opportune targets beyond pistol range. As they come in closer, you reload. As you prepare for your next volley, I'll bring my Colts to bear with two or three shots."

"So our strategy is that I shall handle them afar, and you when they draw close," Eruditus said. "An excellent plan, I must say! Its simplicity belies the intelligence behind it."

"I think we should do a bit less talking and more acting, if you please," Grant said politely.

"Your point is well taken," Eruditus said.

Grant continued to watch the horsemen coming at them. "I expect they will try a ride-by at first before actually attempting to charge into us."

By the time their brief conversation ended, there was no time for anything but action. Eruditus aimed his musket over his horse Plutarch into the now close-packed formation of attackers. He fired, and could see one fall to disappear into the dust kicked up by the horses' hooves. A second shot sent one of the attacker's mounts crashing to the ground. The older man immediately turned to the task of reloading.

Now Grant waited a few moments to let them draw in a bit closer. Kneeling behind his mount, the captain raised the revolver and fired two evenly spaced shots as they swept past. One more attacker slammed into the desert floor. "Get ready, Eruditus! They'll be charging directly into us the next time!"

Eruditus, with both long guns loaded, held his trusty musket. "Sum paratus et maneto — ready and waiting!"

"I see you have your Latin back," Grant remarked as he did his own reloading of the revolver cylinder.

"It may seem incredible, but many times, physical danger inspires the intellect," Eruditus said. Laughing loudly in desperate humor, he added, "We need a death song like the Indians have. A nice, dark ditty!"

Grant also laughed uproariously in the nervous excitement he felt. "Sorry! I haven't time to compose one at the moment." The combined exultation of anger and fear brought robust emotions to the surface as the two men faced what would be their last battle.

"You realize, of course, that we are both mad!" Eruditus observed.

"I've always found that a bit of insanity helps in situations like this," Grant said with a vicious grin.

"We are not only mad, we are doomed!" Eruditus said.

Grant laughed. "We are mad, doomed, and damned!"

"Amen!" Eruditus echoed.

The riders galloped far beyond the two defenders before coming to a halt. It was obvious as they milled around that they were forming up for a coordinated attack.

Grant watched the conduct of the attackers. "I swear to God!" he exclaimed. "Those are soldiers. They must be."

"Either that or well-drilled bandits, hey?" Eruditus remarked.

"I don't suppose we'll ever be able to find out," Grant said.

Eruditus reached down and patted Plutarch's shoulder. "Patience, old fellow. Soon you'll be in equine paradise where there are no such things as saddles, bridles, or the violence of men."

"Just lush meadows," Grant added. "And mares in a permanent state of heat."

"I wonder what awaits us in the afterlife," Eruditus mused. "Oh, never mind. We shall soon know." He glanced at his companion. "Unless you are considering surrender, friend Grant."

"To be quickly executed?" Grant asked.

"Perhaps slowly rather than quickly," Eruditus remarked.

"Either way, I think not, friend Eruditus."

"I agree one hundred percent," Eruditus said. He pulled one of his single-shot pistols from his belt and handed it to Grant. "Take this one and I shall keep the other. When the final moment comes, we can decide whether to take down another of the attackers or put a ball into our own brains. Bandidos can be as cruel to captives as Apaches."

"Thank you, friend Eruditus," Grant said taking the single-shot pistol.

A movement by the horsemen caught Eruditus' attention. "Here come the blackguards!" he exclaimed.

The attackers swept forward in well-formed ranks. Now Grant and Eruditus could see that four of the men in the front had lances.

"By God!" Grant exclaimed. "Those sons of bitches are sure as hell soldiers not bandidos! Look at their formation! All they lack are uniforms and banners."

With no time for comment, Eruditus took aim at one and fired. The man jerked as the musket ball slammed into his body, but he managed to keep to the saddle and to pull his horse to one side although he dropped his lance. Now, using Grant's carbine, the older man waited a couple of seconds then fired again. He cursed as he missed and, ignoring the thundering hell bearing down on them, turned to his reloading chores.

Grant picked out one of the lancers. He waited, holding his breath, as the riders roared at them. At the last moment, he aimed the Colt and squeezed the trigger three times. The closeness and density of the attackers made it impossible to miss. Two men went down, the latter a lancer whose weapon struck point face into the earth a few yards away as the man pitched over his horse's head.

The closeness of the attackers' horses disturbed Plutarch and Grant's army mount to the point they forgot their training. Neighing in excitement and fear, they lurched to standing positions. Both men grasped desperately at the reins, but the animals galloped out to join the horsemen before their owners could react. But within moments, other instincts took over and the two animals turned north toward the dragoon camp still far away. The homing instinct was strong enough in their limited equine intellects to overcome the raw fear they felt.

"We have been deserted!" Eruditus exclaimed.

"At least those poor beasts will survive," Grant said.

As the attackers regrouped for another assault, the army officer took advantage of the brief lull. He ran out and retrieved the lance. He went out a few more yards and grabbed the second belonging to the man Eruditus had wounded. Running fast, he returned to their defensive position.

Eruditus had just finished shoving powder and ball down the musket barrel. As he tamped it down with a ramrod, he said, "I am sure you have a reason for picking up those weapons, Grant. Just what do you plan on doing with them?"

"Waterloo," Grant answered breathless from his run. "British square—French cavalry."

Eruditus cocked the hammer and placed a cap in place. "Not much of an explanation, old friend, but I shall trust to your reasoning."

Shouts from the riders preceded the next attack. Eruditus, with the carbine ready waited for them to come back close enough to fire. At the right moment, he let loose a shot that sent another rider sprawling to the sand.

"Well done!" Grant shouted.

Eruditus's second firing, done with the carbine, unseated the third lancer. "That's more like it!" he shouted as he grabbed his powder horn.

Grant, now firing, got the fourth and last lancer, but his other shots missed as the thundering group of attackers again passed by. He glanced over at Eruditus. "How stands your powder and ball, my friend?"

"I fear that particular well is going dry," Eruditus said. "I can only fire each weapon twice more."

"My predicament too," Grant said. "I count that we've killed seven and wounded two. I've finally managed to gauge their strength."

"I would say our defense has been quite good so far," Eruditus said.

"But not good enough," Grant remarked.

"Again, I must agree with you. There are a dozen of the rotters left," Eruditus said. "I, too, have been keeping score. Even if all our remaining shots counted, there would still be eight survivors to dispatch us to Valhalla. We cannot win."

"I did not see a victory to begin with," Grant said. "We are outnumbered, cut off, and without much cover. The only thing that has been working for us is their misplaced bravery so common in Mexican soldiers. Whoever is commanding them is more exuberant than prudent. He is wasting the lives of good troopers. I saw a lot of that during the war."

"I've always felt the Mexican people deserved better leaders than they have been burdened with," Eruditus said.

"That goes double in their army," Grant said. "I believe these particular troops belong to our old and dear friend General De La Nobleza. There is no other military command in this region."

"I am inclined to agree, though with sadness and reluctance," Eruditus said.

"That means we could never surrender and expect honorable treatment even if they are not bandits," Grant said.

"Of course not," Eruditus said. "We would be immediately executed to cover up General De La Nobleza and his scalphunters' illegal excursions into Arizona." He looked outward. "No time for further conversation, Grant. They are coming at us once again!"

The shouted commands in Spanish could barely be heard in the gusts now whipping across the desert. The Mexicans charged forward in another coordinated attack, their ranks properly aligned.

Eruditus aimed carefully and squeezed off a shot. He gritted his teeth as he missed and grabbed the carbine. It helped that they were closer and he managed to drop another as the horsemen closed in. Grant followed with a couple of shots, but could bring none down.

"Their thinning ranks have reduced targets of opportunity," the army captain remarked.

Another charge followed with the same results. Grant and Eruditus fired their final shots from the Colt and long guns as the attackers once more thundered past their position.

Grant picked up a lance and tossed it to Eruditus. "Keep this on the ground beside you. Act as if we still have ammunition, but when they close in, plant the butt of the lance on the ground and point it upward at about a forty-five degree angle toward the horses' chests. At the moment of collision, roll away or be trampled!"

"Is this what the British infantry did to the French cavalry at Waterloo?" Eruditus asked. "I am not particularly well-versed in that period of history."

"Yes," Grant said. "Except the British used bayonets on the end of muskets rather than lances. Of course they were much more numerous, and formed into squares."

"We must do what we can," Eruditus said positioning the bladed weapon beside him.

The Mexicans now abandoned all pretense that they were common bandidos. A bugle sounded as more commands were shouted to the assembled soldiers. A drop in the wind made the officer's order easy for Grant and Eruditus to hear:

"Al ataque!"

Both defenders, to give the appearance they still had powder and ball, aimed a useless long gun at the men bounding toward them. Grant judged the distance as best he could. When he was ready, he shouted, "Now!"

The younger and older man each grabbed a lance and

planted the butts into the ground. Using hand-held weapons put the fight in an entirely new perspective for Grant and Eruditus. The Mexican horses looked twice as big and the pounding of their hooves seemed like thunder.

"Oh, my God!" Eruditus exclaimed. "We are going to die!"

"Be brave!" Grant shouted as contact with the charging beasts was but a split second away. "Raise the blades!"

They pulled up the lances so the heads aimed straight at the horses' chests. When contact was made, the shafts of the weapons bent, then broke on contact as the horses ran themselves straight onto the lances. Both animals neighed in pain, lurching and stumbling. Their riders, bellowing in furious surprise, crashed to the ground.

One of the Mexicans, unhurt, got to his feet and swung his carbine around to fire. But Grant rushed toward him, slamming him hard across the head with the barrel of his Colt. The man's skull cracked open under the blow and he rolled to the ground, twitching as he died.

The second rider, a bit slower and dazed, managed to struggle to his knees and fire at Eruditus. He missed, but Grant grabbed the other attacker's carbine and shot the man dead.

"Look!" Eruditus exclaimed pointing to the surviving riders. "They know we have no more ball or powder."

"Except these," Grant said indicating the single-shot pistols.

"I'll not take my own life. I elect that we kill a couple more of them, then go to our Maker vanquished but unbowed," Eruditus said.

"Very well, friend Eruditus," Grant said pulling the one-shot weapon from his belt. "Let us go out in a blaze of glory."

Eruditus licked his lips. "Now that the final moments are here, I must confess to a rather sharp stab of fear, Grant.

What exuberance I felt before has melted like snow under a hot sun."

"I feel the same," Grant said. "But I'll be damned if I'll let those sons of bitches know it." He forced a grin. "Besides, this won't take long."

"That is not a particularly cheerful thought," Eruditus said pulling back the hammer on the pistol and checking its percussion cap.

The Mexicans, less than fifty yards away, now laughed and shouted at the two Americans.

"Digan sus ultimas oraciones!" one yelled.

"He is bidding us to say our last prayers," Eruditus translated.

The Mexicans leisurely formed up for a final charge. They drew out the maneuver, making it last as long as possible. They hooted and whistled at the two forlorn figures who awaited their last moments on earth.

A shot, fired from a distance sounded, and one of the riders jerked backward, then crashed to the ground from his saddle. Other reports detonated and two more of the attackers went down. The survivors wheeled about, then suddenly jerked the reins of their horses and galloped off toward the east.

Grant and Eruditus stood in astounded silence for a moment. Then they noticed a nearby cloud of dust kicked up by numerous horses approaching. As the riders drew nearer, their identity was easy to discern.

"Dragoons!" Grant shouted. "By God, those are Dragoons!"

Moments later a detachment, led by Sergeant William Clooney,. rode up. The troopers had Plutarch and Grant's mount with them. The sergeant quickly dismounted and saluted.

"We heard the shooting about a half hour ago and wasn't sure where it came from 'til these two animals came loping

137

towards us," he said. "We traced their tracks back and finally got on the right trail." He looked at Grant and Eruditus. "Are yez alright then, sir?"

"We are fine, by God, Sergeant!" Grant said. "And extremely happy to see you."

"I've been patrolling out toward the border since yez left, sir," Clooney explained. "I reckon I never felt easy about this whole thing."

"I'm very happy you took precautions," Grant said. "We've run out of ammunition and fought off the last charge with lances."

Clooney looked at the Mexican horses, now dead, lying a few yards away with the remnants of the spearlike weapons protruding from their chests. He also noted the two remaining lances lying side-by-side in the sand. "At this point, sir, I'd say it was a good thing this patrol didn't tarry after we discovered yer mounts."

"Indeed!" Grant said. He took a deep breath. "At least we can rest a bit easier now, hey, Eruditus?"

"It would seem so, Grant," the older man said.

"Begging yer pardon, sir," Clooney said. "But ye can expect more trouble up there on the Vano Basin."

A feeling of cold dread replaced the one of near euphoria Grant experienced at being rescued. "Now what has transpired during our absence?"

"We've discovered several dead Apaches, all scalped, a few miles to the north of here," Clooney reported. "They was a hunting party o' sorts, and they was definitely Chirinatos."

"All scalped you say?" Grant asked.

"It was the sun reflected off'n the top o' their skulls that attracted us to the spot, sir," Clooney said. "There was plenty o' hoof marks around—hoofs wit' horseshoes, sir. We was going to follow the trail, 'cept yer mounts come into view."

Eruditus asked, "Am I to assume the trail left by the murderers is easy to follow?"

"That it is, Mister Fletcher," the sergeant responded. "Them murdering devils is pretty sure of theirselves."

"Do you have enough ball and powder in the patrol to supply Mister Fletcher and me?" Grant asked.

"Yes, sir!" Clooney answered. "I come out here expecting big trouble, sir."

"Excellent!" Grant exclaimed. He laid a hand on Eruditus's shoulder, "Do you feel like another battle, my friend?"

"With the scalphunters? I most certainly do!" Eruditus replied with feeling.

"Then this day of fighting hasn't ended," Grant said. "Sergeant Clooney! Take us back to the bodies. We're going to find those killers and put an end to their degradations today!"

The nearby dragoons listened grimly, knowing that before that day's sun set, more blood would be spilled on the Sonoran Desert.

Chapter Thirteen

The dragoon patrol could see the circling buzzards in the sky for a long time before they reached the place where the bodies of the seven scalped Apaches lay scattered and violated under the broiling sun.

Sergeant Clooney looked up at the loathsome birds floating on the air currents. "There'll be more of them rotten-meat eaters on the ground than in the sky," he said. "It's gonna be a hell of a sight when we get there."

"We can take comfort in one thing, however," Eruditus said. "The fact that those scavengers are there means the dead have not been discovered and removed by the Chirinatos."

"They'll find out about this eventually, but at least we won't have a war yet," Grant said. He turned to his men and ordered in a loud voice, "Gallop, ho!"

The column broke into a faster gait, quickly covering the ground to where the crime had been committed. Upon arrival, they found the Indian corpses lying in undignified positions from the rolling and twisting done by the scalphunters during the mutilation. Hunks of flesh had been torn from the cadavers by the strong, sharp beaks of the buzzards.

Eruditus slid from his saddle and hurried over to the dead men, kicking and swatting at the birds who fed on the dead men. "Fly! Fly! Filthy fowls! This is not carrion! These are dead people!" He watched the buzzards, squawking in anger, take to the sky. The old man gestured at them in an apologetic manner. "Ah, forgive me, feathered ones. You are only doing what the Creator has meant for you to do." Then he turned his attention back to the dead people, immediately recognizing a couple of them.

While Eruditus inspected the cadavers, the dragoons, under Sergeant Clooney's supervision, spread out and formed a defensive perimeter in case of trouble from an appearance by Indians or the return of the scalphunters. The soldiers' expressions were tense as they kept a sharp lookout.

Eruditus Fletcher could not take his sad eyes from the dead warriors. He shook his head, muttering, "I know three of these fine fellows. Their losses will be keenly felt by the Chirinatos. This means a plethora of grief and anger among the tribe. I fear Lobo Cano will have trouble containing any angry reaction on their part."

Grant had dismounted and joined him. "Let us hope we can catch the scalphunters and avert any rampant vengeance against innocent travelers," the captain said. "How does the trail look?"

Eruditus examined the ground. "Sergeant Clooney was correct. The arrogant rascals made no effort to cover their tracks at the site. We shall have to see if they took precautions later on."

"Lead on, Eruditus, my friend," Grant said. "But be cautious. Those fellows are no fools. We don't want to stumble into an ambush."

"Perhaps if a stalwart dragoon were to accompany me, and stay close he could keep watch on the surrounding countryside while I study the ground," Eruditus said.

"Sergeant Clooney!" Grant said. "Dispatch one man to escort Mister Fletcher."

141

"Yes, sir!" Clooney pointed to a dragoon. "Donegan! Cover Mister Fletcher while he reads sign."

"Yes, Sergeant," Donegan said. The old soldier rode forward and dismounted beside the scout. He winked at Eruditus. "Sure now, Mister Fletcher, and I'll keep them devils off'n yer back then."

"I appreciate that, Mister Donegan," Eruditus said. "We may be a hoary pair, but we'll do our job proper enough."

"Right y'are," Mister Fletcher," Donegan agreed.

"Then let us go straight away and find the rotters as quickly as we can," Eruditus said.

"After you, sir," Donegan said.

Eruditus walked around the bodies, studying the ground. "There're possibly a dozen of them," he called out. Finally he pointed to the northwest. "They've gone in that direction."

"Then so shall we," Grant said.

Eruditus swung back into his saddle and rode slowly forward, his head bent down as he noted the tracks. Private Donegan, quickly assuming his duties, rode directly behind the scout. The dragoon's carbine was at the ready as he scanned the surrounding terrain for any sign of possible trouble.

Grant organized the patrol so that one man rode on each flank, charged with keeping an eye to the right and left. Another pair, working together, watched the rear. The rest of the horse soldiers followed behind Grant and Sergeant Clooney in the main column. They maintained a distance of some fifteen yards from Eruditus.

The experienced old scout had been correct in assuming the scalphunters would take care not to leave a trail when they had gotten out a ways from the scene of the murders. After traveling a bit less than a mile, they had left the soft, sandy areas to ride across more rocky terrain where their horses would leave no hoofprints. The murderers obviously went out of their way now and then to travel across the more solid ground in an attempt to cover up the direction of their route.

Their tactics did not stop Eruditus. However, in spite of his experience, the old man was slowed a bit. He dismounted and walked slowly along, almost bent double as he studied scrapes on the stones. He noted the freshness and direction of the marks made by horse shoes. Now and then a pile of horse dung gave away the passing of the killers. He also found a spot where someone had urinated. Although the puddle itself had evaporated under the sun's heat, a dampness between the rocks remained. Such signs did not escape Eruditus's practiced eyes.

Finally he held up his hand to signal a halt. Jumping back into the saddle, he returned to the column with Donegan close behind. "We are not closing the distance between ourselves and those devils," Eruditus said. "But we are drawing nearer to the foothills. Because there is a possibility the rascals might lay an ambush, may I take the liberty of suggesting a scouting party take a wide look around while the remainder of the men stand fast?"

"Most excellent advice," Grant said. "I shall put your counsel into immediate operation."

A few quick commands sent four of the dragoons out on a reconnaissance. The seasoned troopers made a wide circuit of the spot where the column waited, taking special precautions when approaching the cover offered in the bottom reaches of the mountains. Two of the men dismounted and, with their comrades covering them, went into the growing vegetation to search out any potential ambushers who might be lurking there. In half an hour, the pair returned to their horses and mounted up for the ride back to the column.

The senior horse soldier reported directly to Grant Drummond. "Sir," he announced saluting. "I can tell ye fer sure that them foothills is as empty as a trooper's pockets the first morning after payday."

"Thank you," Grant said. He nodded to Eruditus. "Shall we proceed now?"

"Yes," Eruditus said. "But alertness is of the utmost importance now. I am of the opinion those mutilators did not think it necessary to go very far into the mountains to rest between their dastardly crimes."

"Excellent!" Grant said. "That means we shall catch them that much sooner! I would like for you to continue your scout with Private Donegan, Eruditus. The rest of us will hang back a bit until you're hot on their trail. Then, depending on the circumstances, we will move in for the attack either on foot or horseback, whichever is the most advantageous for us."

"Very well, friend Grant," Eruditus said. He called over to the dragoon, "Come now, Mister Donegan. Let us seek out the lair of this particular pack of wolves."

"I'm with you, Mister Fletcher," Donegan said cheerfully.

The pair moved out once again. Eruditus, on foot, searched back and forth until he found the track that satisfied him. Then, with the ever-alert Donegan guarding him, he moved into the brush to begin the slight ascent up into the foothills.

Eruditus walked like an Apache, deliberately picking up his feet with each step, and setting them down only when he was sure no twig was present to be loudly snapped or rock to be accidentally kicked into a noisy roll. Close behind, the veteran soldier Donegan did the same, having to take even more precautionary measures because of his heavy boots.

They traveled in an agonizingly slow zigzag pattern, moving approximately fifty yards in one direction before going upward a few feet and heading back in the opposite way.

They continued the activity for an hour before Eruditus suddenly stopped. As Donegan kept a sharp eye around their location, the old man dropped to his knees. He carefully examined the ground, brushing away some twigs and leaves. Finally he noted a pattern in the dirt as if someone had been sweeping back and forth with a crude broom or a branch.

Eruditus smiled to himself. This was attempt to hide tracks.

He got to his feet and turned upward, moving into the brush and finally found what he wanted. A couple of hoofprints, carelessly missed by whoever had swept the earth, showed plainly. A few paces beyond that were more, this time mixed in with some boot markings. He knelt again, motioning Donegan to join him.

The trooper moved quietly, squatting down beside the scout. "Have you found something, Mister Fletcher?" he asked in a whisper.

"I believe our quarry is close by," Eruditus said. "It is imperative that we move as quietly as possible."

"You bet, Mister Fletcher," Donegan said.

Eruditus rose to his feet, but stayed bent over. He moved even slower at that point, taking advantage of all the cover the increasing vegetation offered. Donegan strained his eyes as he peered through the brush in case of an unexpected encounter with the scalphunters.

A cough suddenly sounded up ahead. The noise startled both men, who immediately stopped in their tracks, remaining motionless.

Now approaching footsteps could easily be heard. Then a sing-song, tuneless humming came into earshot as a man wearing buckskins pushed through the brush. He was an ugly, ill-kempt individual who was badly in need of a decent haircut and beard-trim.

"Here's an excellent example of border riffraff," Eruditus whispered to his companion.

The scalphunter held some wadded up paper in his hand showing that an errand of nature had caused him to wander off by himself into the brush. He stopped, fiddled with his trousers, then squatted to tend to his business. He hacked and spit, then loudly broke wind. He followed that with an enormous belch.

"Disgusting!" Eruditus said under his breath.

"He reminds me of my Uncle Elmer," Donegan said with a grin. "The old sinner could fart the leaves off a tree."

Eruditus signaled Donegan to remain still. He drew his Bowie knife from its sheath and moved forward as the pungent smell of feces wafted up from where the man strained and grunted. A quick hand over the mouth and the blade of the weapon across the throat and deep through the jugular vein was followed by some minor thrashing before the scalphunter died and fell over in his own mess.

"No dignity in that death," Eruditus remarked to himself. "And none deserved by the wretch." He returned to Donegan.

"It sounded as if you took care of him, Mister Fletcher," the dragoon said.

Eruditus nodded, saying, "They are very close. I must check the layout of their camp. Wait here for me. If I've not rejoined you in a quarter of an hour, return to the column and make your report to Captain Grant."

"That I will, Mister Fletcher," Donegan said. "Don't you worry none about that."

Eruditus moved off and Donegan began his wait. The old soldier didn't have a watch, couldn't tell time anyhow, and hadn't the slightest idea how long a quarter of an hour would be. He decided to wait until his instincts told him it was time to go. Frowning at the foul odor of the dead man's leavings, he moved off a ways to bide his time.

After a while, insects began buzzing around the corpse not too far away. Donegan consoled himself with the thought at least the mess over in that direction kept the flying bugs off him. He continued to wait, vaguely wondering how many minutes had passed, when a sudden noise caught his attention. Easing back the hammer on his carbine, he waited. Then Eruditus appeared. The old man winked at him and started back toward the column. Donegan followed as they returned with the same caution used on the short trip out.

When they rejoined the dragoons they found the troopers had moved a ways into the brush. Grant, waiting with Sergeant Clooney, smiled a greeting at his friend.

"From the expression on your face, I assume you found those sons of bitches," the captain said.

"That I have," Eruditus said. "The scalphunters are in a narrow draw approximately a mile in. They seem to feel quite secure and haven't bothered to organize any sort of defense. They are quite vulnerable. It even appears as if each fellow sought out a spot he favored and settled in with blankets and belongings without regard to any potential attack."

"Will the terrain allow a silent approach?" Grant asked.

"Only if everyone is exceedingly careful," Eruditus said.

"Then thank God we have veteran soldiers with us," Grant said. "This doesn't appear to be a mission for recruits." He turned and called out, "Sergeant Clooney!"

The sergeant responded immediately, leading his horse up to the captain. "Yes, sir?"

"Hobble the horses and detail two men as guard," Grant instructed. "The rest will follow us in. The enemy is occupying a small draw approximately a mile up into the foothills. Everyone must take care to exercise absolute silence."

"I'll see to it, sir," Clooney said. He left to tend to the job at hand.

In ten minutes the entire column was ready to move to the attack. Eruditus and Grant went to the head of the formation as they slowly entered the foothills and began the short climb to where the scalphunters had camped.

Noise discipline was superb as the dragoons moved through the brush. A half hour of slow travel brought them to a spot where Eruditus signaled a halt. Grant went forward a couple of yards and joined him.

The scout pointed ahead. "You'll be able to see their bivouac from those bushes ahead. Watch your step. There is a rather messy cadaver on the way."

Grant sniffed. "It smells like a latrine around here."

"You'll see why in a bit," Eruditus said.

Grant, every nerve of his being alert, stalked forward. He passed the dead man with his pants down lying in feces. Flies covered both the filth and the body. The captain reached the proper place and took a careful look.

The camp in the draw was informal with no guards posted. It was evident that Eruditus had been correct in his assumption that the murderers felt secure in the combined cover of the brush and the dip in the ground. All it took was a few moments of observation to form a plan in his mind. Then he returned to the column.

Clooney stood waiting for orders. "The patrol is ready, sir."

"Divide the men into three even groups," Grant said. "One for the left side, one for the right, and the remainder to stay with me. We will move forward. When I open fire, the attack will take place. Have the groups on the flanks close in to cut off any escape attempts while we in the center carry the main thrust of the attack."

"How many of 'em is there, sir?" Clooney asked.

"About the same number as we are," Grant said. "But the element of surprise will work quite favorably for us."

"I won't take long, sir," Clooney said.

The sergeant's word was good. Within moments, the attack formation moved forward with Grant leading the way. When he reached his observation point, he was glad to note there was no change in the scalphunters' lack of alertness. He picked out a particularly obnoxious looking fellow, and took careful aim with one of his Colts. The dragoon officer squeezed the trigger and felt the weapon buck as it fired. He was instantly gratified with the sight of the scalphunter lurching, then falling to the ground.

The rest of the patrol responded immediately with both pistols and carbines. The slugs whipped through the undergrowth cutting small branches, kicking up dust, and slamming into bodies.

One man squatting over a kettle of beans took a direct hit in the forehead. Bits of skull were blown through his hat as he sat down then simply fell over on his back. Another, near him, who lay dozing on his blankets, took three shots that rolled him over several times. He was dead before he came to a halt.

Another fellow, instantly full of fight, fired his revolver in the brush although he couldn't spot any of the dragoons attacking the camp. His boldness cost him an immediate slug in the belly. Yelling in pain, he sunk to his knees, but continued to blindly shoot back. A round to the shoulder spun him halfway around on his knees while another ended his life by smashing into the side of his head.

Down at the far end of the draw, Roberto Weismann and Penrod Donaldson scurried to the dubious cover offered by some stunted bushes. With guns drawn, they waited for targets to appear.

"Do you think it's Indians?" Donaldson asked.

"Quien sabe?" Weismann answered. "But I think not. Their firing is too well organized."

Suddenly a shouted command could be heard and a quick volley smashed into a trio of scalphunters who tried to run up one side of the dip in the ground. Two tumbled back to the bottom of the draw, but the third continued on in spite of having to limp badly from a bullet in his thigh. The wounded fellow managed to reach to top when a dragoon showed himself just enough to deliver a vicious buttstroke with his carbine.

The murderer fell back with his nose smashed and bleeding. A couple of shots finished him off.

"Soldiers!" Weismann exclaimed. "Por el amor de Dios! Let us leave this place now."

"I'm with you," Donaldson said.

The two scalphunters had tied their horses to some heavy brush a few yards away as was always their habit. They crawled deeper into the brush before being able to get to their feet and rush to the animals. Although the mounts were unsaddled, the pair took no time to prepare them for a ride. They immediately led the horses away from the one-sided battle until reaching more wide-open terrain. After hastily slipping onto the backs of the horses, Weismann and Donaldson rode away, the sound covered by the shooting.

Back at the draw, Grant shouted, "Cease fire!"

Immediately the well-disciplined troops stopped shooting. An eerie silence filled the glen as the dragoon officer led his men into the camp.

Sergeant Clooney spat. "No survivors, sir."

Grant glanced at Eruditus "It would seem we've solved our own problem in a most unexpected manner."

"Perhaps so, Grant," Eruditus said. He found a leather bag and opened it. "Oh, my sweet God in heaven!"

"What is it?" Grant asked.

"Fresh scalps," Eruditus said.

"We shouldn't have any more of that now that we've destroyed this band of murderers," Grant said.

"Let's not forget the Chirinato Apaches, Grant," Eruditus cautioned him. "If we can keep them from making any vengeance raids on travelers, then we will have finally brought peace to the Vano Basin."

"These bodies should satisfy our Indian friends, should they not?" Grant asked.

"I sincerely hope so," Eruditus replied.

Grant holstered his Colts with a smile. "This could well be the last blood shed in this part of Arizona."

Meanwhile, now out on the desert, Roberto Weismann and Penrod Donaldson held to their precarious seats during the wild bareback ride toward the hacienda of His Excellency General Antonio Eduardo San Andres De La Nobleza.

Chapter Fourteen

The condemned man sat in the corner of the bare, unfurnished cell. The only thing between himself and the cold stone-slab floor was a thin blanket.

The day before he had been concerned with saving his life. During the court martial he'd pleaded as eloquently as possible, damning his lack of formal education, as he gave his side of the situation. But his case was weak, the capital charges he faced were numerous, and the prosecution strong. All that made the outcome of the trial inevitable.

A few years previously, when he'd been promoted from the ranks to a lieutenancy, the prisoner had never dreamed one day he would be sentenced to the firing squad for botching a battle. Particularly one in which the men he commanded outnumbered the enemy by more than ten-to-one.

The man, named Montoya, cursed his bad luck, muttering, "Madre de Dios! Chinga la mal suerte que me plaga!"

General Nobleza himself had ordered Lieutenant Montoya to take two sections of soldiers dressed in civilian clothing to chase down the American officer and the old Gringo who had come to visit at the hacienda. The orders were terse and to the point: Track the foreign pair and kill them.

To be chosen for such a mission was a great honor and he'd wasted no time in telling his proud wife how the general had such confidence in him.

"Surely you will soon be a capitan!" she had exclaimed.

"With a capitan's pay and the opportunity to earn some extra from bribes and other undertakings, we will be rich!" Montoya told her.

Happy in the thought his life was about to get better, Montoya took his platoon out and tracked down the Gringos, finally running them to ground after a weary chase. Cocky and self-assured, Montoya had seen the action as a chance to give his men some good sport by having them charge back-and-forth past the two Americanos to enjoy some shooting at live targets before delivering the final blow.

But the pair had fought back stubbornly and well, finally reaching a point where they staved off a final charge with the lances of Montoya's own men.

Then, at almost the exact moment he was ready to order the final killing charge, the American dragoons arrived on the scene and drove the Mexicans away. This resulted in the embarrassed lieutenant having to report to His Excellency that the easy attack had been routed. General De La Nobleza was furious, ordering an immediate court martial and sentence of death in one breath.

"Please, Excelencia," Montoya had begged. "Give me one more chance! I will die before I fail again!"

The general thought that funny. He laughed and said, "That is a certainty." Then, with a snap of his fingers, he had called two guards to make the arrest. "Take him away for the punishment he so richly deserves."

Now, with his execution only a short time away, Montoya was no longer concerned with any futile hopes of survival. All he worried about now was dying well. Several of his acquaintances were on the firing squad, and he wanted them to be able to tell his four sons that their father had died bravely. He shrugged with resignation as he thought of his wife. Within six months she would be the woman of another officer. But that was only right. After all, she was young and very pretty.

The sound of marching feet interrupted his thoughts. Montoya wasted no time in standing up. He wanted them to find him at a dignified position of attention, looking soldierly in spite of the spoiled uniform he wore that had been stripped of all buttons and insignia. Better that than cringing in the corner of the cell looking like a whipped dog.

The door opened and Captain Ricardo Perez stepped inside. He nodded in approval at the sight of the courageous prisoner. "Buenos dias," he greeted him.

"Buenos dias, Capitan," Montoya responded. At least having General De La Nobleza's personal adjutant in charge of the firing squad was an unexpected honor. Montoya almost thanked him.

"Listo?" Perez asked.

"Yes," Montoya answered. "I am ready."

The prisoner marched outside and positioned himself between the double row of riflemen who would soon be blasting the life from his body. He dully noted that the sun had just began to rise, casting the hacienda compound in a weak, reddish light. Not a cloud showed in the sky.

"It looks like another hot day, muchachos," Montoya said with forced bravado. He laughed. "If it stays this way my widow will have to spend a lot of time watering the flowers on my grave, eh?"

"Que hombre!" one of the soldiers exclaimed in unabashed admiration.

Perez wanted to get the job over. He barked orders and the group paraded from the guard house across the width of the open area to a bullet-pocked section of wall. This wasn't the first time that particular part of the hacienda had been used to dispatch a condemned man, nor the first time for the priest waiting there to hear the last confession.

The firing squad halted and the prisoner went forward. He knelt by the priest and tended to the final religious ceremony of his life. After receiving the blessing, he got to his feet, keeping his shoulders back. He turned and faced the firing squad.

"Do your duty, soldiers," Montoya said in a firm voice.

The priest made the sign of the cross over the doomed prisoner while Perez brought the firing squad into the proper formation.

Waiting until the padre had moved out of the way, Montoya asked, "May I have the honor of issuing the commands?"

"Por su puesto," Perez said without trying to hide the admiration in his voice. "Of course."

Montoya took a deep breath. "Atencion!" he spoke in a loud clear voice. "Preparan!"

The half dozen soldiers brought their muskets up and pulled back the hammers.

"Apuntan!" Montoya ordered.

The squad raised their weapons to their shoulders and aimed at the prisoner's chest.

Montoya hesitated only a moment before taking another deep breath and shouting, "Fuego!"

The six muskets blasted, the balls striking true. The force of their impact hurled the condemned man against the wall. He bounced off and toppled to the ground.

Perez pulled his pistol from its holster and approached the body. He knelt down to arrange the corpse in a more dignified position, then put the barrel of the weapon behind the dead man's ear. The coup de grace seemed louder than the musketry as Montoya's head jerked under the force of the shot.

Perez stood up and walked toward the hacienda's main

building as some specially hired peones carrying a wooden casket rushed from the shadows to pick up the cadaver.

Perez went past a sentry, going into the rambling adobe structure to walk down a long hall to the dining area. He found General De La Nobleza eating breakfast with his faithful servant Luis standing by to serve him.

"Lieutenant Montoya has been executed, Excellency," Perez said.

"Former lieutenant," De La Nobleza corrected him. "If you recall, we stripped him of his rank at the court martial."

"Of course, Excellency," Perez acknowledged.

"At any rate, I heard the shots," De La Nobleza said enjoying a sweet roll. "How did he die?"

"He asked to give the commands himself," Perez said. "His last moments were those of courage."

De La Nobleza smiled. "Ah! All my officers and soldiers are brave men. It makes me proud!"

"The entire battalion will speak of his valor," Perez said. "Montoya set a good example."

De La Nobleza scowled. "You should say his death atoned for his stupidity in letting the Gringos escape."

"Of course, Excellency," Perez said. "I did not mean he was undeserving of being executed."

"Make sure the men understand that," De La Nobleza said. "I will have no martyrs in my command unless they benefit me personally."

"Yes, Excellency!"

"Very well," De La Nobleza said. "Now sit down and have a cup of coffee. The present situation about the Apache scalp bounty must be discussed."

Luis stepped forward and served a cup of the hot brew to the officer as he settled into a chair at the table. Then the servant returned to his station by the door and waited until he was needed again.

Perez scooped several generous spoonfuls of sugar into

the coffee. "Do you think the Gringo officer was fooled into thinking bandidos had attacked him and the old man?" Perez asked.

"I do not know," De La Nobleza answered. "They were dressed for the part, were they not?"

"Yes, Excellency," Perez answered.

"Whether they were duped or not makes little difference," De La Nobleza said. "If the situation is handled correctly, we will still be able to earn silver pesos from the scalps of those Arizona Apaches."

"You are correct, of course," Perez said. "Provided nothing happens to Señor Weismann."

"I have faith in Don Roberto," De La Nobleza said. "There are many Chirinato Apaches scattered about El Vano. The chance to earn much money will sharpen his skills and intelligence."

"I hope so," Perez said taking a sip of coffee.

De La Nobleza frowned. "You do not seem optimistic, Capitan."

"Perdoname, Excelencia," Perez said. "But the American impressed me as an excellent soldier. The fact that he and the old man managed to hold off an overwhelming number of our men until help arrived makes me cautious about the campaign to lift Apache hair in Arizona."

"He has a small force," De La Nobleza said dismissing the other officer's worries with a wave of his hand.

"But how do you know that, Excelencia?" Perez asked. "Con permiso, but this is a question that must be asked."

"I appreciate your candor about sensitive issues as this one, Capitan," De La Nobleza said. "But do you not think that if the Gringo had a large, strong force he would bother to come here to ask me to help in controlling the scalphunters? He would have dispatched his troops to search out and destroy any interlopers in that land the Gringos have taken from us."

"I think I understand, Excelencia," Perez said. "You are correct, of course."

De La Nobleza smiled. "That is why I am a general and you are a captain."

"Yes, Excelencia," Perez intoned respectfully.

A hard knocking at the door interrupted further conversation. Luis strode over to the portal and answered the summons. Moments later he hurriedly returned. "It is el sargento de la guardia, Excelencia," Luis said. "He wishes to inform you that Señor Weismann and Señor Donaldson are outside requesting to see you."

"Send them in immediately!" De La Nobleza ordered. "Madre de Dios! This can only mean trouble!"

Captain Perez finished his coffee, secretly smiling to himself with the knowledge that Captain Grant Drummond had evidently not waited long to strike the scalphunters. Perez was smart enough to keep his satisfaction of being right while De La Nobleza was wrong, undetectable. His mind told him, "Al infierno con el general! To hell with the general! He is mistaken in his judgment of the Gringo officer. That Captain Drummond will not be an easy man to do away with."

Luis fetched the two unexpected visitors, admitting the pair of disheveled, nearly exhausted men into the presence of the general. Roberto Weismann wasted no time in speaking.

"Where in hell did those Gringo soldiers come from?" he demanded to know.

Such impudence from anyone else would have sent General De La Nobleza into a rage. But his admiration and respect for Roberto Weismann helped him to keep his temper under control. "An unfortunate incident, Don Roberto. And I fear it was brought about through the incompetence of one of my own officers."

Perez quickly added, "Who was summarily executed less than an hour ago."

Penrod Donaldson smirked. "Was that the funeral going on outside the walls there as we rode in?"

"It was," Perez said coldly. He still did not like the Gringo.

Donaldson, despite being dirty, rumpled, and tired, chuckled. "I could see some of your officers already giving the grieving widow some admiring glances." He laughed aloud. "I got to admit she was a pretty sight in that black dress and shawl."

"Perhaps widows appeal to you because they are unprotected women without men," Perez said in cool anger.

"Damn right!" Donaldson said.

"Luis!" De La Nobleza barked. "Do not stand there like a stupid burro. Fetch refreshments for Don Roberto and Señor Donaldson."

The sarcastic grin hadn't left Donaldson's face. "So I'm Señor Donaldson and not Don Penrod, eh?"

"Correcto!" De La Nobleza said. "The title of don is reserved for gentlemen."

"Well, now, I've never claimed to be that," Donaldson said sitting down before being invited. "Manners and all that shit is just something that ain't part o' my nature."

Luis quickly saw to it that coffee and rolls had been provided to the pair of scalphunters. He turned to the general. "Shall I have rooms prepared for Don Roberto and Señor Donaldson, Excellency?"

"Of course!" De La Nobleza said. "From the looks of them, they have come through a most unhappy experience."

"We damn near got kilt," Donaldson said. "We even had to ride hell-for-horseflesh bareback to get outta there in one piece. Ain't that right, Roberto?"

Weismann nodded. "And we were forced to leave seven male Apache scalps behind."

"Que paso?" Perez asked. "What happened?"

Weismann spoke while Donaldson downed his coffee and roll with loud slurps and smacking of his lips.

"We had bivouacked in a draw located in the foothills of the Culebras," Weismann said. "A couple of hours previously we had ambushed and scalped a hunting party of seven Chirinatos."

"All men like Roberto told you," Donaldson interrupted. "That was a loss o' seven hundred pesos, by God!" He punctuated his anger with a loud belch.

Weismann continued, "We were all very tired and since there was no other sign of Indians in the vicinity it seemed safe enough to rest up for a day or two. The concealment in the area was excellent. We had found a small barranco — a ravine."

"Lucky for me and Roberto we was down on the far end from the attack," Donaldson said.

"Most of the men had settled in and were napping or playing cards when the charge was launched," Weismann said. "It was handled very expertly. Fire came at us from the center and both flanks. Most of the muchachos were caught and killed without realizing what happened," Weismann said. "Those that fought back did not last much longer."

"Were all your men killed?" De La Nobleza asked.

"All were hit," Weismann said. "I do not know if all died."

"That means Capitan Drummond might have a prisoner or two," Perez remarked.

"Capitan Drummond?" Weismann asked. "Who is he?"

"The Gringo commander," Perez said. "He had come here asking us to help in ending the scalphunting."

Donaldson burst into laughter. "Now ain't that a caution!"

"He did not know His Excellency was involved," Perez said. "But if he has captured any of your men alive, he may well know now."

Weismann glanced at De La Nobleza. "He will send a message to that effect to his headquarters."

De La Nobleza reached over and nudged Perez. "Dispatch a half-dozen men up to El Vano. Have them watch the area of the Gringo camp. They are to intercept and kill any dispatch riders either in or out of that place. I suggest you send Lieutenant Montoya."

"We have just executed him, Excellency," Perez said. "I suggest Sergeant Valverde. He is an excellent scout and tracker."

"Very well," De La Nobleza said. "Remember to have them wear civilian clothing. Now see that it is done, Capitan!"

"Inmediatamente!" Perez said getting to his feet. He rushed off to tend to the matter.

Weismann, who had yet to touch his refreshments, finally took a sip of coffee. He was silently thoughtful for several long moments. After awhile he asked, "How many Gringo soldiers are there in El Vano?"

"Not many," De La Nobleza said. "That is why he came here seeking assistance from me in ending the scalphunting."

"Of course," Weismann said. "That makes sense. His force probably wasn't much larger than my own. The element of surprise weighed in his favor."

"He prob'ly figgered there was only a dozen or so of us when he tracked our happy bunch to that ravine," Donaldson said.

"The Gringo will not do that to me again," Weismann said.

De La Nobleza's worries had begun to melt away as he noted that Weismann gave no sign he was beaten. "You are thinking over the recent developments, are you not, Don Roberto?"

"I most certainly am," Weismann assured him. "I believe the situation is salvageable. Or at least we can keep things going our way long enough to get plenty more scalps before a larger force of Americanos shows up to force us to withdraw."

"What is it you wish to do, Don Roberto?" De La Nobleza asked.

"I need money to recruit more pistoleros in Juntera," Weismann said.

Donaldson snapped his fingers at Luis. "Mas cafe, damn it! More coffee!" He turned to Weismann. "You ain't gonna get enough gunslingers there to fight soldiers, Roberto."

"I realize that," Weismann said. "That is why I will need some soldiers from here to augment the force. If the Gringo camp is kept isolated, we can wipe them out."

"Right!" Donaldson said. "Then we can turn on them goddamned Injuns and scalp 'em down to the last yowling papoose!"

Perez returned and reported, "Sergeant Valverde and six good soldiers will be on their way to El Vano within the hour, Excellency."

"Thank you, Capitan," De La Nobleza said. "Now I have another job for you. Take command of the Second Company. You and those soldiers will also dress as civilians. You are going to to El Vano to attack the Gringo soldiers."

Perez smiled and clicked his heels. "With pleasure, Excellency."

"You will accompany Don Roberto and Señor Donaldson to Juntera where they will hire more gunmen for the expedition," De La Nobleza continued.

"I am pleased to hear that," Perez said. "I appreciate having even more men under my command."

"They will not be under *your* command, Capitan," De La

Nobleza said. "You, the soldiers of the Second Company, and the hired gunmen will *all* be under the command of Don Roberto."

"I must protest, Excellency!" Perez exclaimed. "I am an officer in the army!"

De La Nobleza's expression turned sinister. "Do you recall what happened to the last officer in the army who displeased me, Capitan?"

Fresh memories of Montoya being shot by the firing squad flooded Perez's mind. He swallowed hard. "I will be most happy to serve under Don Roberto, Excellency."

Weismann got to his feet. "Let us get moving! There are Gringo soldiers to kill."

He hurriedly left the dining room with Donaldson and Perez on his heels.

Chapter Fifteen

The hooves of the horses kicked rocks loose, sending the stones clattering down the narrow trail as the dragoons slowly made their way into the higher reaches of the Culebra Mountains.

Now and then an abrupt, angry expletive was uttered when someone accidentally allowed a limb to snap back and hit another trooper in the face.

"Watch it!" Sergeant Clooney snapped. "We're moving slow enough for yez to watch out fer the man behind."

The column's lack of speed could be attributed to the fact that each man in the formation led a second horse. These extra animals bore not only the cadavers of slain scalphunters across their backs, but also the dead men's belonging which had been quickly stowed into the saddlebags of the former owners. The only items not packed for this trip were the firearms and shooting accoutrements found in the camp, along with any liquor.

Nine horses carried these gruesome burdens. The tenth dead man had been left where he died. He was the one caught in the act of defecating, and knifed to death by Eruditus Fletcher. This particular fellow was left to rot in his own filth. Not even Sergeant Clooney, who had no problems with ordering troopers to perform disagreeable chores, would force one of his men to take charge of that mess.

This particular corpse's belongings now rode atop those of another deceased scalphunter.

There had been no survivors among the scalphunters after the attack. All had fought to the death. The one exception had been found inside his tent. To everyone's surprise, a quick investigation revealed this death to be a suicide. He had evidently shoved a pistol in his mouth and fired it, splattering the inside of the canvas shelter with blood and brains.

"I would assume he thought their camp had been attacked by avenging Apaches," Eruditus told Grant after examining the self-inflicted wound. "No doubt he preferred a quick death to the slow, drawn out agony the Indians would have forced him to endure."

"That's a shame as far as I'm concerned," Grant said. "Not out of any misguided pity, I assure you, but I could have used a prisoner for interrogation. We are woefully lacking in information about this scalphunting situation."

"I hope we have ended these unhappy circumstances here and now," Eruditus said. "To assure this, I have a most strong suggestion. We must take these dead and show them to the Chirinatos. They will be impressed if they see we have already avenged their dead."

"Yes," Grant agreed. "Perhaps any young hotheads among the warriors can be dissuaded from attacking innocent travelers crossing the Vano Basin if they see we have already taken prompt action."

"We should also turn over the belongings of these wretches to the Indians," Eruditus said. "Such an act will go a long way in soothing angry grief."

"Then we shall," Grant said. "An excellent suggestion as usual, Eruditus."

"Only too happy to help," Eruditus replied with a smile.

After loading the scalphunter dead and their possessions on extra horses sent out from camp, the column left the scene of the attack to meet with the Apaches. Upon reaching the place where the scalped Chirinatos had been found, the dragoons discovered the bodies had been removed during the time of the attack on the murderers' camp.

Eruditus had been worried. "Now it is most imperative that we speak with the tribal council. If the tribe does not hear about our killing of the mutilators, they will go to war en masse."

"You are right, of course," Grant said. "And time is of the essence. Meanwhile, I am going to dispatch a rider back to departmental headquarters at Santa Fe to request additional men and supplies. At least that way we shall be able to handle any more trouble that might be forced on us."

"Excellent!" Eruditus said in approval.

"I want you to ride ahead and make arrangements for us to meet with the tribal council," Grant said. "For God's sake! Tell them we've killed the men who murdered their clansmen."

"Of course," Eruditus said. "I'll waste no time at all in taking care of that matter. I shall be sure to mention the presents we have for them and where the gifts came from."

"Have them meet with us in the same place we met before," Grant said. "It is an easy spot to find."

"I shall!" Eruditus said.

"I'll have the column with the bodies up there as quickly as I can," Grant said.

Eruditus, after giving a wave to the officer and dragoons, rode out to meet with his Indian friends.

Now, with Eruditus already in the mountains, and the messenger heading toward New Mexico Territory, Captain Grant Drummond rode at the head of the formation. He controlled his horse to make sure he didn't outpace the men with the extra mounts.

Grant reached the summit of the climb and wheeled

aside to wait for the rest of the detachment. Sergeant Clooney quickly appeared. Then the nine dragoons leading the horses bearing the corpses followed. The dead men bounced and swung grotesquely in movement with the animals on which they were tied. Finally the three-man rear guard led by Corporal Rush came into view.

"Ever'body's present, sir," the corporal reported with a salute. "No stragglers back there."

Pulling on his mount's reins, Grant turned and cantered up the column to the head. Once again he led his men into the wooded area as the trees grew thicker and taller with each ten to fifteen yards of increased elevation.

"Grant!" Eruditus Fletcher's voice sounded in the thickness of the woods. "Ho, Grant!"

"Ho, Eruditus!" Grant shouted back.

The old man rode up to him and reined in. "The council is waiting. As we suspected, they had already recovered the bodies. I feel it is imperative we talk to them as quickly as possible to avert any bloodshed in the Vano Basin." He glanced back at the column. "It is a good thing you are bringing those bodies and the gifts with you. It should save valuable time."

"Don't be modest about your valuable contributions in this sad situation, my friend. It was your idea," Grant said. "Your value on this mission seems to increase daily."

"I thank you for those kind words, but we mustn't tarry," Eruditus said.

The scout led them up to the former spot where the dragoons had picketed their horses. This time, after dismounting, the rear guard took care of the mounts, while the troopers who manned animals with corpses led them forward under Eruditus's instructions.

The Chirinato council, with a good deal of the tribe standing behind them, rose to their feet as the grisly parade appeared. Lobo Cano, the chief, stepped forward and went to each body examining it to satisfy himself of the revenge that had already been taken.

Eruditus's old friend Aguila grabbed the hair of cadavers and lifted up the heads to gaze into the blank features of death. He then checked out the knives the dead men still had in their scabbards.

"Ayee!" he turned to the assembled tribe, crying out, "These are scalphunters! No doubt! The soldiers have killed them!"

Grant stepped forward holding a greasy, leather bag. "Here are the scalps of the seven dead members of your tribe. We bring them to you for the proper ceremonies to honor your departed clansmen."

"Yes," Aguila said. "I must do that because my brother Nitcho has already died under these evil ones' knives." Then he added under his breath, "We have no medicine man because of these dogs." He spat on the nearest body.

Eruditus immediately went to work as a translator for both sides of the meeting.

"You have explained this loss of spiritual guidance to me before," Grant said. "It made my heart heavy when I heard of Nitcho's death. But now I laugh with joy that my men and I could kill your enemies who caused you this grievous loss."

Lobo Cano asked, "Did you kill all of them?"

"We think we did," Grant said. "If some escaped, they will not be many and they will run away back to Mexico. I do not think they will ever be back. There are also the belongings of these killers for your tribe to have. There are blankets, knives, saddles, tobacco, and many other things."

The warrior Quintero shoved his way through the crowd. A furious expression twisted the features of his face. "Where are their guns?" he demanded to know in a loud voice. "Where is their powder and balls and caps?"

"They are for the Big Chief of the Americans," Grant answered through Eruditus. "He wants those things for himself."

"Did they not have whiskey?" Quintero asked.

Eruditus said, "The soldiers took the whiskey. They killed the scalphunters, so they have a right to something."

"Bah!" Quintero spat.

"Why do you want whiskey, Quintero?" Eruditus asked. "I know you do not approve of it or mescal or tequila for Apaches. Do you want to give it to Chirinato warriors so they will get drunk and crazy and follow you to kill people on El Vano?"

Quintero glared at the old man, then spun on his heel and returned to the crowd where his friends waited for him.

Eruditus decided to lighten the situation which had grown darker because of Quintero's words. "We left one of the dead coyotes back where he died," he explained. The old man told of killing the man while he squatted and strained to relieve himself.

The Chirinatos, always appreciative of what tickled their humorous sides, laughed.

"We are glad you did not bring the messy one with you," Aguila said. "He would stink up the whole of the Culebra Mountains."

The Indians renewed their laughter.

Now Eruditus saw an opportunity to hold the center of attention. He walked directly in front of three of the four Apaches who made up the council. Aguila went about carefully examining each of the dead scalphunters.

Eruditus began his talk by saying, "My friend Grant and I went to Mexico to find out who paid the scalphunters to kill Chirinatos."

Zorro, a member of the Apache group, spat. "It is the Mexican soldier chiefs who buy our people's scalps."

"Yes," Eruditus said. "But they are not supposed to do that in El Vano because that is no longer Mexico."

"It never was!" Quintero called out from the crowd. "That is Chirinato land."

Eruditus turned and explained what had transpired to Grant. "This calls for much diplomacy, my friend," he said after the interpreting chore.

"Tell Lobo Cano that the Big Chief of the Americans has told the Mexicans to leave the Chirinatos alone in the Vano Basin," Grant said. "They disobeyed him, so my dragoons and I were ordered to kill them. This we did. The proof of the Big Chief of the Americans' love for the Chirinato people is on the backs of those horses."

Eruditus translated the words to the Apaches, adding, "Now do you believe the Big Chief of the Americans cares for his Chirinato brothers?"

"That is good," Lobo Cano said.

Aguila, who had spent considerable time with the dead scalphunters, walked back to join the group. "But how do we know the Mexican soldier chief will not send even more scalphunters than ever before to come up here?"

"Because they will be afraid," Eruditus said.

"How do we know that?" Aguila asked sitting down with the other three members of the council.

"You will know after I tell you of a great fight my friend Grant and I had with Mexican soldiers sent after us by their chief," Eruditus said. "Everybody sit down."

The Indians all took seats as Eruditus had bid them. The Chirinatos had a tradition of storytelling. They loved to sit and hear the old ones spin yarns involving ancient adventures, battles, and myths of their people. Many of the tales had been heard over and over again, yet they never tired of them. The Indians were especially excited with this opportunity to hear something brand new. Even the ones who had been hanging about at the edges of the discussion pressed forward so Eruditus could tell of the recent battle.

The old man, well-versed not only in the Chirinato lan-

170

guage, but the methods of putting real feeling and emotion in the guttural words, dramatized the tale of the fight with suspense, horror, and even a bit of humor as he dragged out the facts of the incident until the telling took almost as much time as the actual fighting.

His friend Aguila, along with Chief Lobo Cano, Zorro, and Terron of the council, was as spellbound as the other listeners. Each description of the charges of the Mexicans, exchanges of gunfire, and mutual taunts and insults of the fighters brought cries and yelps from the assembled Apaches.

"We stood alone," Eruditus said. "In the middle of the desert completely surrounded by Mexicans. All our bullets were finally gone. We were like two small rabbits facing a pack of coyotes." He gestured at Grant. "But I drew courage from my brave friend. Nothing frightens him. Nothing!"

Grant, unable to understand the words, was a bit confused by the approving grunts and glances thrown his way. He merely smiled and nodded.

Eruditus took extra effort in reciting the details of meeting the final assault with lances. He was particularly flattering of Grant's fighting prowess as he told of how the captain used an ancient method of meeting galloping horses face-to-face with only a stabbing weapon. This was particularly impressive to Chirinatos whose legends were filled with extraordinary deeds performed in hand-to-hand fighting with primitive weapons.

"We knelt there, with the butts of the lances in the dirt and the blades pointing skyward," Eruditus exclaimed. "I think there was fire coming from the nostrils of the Mexicans' horses, my brothers. Those animals wanted us to die as much as their owners."

The part where Sergeant Clooney and the patrol showed up consisted of portraying the Mexicans as cringing before the spiritual bravery of the Americans who, knowing that their Big Chief was behind them, had almost magical fighting qualities. The surviving enemy fled in ignominious defeat and disgrace.

By then Eruditus was enjoying being the center of attention so much that he couldn't stop. He told of discovering the bodies of the seven scalped Chirinato hunters. Even the stoic Apaches wiped at tears as the old man described the anguish of the dragoons at the awful sight.

"Captain Grant howled his grief to the sky," Eruditus said. "Because he knew how his Big Chief would weep when he heard the news of the seven dead warriors." He paused for effect. "Then the anger over came him. Slowly at first, then like the torrent of a flash flood rolling across the desert floor. He bellowed for the blood of the scalphunters!"

The Apaches shouted and yelled so much that Grant and the dragoons became alarmed. Only Eruditus's continued narration showed them all was well.

Eruditus finally brought the story to a finish, orchestrating the tale right up to that same moment as he stood there finishing it up for the most appreciative audience. When he ended, the Apaches began talking among themselves, telling of how much they had enjoyed hearing the man they called Erudito speak to them of those things both wondrous and terrible.

Meanwhile, the old man turned to Grant and gave him a brief description of what had transpired. "Now, my friend," Eruditus said. "You must make appropriate closing remarks. Be sure and mention the dead have been avenged and the Chirinatos do not have to go out to murder any white for revenge."

Grant stepped forward with Eruditus standing slightly behind him. As the army officer spoke, the old scout broke in at appropriate times to translate the words into the language of the Chirinato Apache tribe.

"My brothers," Grant said. "It is my fervent hope that peace will now come to the Vano Basin. It will be good if travelers going to the big waters to the west are able to pass through without trouble. And it will be good if Chirinatos can roam and hunt on the land of the ancestors without worry about murderers killing them for their scalps."

A few of the Indians, mostly the elder, voiced agreement with nods of their heads and low-voiced grunts.

"With no more killings of innocent Indians, there will be no reason for trouble between us," Grant continued. "The Big Chief of the Americans will not be angry with his Chirinato brothers so long as none kill the travelers or make war against us soldiers at the Pool-Beneath-the-Cliff."

The young warrior named Quintero suddenly cried out, "What if we go to Mexico to steal cattle? What will the Big Chief of the Americans think of that?" His friends Chaparro, Bistozo, and Zalea remained close to him.

"He wishes peace between you and the Mexicans," Grant said. "But what you do in their land is between yourselves and them. If they kill you in Mexico, the Big Chief of the Americans can do nothing about it. If you kill Mexicans, he can do nothing about it. But if you kill Americans, he will be angry. He is concerned about peace here in the Vano Basin and across the great desert." Grant paused, gauging the Indians' reaction to his words. He was satisfied. "I have spoken."

Lobo Cano stood up. "I like what the American soldier chief has just said. I think there will be no trouble in El Vano. We know the Big Chief of the Americans has powerful medicine. He has defeated the whole of the Mexicans and made them stay out of places like El Vano. We will be at peace with him because we have learned to trust him."

"That is good," Grant said after Eruditus's translation.

"But if more of our people die, I do not know what will happen," Lobo Cano warned. "The Big Chief of the Americans must make sure the Mexicans and their scalphunters stay away from us."

Quintero, the hot-headed warrior, swaggered forward and lifted his musket in the air. "If one more of our tribe dies by the hands of scalphunters, we will fight everybody! White travelers and white soldiers and Mexicans and everybody outside our tribe along with the scalphunters will be killed!"

Eruditus leaned toward Grant and whispered in his ear, "If you recite prayers at night, my friend, beseech the Almighty to keep General De La Nobleza and his men out of Arizona!"

Chapter Sixteen

The outlaw community of Juntera in northern Sonora was generally a quiet place. The oppressive, heavy, strength-sapping heat of the desert kept most physical activity to an absolute minimum. Because of this, occasional, thundering but brief outbursts of violence marred the long periods of silence in the sun-baked desert town. These disturbances were generally between a few men who had old scores to settle or who, during a wild, brain-boiling drunk, became enraged over an insult or a gambling incident where cheating had occurred.

But a lasting hubbub of activity had been going on in the settlement for more than three days since Roberto Weismann and Penrod Donaldson showed up with more than a hundred and fifty Mexican horsemen. Those unusual riders caused plenty of curious stares, but it didn't take long before the wily people in the village figured out the unusual behavior of the riders, such as setting up an orderly camp and following a routine of waking, eating, and chores was due to the fact they were soldiers in the Mexican army dressed in civilian clothing. Once that was established, everyone began trying to figure out why.

A couple of hours later it became well-known in that small metropolis of sin, that among those troopers was a full captain. Juntera's gossip mill kept grinding at full speed until it became common knowledge on the street that the officer was a rather grumpy young man called Ricardo Perez.

That bit of local intelligence at first caused great concern among the population of mostly temporary inhabitants. Quite a few nervous fellows, wanted for lawbreaking on both sides of the border, suddenly lit out with the fear that the cavalrymen were there to make arrests. The exodus would have been greater, but when the word finally got around that Weismann and Donaldson were part of the group, relief set in quickly. Anybody that knew anything about those two realized they would never be involved in any law enforcement activity.

That knowledge preyed on everyone's curiosity, causing plenty of conversation regarding just what in hell Weismann and Donaldson had to do with the Mexican army. This interest increased a hundred-fold when it became known that Weismann was actually *in command* of the cavalrymen, including the petulant officer!

All the flying rumors and suppositions caused plenty of anxious and excited talk in the cantinas and bordellos of the desert community. The prevalent prattle was that a revolution or mutiny within the Mexican military was in the offing and there existed a very strong possibility that Roberto Weismann was a general in what could only be a planned coup d'etat against Mexico City. Only God knew who might be the power and money behind the plot.

Weismann damned the talk, keeping his reasons for visiting Juntera to himself at first. The scalphunter chief went as far as threatening a couple of particularly nosy inquirers. He did not want to begin a general hiring of pistoleros immediately. Instead, the scalphunter chief and Donaldson — along with Capitan Perez as company — walked Juntera's streets, visiting the cantinas, as the scalphunters noted what particular outlaws had made stops in the town. After spending an entire day simply looking around, the trio retired to a popular cantina to discuss the situation.

When their drinks were served and they were left alone at a corner table, the captain grumbled, "We are wasting time, Don Roberto."

Donaldson shook his head and interrupted, speaking in a scornful tone. "No we ain't!"

"I am not speaking to you, Donaldson," Perez said. "So keep your mouth shut."

The American slapped at his scabbard and had his fighting knife out in an instant. He stretched out his arm so that the point of the weapon was but inches from Perez's throat.

"I don't give a damn if'n you call me Don Penrod or not," he growled. "But, by God, you're gonna call me Señor Donaldson, or I'll cut your damn gizzard out and feed it to the dawgs on the street."

Donaldson waited to see the reaction to his words. When Perez remained stony-faced and impassive at the threat, the American could see he was dealing with a man who wouldn't be intimidated. He replaced the knife in its leather holder.

"You'll speak polite to me too," the American said.

Perez was a brave man who would not back down from anybody under any circumstances. "I lose no sleep in worrying about any threats from you. Comprendes? Therefore, I shall speak to you in any manner that pleases me, Gringo!"

Donaldson leaped to his feet, drawing his pistol. He meant to bring the affair to an end then and there. "Then you'll die in any manner that pleases *me,* Greaser!"

Weismann spoke. "Sit down." His voice was low and calm, but the threat in it was as obvious as a rattlesnake's warning buzz. He said again, "Sit down."

"This feller's giving me more shit then I can take," Donaldson complained.

177

"I don't think the general would be very happy with you if you shot his captain," Weismann pointed out.

"That general don't worry me none," Donaldson said.

"Killing Perez would also upset me," Weismann said in a calm voice.

"I understand, Roberto," Donaldson said. He reholstered his pistol and plopped back in the chair.

Weismann turned to Perez. "You will address him as Señor Donaldson."

Perez started to protest, but the danger he read in Weismann's cold, green eyes caused him to change his mind. "As you wish, Don Roberto."

"That will not be difficult, I think," Weismann said. "It is only a little thing, is it not?"

"Certainly," Perez said.

Weismann began speaking again as if nothing had taken place. "I am not wasting time, Capitan Perez. I have been walking the town to see not only who is here, but what sort of fellows I can expect to hire for the dangerous trip up north."

"Esta bien, Don Roberto," Perez said. "I understand. After all, this is what you get paid for."

"Exactly," Weismann said.

Donaldson took a deep swallow of his tequila. "There was one feller you might not have noticed," he said. "A big'n wearing buckskin and toting a shotgun."

"You mean the one with the red beard?" Weismann asked. "I noticed him."

"Well, Roberto, that is one of the meanest son of a bitches that ever trapped in the Rocky Mountains," Donaldson said. "I don't know him personal, but he used to bring furs into the trading post where I worked and I seen him a time or two at the rendezvous we had up there."

"Que quiere decir 'rendezvous?' " Weismann asked. "I don't understand what that is."

"It's a big get-together when the trappers, traders, Injuns, and mountainmen of all kinds from hunters to wanderers, have a big meet," Donaldson explained. "There's business conducted, drinking, fighting, dallying with Injun women, and anything else that a group a crazy people who been locked away for months in the winter snows can think of doing."

"So you used to see this fellow at those rendezvous, eh?" Weismann asked.

"Yeah," Donaldson answered. "He was a ring-tailed terror, let me tell you. He's never forgive a grudge and if he heard tell of somebody wanting some trouble, then he'd go looking for him. No reason a'tall, 'cept to kill somebody. Even the Injuns was leery of him."

"He sounds perfect," Weismann said.

Perez wasn't so sure. "Are you sure he can be kept under control? We cannot have somebody going about doing as he damn well pleases."

"I reckon the opportunity to earn silver pesos will make him toe the line," Donaldson said. "He always worked hard with other fellers when it come to trapping for fur."

"What is his name?" Weismann asked.

"He's knowed as Wild River Garvey," Donaldson answered. "You want me to go fetch him?"

"Yes," Weismann answered. "I think it would be worth our while to speak with this man." He chuckled in his throat. "Wild River, eh? Rio Cimarron in Spanish."

"I'll be back directly with him," Donaldson said. He got up and hurriedly strode from the bar to search out the strange man called Wild River.

Perez signaled to the barkeep for another round of drinks. "Do you think it really necessary to hire these uncivilized rascals?" he asked Weismann.

Weismann eyed the officer. "Would you and your men prefer to remove the scalps of Apaches?"

"Of course not, Don Roberto," Perez said. "My men are professional soldiers. They have too much honor to—" He suddenly stopped speaking as he realized he was about to insult what Weismann did for a living.

Weismann, however, was not angry. "Soldiers live by a code and scalphunters live by a code," he said. "I would not expect my men to put themselves under military discipline like your troopers. Their jobs are different. Yours are with me to fight other soldiers."

"I am glad you understand what I mean, Don Roberto," Perez said. He took a quick drink of the tequila. "Very glad."

"Then do not worry yourself about such matters," Weismann told him. "Or what sort of men are hired."

"My real concern is that General De La Nobleza be pleased with the outcome of this undertaking," Perez said.

"After seeing that fellow buried outside the hacienda, I can very well appreciate your careful interest in how I handle our operation," Weismann said. "As for me, I am like Penrod Donaldson. I do not fear the general. In fact, someday he may try to hunt me down for some future activity I become engaged in. What I do, I do for money. Do you understand, Capitan?"

"Yes, Don Roberto," Perez said.

"Do not worry, Capitan," Weismann said. "You will not go al paredon—to the wall."

Perez only nodded in reply. The longer he stayed in the scalphunter chief's company, the less he cared for the situation. He had taken on an army commission for glory, to serve Mexico, and to make a small fortune for himself. At least enough to own his own rancho and a nice herd of cattle after a few years of service.

Instead, he now found himself placed most unwillingly under the control of a man who casually murdered men, women, and children, then brought in a portion of their anatomies in order to collect money. Perez remembered peones doing that with coyotes, producing tails as proof of kills. The bad thing was that while it was impossible to work out any agreements with coyotes about killing cattle and sheep, at least an effort could be made to have a treaty with Apaches. Perez certainly harbored no secret affection for those natives of the desert, but that didn't mean it pleased him to kill and mutilate them. His idea to handle the situation of marauders was to meet with the tribal leaders and work out an agreement in which the Indians would be paid with animals to butcher and eat. That left plenty of energy and opportunity to protect the herds from natural enemies.

Weismann and Perez drank slowly and silently for another quarter of an hour. Then the door opened and Donaldson came back into the cantina in the company of another man. The fellow was tall, well over six feet in height, and slim. His long hair and full beard were striking in the bright redness of their color. He was dressed in greasy buckskins, wearing a wide-brimmed, slouching hat that almost covered his heavily bearded face. He wore a couple of haversacks criss-crossed across his body and he sported a shotgun carried casually in the crook of his left arm.

Donaldson led him up to the table. "Roberto, this here is Wild River Garvey."

"Howdy," Garvey said. He spoke broken, but passable Spanish. "This feller tells me I can earn money by killing Injuns. Is 'at right?"

"You must scalp them as proof of the kill," Perez interjected.

Garvey glared at him. "Who'n' hell are you?"

"I am Captain Perez of the Mexican Army," Perez said thinking that another fellow exactly like Donaldson had joined the group. "I work directly for the man who buys Apache scalps."

"I've traded in beaver, squirrel, bear, and buffalo," Garvey said. "But this is the first time I've dealt in human hair." He laughed. "By God, the pay's a little better. I never got no hunnerd silver pesos fer a male beaver."

"There is more to it than that," Weismann said. "A group of American soldiers will be trying to stop us. Captain Perez's men will deal with them, therefore, we outnumber them by a tremendous amount."

"Could there be an outside chance we might have to fight 'em too?" Garvey asked.

"Perhaps," Weismann admitted. "But not likely."

Donaldson looked at Garvey. "You ain't got no objection to shooting at the U.S. Army if you have to, do you?"

"I done it before," Garvey answered. "But what're they doing in Mexico?"

"They ain't in Mexico," Donaldson said. "They're in Arizona Territory."

"Ain't that part o' Mexico?" Garvey asked.

"No more," Perez said. "The United States won that as a concession after defeating Mexico in the war."

"What war?" Garvey asked. "Has there been a war?"

"Sure, Wild River," Donaldson said. "The United States and Mexico went at it hammer-and-tongs fer a coupla years."

"What about New Mexico?" Garvey asked. "I spent me some time in Santa Fe. That's where I picked up some of that there Español lingo."

"That is now part of the United States too," Donaldson said. "And so is Californy."

"Californy? Well, I'll be damned," Garvey said. "I reckon I've been up in them mountains too long."

Perez asked, "What brought you down from the high country?"

"None o' your business," Garvey said. He was a bit upset about the lack of courtesy in the question. Prying into someone's past or present life was a faux pas of extreme proportions on the American frontier.

Perez seethed inside. Under normal circumstances, he would have had the arrogant lout whipped half to death then shot. But this latest assignment from De La Nobleza prevented that.

Weismann grew tired of the drawn-out conversation. "Are you with us, or not?"

Garvey grinned. "Sure, Boss."

"Sit down and have a drink," Donaldson said. "You can pick up your stuff and camp with us tonight."

"I got all my stuff on me," Garvey said sitting down.

"Cantinero!" Donaldson hollered to the bartender. "More tequila!"

The drinks were quickly served and the saloonkeeper went back to his post. Something about the four men at the table made him uneasy. He went to stand by his friend at the end of the bar.

The friend looked at Weismann, Donaldson, Perez, and Garvey. He instinctively experienced a slight shudder. "Quienes son?" he asked in a nervous whisper.

"Estos son diablos," the barkeep answered. "They are devils, I think."

Even his experiences with the worst of the border riffraff had not prepared him for the quartet he now served. For this first time since he opened the establishment, he wished he had a crucifix hanging somewhere in the cantina.

The four men had no more than a couple of more rounds of drinks before leaving the bar. Perez returned to the cavalry camp while the other three went down to a flea-infested adobe inn to work out the hiring routine for the next day.

After paying to have a local harlot leave her crib for a bit

183

and visit them, the three exhausted themselves on the tireless woman who went away with a handful of pesos for her trouble. That had been Roberto Weismann's treat. Donaldson and Garvey, who didn't have enough money between them to hire the oldest, most disease-ridden whore in all of Mexico, appreciated the gesture though they had to wait their turns until the boss had satiated himself.

The next day saw the actual hiring begin. A return to the cantina for breakfast brought the opportunity to speak to a couple of likely looking candidates who stood drinking at the bar. These were typical hardcases who could be counted on to kill. One was a Yaqui halfbreed named Osito and the other a Mexican who identified himself only with the nickname of Costuron. This obviously came from the deep scar that ran across his nose which was the result of somebody trying to remove it.

"Did Injuns do that?" Donaldson asked pointedly.

"It was about another man's woman," Costuron said.

"Damn!" Garvey said. "I hope the gal was worth it." He laughed. "You musta really been in love."

"No," Costuron said. "He had paid for her and I sneaked in first. This was in —"

"You can swap tales later," Weismann interrupted. "I want you and Osito to get out on the street and tell every pistolero or riflero you see that I'm hiring scalphunters under legal contract to General De La Nobleza. If they are interested, they will find me here."

Thus began a day-long activity of speaking with gunmen looking for chances to make money. Some, obvious drunks with more bluster than guts, were sent hurtling through the batwing doors, propelled by Donaldson and Garvey. Others, like one poor fellow who had taken a couple of hits in some previous gunfight, were considered too beat up and crippled for what would be demanded of them in Arizona.

But a few filled the bill and were signed on to serve in Roberto Weismann's small army.

Among them was an American who called himself the Mississippi Kid. A slim young Southerner, his manner of speech showed him to be an educated and even cultured man. Some misdeed or crime had driven him to Juntera. The fact that he survived was enough to impress Weismann and the other Americans.

Another fellow from north of the border was an African named Mjeledi. "That is my name in Africa," he said. "I make my living long time before by catch the fellers in the jungle and sell 'em to the ship cap'ns on the beach. One day I make trouble because the cap'n feller cheat me. His men jump on me and beat me up. They take me to be sold too."

"You shoulda stayed away from that beach," Donaldson said with a wink. "Or at least not argue with no ship cap'ns."

"They bring me to America and I work on the plantation," he said with a long look at the Mississippi Kid. "I stay 'til I bash in the head o' massa's overseer and running away."

Mississippi, understanding the situation, only shrugged. "Most of those overseers could do with a head-bashing now and then."

The rest of the day was filled accepting and refusing candidates until five more Mexicans had been added to their ranks: Martinez, Garcia, Toledo, Jacumba, and a particularly nasty fellow whose name of Bendito meant Blessed in English.

Donaldson thought that hilarious. He could barely contain his laughter as he asked, "Are you sure it ain't Bandido?"

"That is no name," Bendito answered. "That is a profession."

"You'll do," Weismann said. "You are hired."

The final activity of the day was the arrival of Sergeant Valverde whom General De La Nobleza had ordered out to intercept and kill any dispatch riders coming from the dragoon camp in the Vano Basin.

He found Perez in the bar. In spite of his dusty, civilian clothing, the sergeant marched up and rendered a salute that would have done honors on a formal parade field.

"Mi Capitan," he said. "I have the honor to report that we intercepted the dispatch rider just north of Agua Prieta. He made an attempt to escape, but he was shot and killed." The sergeant dropped a heavy dispatch case on the table. "This was what the Americano carried."

Perez opened the container and pulled out a sheaf of papers. After discarding the routine administrative and supply documents, he found what he was looking for.

"Ah ha!" the captain exclaimed. "Here is a message requesting reinforcements from the Gringo headquarters in Santa Fe. According to this, Capitan Drummond has no more than two dozen men in his command."

Weismann was satisfied. "No wonder he requested help from General De La Nobleza in ridding him of scalphunters. With your soldiers, we outnumber him four-to-one."

"Yes," Perez said. "Now the Gringos are completely isolated and at our mercy."

"Excellent!" Weismann said standing up. "Then tomorrow we ride for Arizona."

Chapter Seventeen

"It's about bluddy time!"

The words were uttered in a combination of relief and impatience by the tough old Irish trooper named Donegan. Looking through the predawn darkness he could see the silhouettes of the approaching corporal of the guard and a sentry showing against the weak glare of a campfire.

"Now don't be dragging yer feet then!" he implored the two in a hoarse whisper to himself.

Donegan was finishing up his stint of guard duty and was eager to return to that same fire where a steaming pot of coffee waited for the men coming off duty. It was too damned hot during the day to enjoy a boiled brew of the caffeine-impregnated beans. But the early dawn was a wonderful time to imbibe the hot liquid.

The old dragoon straightened up and threw his shoulders back. At the correct moment he assumed the on-guard position with his bayoneted carbine pointing toward the men marching up to him.

"Halt!" Donegan called out. "Who goes there?" He grinned and said to himself, "As if I didn't know!"

"The corporal of the guard and new sentry," came the proper reply from Charlie Rush.

"Advance and be recognized," Donegan ordered.

The two soldiers marched toward him in the gloom.

"Halt!" Donegan said. He peered at them. "Now if yez ain't a pretty sight."

"Mind yerself, Donegan!" Rush warned him.

Donegan came to the position of order arms. "Private Donegan, Post Number One, all's well," he reported.

"Are there any special orders for this post?" Corporal Rush asked.

"The sentry on this post is to be especially alert and keep a sharp lookout toward the open country of the desert," Donegan intoned. "Any civilian travelers who arrive are to be halted and the corp'ral of the guard called afore they're allowed to enter the camp."

The corporal turned toward the other sentry, a cynical fellow named Brawley, and said, "D'ye understand the special orders of this post?"

Brawley almost sneered. "This is the second time I've walked this goddamned post tonight. And I been walking it ever since we got here. O'course I understand the special orders. Ain't I heard 'em enough?"

"Shut yer yap, Brawley!" Rush snapped. "Don't take no hints from Donegan on how to act. Fifteen years of service and he's yet to sport chevrons on his sleeve. This here's the reg'lar army, not some sloppy militia outfit. Now answer up good and proper or I'll see to it you have some digging in the sumps to keep you busy this afternoon."

Brawley sighed, but said, "Yes, Corp'ral. I understand the special orders o' this post and will comply proper."

Charlie Rush turned to Donegan. "Ye're relieved of yer post, Sentry. Shoulder arms! For'd, ho!"

Brawley watched Donegan and Corporal Rush march off into the dim light. Bored and tired, he angrily kicked the sand.

"Corp'ral Rush is right, damn his eyes! I ain't doing no better'n Donegan. This is what I get for not learning a trade!"

The dragoon turned and stared out into the darkness of the desert. The sky, high and black, glittered with stars that showed through the purity of the air like millions of distant candles. The country over which they hung was wide and empty, having nothing but cacti and sand.

"God! This is a lonely place," he said despairingly.

To anyone who had not been out on that desert for any amount of time it would have seemed hot. But to Brawley and his messmates, after weeks of living in the burning atmosphere, the hours of darkness were a godsend with lower temperatures that didn't sap a man's strength and wring the sweat out of him.

He spent the first hour of his duty deep in thought about Donegan. Just because that old soldier was happy being a professional private didn't mean Brawley was. Then and there he decided it was time to put some serious work into bettering himself. He began forming plans to work for a promotion. To begin with, he'd stop talking back to the noncommissioned officers and getting into fights when he got drunk.

"Sure!" he told himself. "It makes all the sense in the world."

If he could just make corporal, his life would be much more bearable. Then, instead of treading a sentry's beat, it would be him who posted other men to spend two to four hours walking tours of vigilance while he sat back at the fire and sipped coffee. He wouldn't have to do any more manual labor either. That was beneath a noncommissioned officer. As a corporal, he would yell at some poor wretch of a private and make him move lively whether the job was shoveling manure on stable duty, digging sumps, or some other muscle-cramping chore that needed doing.

The false dawn lit things a bit just as Brawley made a personal vow to start soldiering better and earn his stripes.

He heard the report of the distant musket only a second or so before the ball crashed into his skull, blowing out his brains and any hopes of advancement in a military career now ended by his sudden death.

Back at the guard fire, Corporal Charlie Rush leaped to his feet. He ran to the sleeping duty bugler and dragged him off his blanket, yanking him upright.

"Sound *To Arms!*" he yelled.

The trumpeter, a veteran soldier, had blown the first three notes through his bugle before even coming completely awake. Then he begin repeating the call rapidly as he played to every corner of the camp.

Meanwhile Donegan had dropped his cup of coffee, turning to kicking the other off-duty guards awake. The sergeant of the guard appeared from the tent with the other two corporals. He immediately took command, forming up the sentries and rushing them forward in the direction of the rifle pits that had been so laboriously dug the first day they arrived in camp.

Charging toward the edge of camp as skirmishers, the line of troopers hadn't gone twenty yards before coming under heavy fire. Three men dropped to the sand before the sergeant wisely ordered the small force to pull back out of harm's way.

Captain Grant Drummond and Sergeant William Clooney joined up in front of the officer's quarters. Both, although only moments out of their blankets, were wide awake and ready for whatever had happened. They were also fully armed and prepared to fight back at those who had attacked the camp.

Eruditus hurried up to them, fully dressed with his musket and pistols at hand. "What's the disturbance?"

"I can't determine exactly what is happening," Grant said.

Clooney glanced about. "It's hard to tell even *where* the trouble is."

Grant looked toward the sentries' area. "Sergeant of the guard!" he called out. "To me!"

The noncommissioned officer wasted no time in racing across the camp. He came to a halt and saluted. "Sir, we came under attack from out on the desert. Looks like right over Post Number One, but no alarm was yelled out by the sentry there."

"Thank you, Sergeant. Relieve the rest of the guards of duty and order them to report back to their squads," Drummond said. "Then get back to your section and take command."

"Yes, sir!"

Sergeant Clooney, in his role as the detachment's senior sergeant, hurried him on his way, saying, "Make sure them lads don't fire unless there's good targets."

"That I'll do, Clooney!" the sergeant assured him.

He rushed through the tents, dodging back and forth in case some attacker had him in a musket's sights.

Incoming bullets splattered around the camp, forcing everyone to duck down. A ragged fusillade of shots now erupted from the bivouac as the dragoons returned fire as best they could.

"We got to get to them rifle pits, sir," Clooney said. "If'n we don't, whoever's out there sure will. We'll play hell trying to pry them outta them holes."

"You're right," Grant said. He spotted a nearby squad of dragoons. The captain ran to them with Eruditus and Clooney both on his heels.

"I'll watch your flank, friend Grant," the old man said.

"Well appreciated," Grant said. "Sergeant Clooney! Gather up another group of men and follow me."

"Yes, sir!"

The captain gave the troopers his full attention. "Form up," the captain ordered. "As skirmishers! You'll fire on my orders! Advance!"

The half dozen troopers went forward. The bullets whizzing around their heads increased as they closed in on the
site of the rifle pits. Up ahead, a full dozen Mexicans appeared out of the battle smoke heading for the same destination.

"That son of a bitch De La Nobleza!" Grant cursed
under his breath. "Those bastards belong to him!"

"None other!" Eruditus agreed.

The group went another ten yards before Grant gave any
more orders. "Halt! Kneel! "Aim!"

The disciplined dragoons reacted instantaneously.

"Fire!"

A bellow of smoke roared out from the volley.

"On your feet!" Grant yelled. "Advance!"

They charged through the smoke and could see the tumbled bodies of the Mexicans who had taken the brunt of
their fire. The soldiers reached the rifle pits and jumped in.

"Look!" Eruditus yelled out. "More of them coming at
us!"

The men in the pits frantically went through the ordeal
of reloading their pieces. Sergeant Clooney, following orders to the letter, quickly appeared with the skirmishers he
had been ordered to organize.

"Halt! Kneel!" the sergeant bellowed. "Aim! Fire!"

The second group of attackers were slammed by the volley fire. Grant crawled from the pit in which he'd dived.
"Take charge of this area, Sergeant Clooney. For God's
sake! Hold on here as long as you can!"

"Yes, sir!"

Grant and Eruditus rushed back to the main group of
dragoons. They stumbled over the body of the sergeant of
the guard. He had died at almost the same instant he'd
taken over his section. Now the group was under the command of Corporal Charlie Rush.

Grant formed a secondary line of defense to give fire

support to Clooney and the men in the pits. Sporadic firing and two more volleys blasted out toward the attacking Mexicans.

Then all was silent.

"They've pulled back," Eruditus said now able to see clearly in the morning sun.

"Not for long," Grant said.

"We've been through this before together, haven't we?" Eruditus remarked.

"We certainly have," Grant said. "I hope it doesn't become a habit. We're pinned in here with our backs to that cliff. They're forming up for a real attack now."

A full minute had barely passed when orchestrated shouting outside the camp burst out. A ground-shaking thunder of hooves followed as several ranks of horsemen bore down in a well-formed cavalry charge toward the dragoons.

Grant took a breath and hollered in a voice so loud that every dragoon could hear him:

"On my command! First and Second Squads! Fire!"

A volley burst out from the dragoon ranks, smashing into the first rank of horsemen. Men were blown from their saddles while horses whirled and crashed to the ground.

"First and Second Squads! Load!" Grant bellowed. "Third and Fourth Squads! Aim! Fire!"

The second group of Mexican riders suffered the same fate. Obeying orders from their sergeants, the survivors wheeled to the side and galloped off to safety.

"Cease fire!" Grant said. "Third and Fourth Squads! Load! Detachment! Stand fast!"

Once more an eerie sort of silence settled over the area. Only the groaning of wounded men could be heard as the sun continued to climb, its heat increasing with each passing minute.

Sergeant Clooney left the rifle pits and hurried over to

join Grant and Eruditus.

The sergeant reported, "They are forming up again, sir. But taking their time."

"How many casualties have we taken, Sergeant?" Grant asked.

"We got a total of five kilt, no wounded," the sergeant answered. He spat. "Y'know, I think those bastards out there is soldiers. They sure as hell fight like disciplined men."

"They *are* soldiers, Sergeant," Grant assured him. "They're under the command of General De La Nobleza. Or at least, at this moment, being led by one of his trusted subordinates."

"Ain't that the gen'ral you and Mister Fletcher went to see?" Clooney asked.

"I'm afraid so," Grant replied. "It's not too hard to figure out he's behind the scalphunters and wants to continue the activity. So, in truth, we're being attacked by the Mexican Army."

"They are dressed as civilians to hide their illegal excursion into Arizona," Eruditus said.

"But they're still Mexican soldiers, eh?" Clooney wanted to know.

"They are troops of the Mexican Republic," Grant said. "Of that, there is absolutely no doubt."

"Fighting the Mexicans is like old times, eh, sir?" Clooney said. "I tried to figger out how many of 'em there is, but I can't see 'em all. They ain't hit us in a big group yet."

"They will," Grant said.

"I reckon ye're right, sir," Clooney allowed. "I hope tha dispatch rider gets through to headquarters in Santa Fe We're gonna be needing all the help we can get."

"Santa Fe offers our only chance," Grant said. "But let keep that between us, right, Sergeant? I don't want an loose talk causing unnecessary worry among the men."

"Yes, sir," Clooney said. "Well, by yer leave, I'll be getting back to my post."

"Dismissed, Sergeant," Grant said. After exchanging salutes with the departing sergeant, the captain looked at Eruditus. "It's going to be a long day, I'm afraid."

"I'm afraid it might be rather short, Grant," Eruditus said. He pointed outward. "Look!"

A couple of hundred yards beyond the camp, the sight distorted by dancing heat waves, what appeared to be two entire troops of cavalry had formed up. Distant, barely audible shouts of officers and noncommissioned officers could be heard as a bugle sounded.

"Now they've become serious," Grant said. "They want to end this fight here and now."

"I'm not a professional military man," Eruditus said. "What are their chances of fulfilling that intention?"

"If I were their commander, I would be feeling quite confident about now," Grant said.

"Don't give up hope, my friend," Eruditus said. "Evenunt posse miraculi."

"Miracles can happen, huh?" Grant said. "We shall see, friend Eruditus. We shall indeed see."

Across the way, the Mexicans were in orderly ranks, now silent as well-disciplined men can be. This quiet lasted for a minute before a sudden shout sounded that was followed by the blaring of the enemy's bugle.

They charged!

"Steady! Stand steady!" Grant yelled as loud as he could.

The dragoons, grim-faced and powder-stained, manned their positions without wavering.

"First and Second Squads! Ready!" Grant said after the incoming horsemen had halved the distance. He waited a couple of more moments. "Aim!"

Eruditus fretted. "I am afraid this habit of facing

charging horses is going to wear on my nerves."

"Fire!" Grant ordered. "First and Second Squads! Load! Third and Fourth Squads! Aim!"

Spurts of flame and thick smoke rolled out of the First and Second Squads. The front rank of the enemy went down but there were plenty behind them.

"Fire!" Grant hollered.

Another fusillade roared outward, knocking more Mexicans from their saddles.

"Fire at will!" Grant yelled.

Now individual shots were exchanged between the two sides. The dragoons in the rifle pits held firm because of their protected position. The other squads gave in a bit to the pressure of the enemy horsemen, causing the defensive line to bend. The Mexicans, hoping to take advantage of the situation pushed into the emptying area. But rather than create an advantage for them, it inadvertently resulted in a murderous crossfire smashing their ranks from the entrenched dragoons in combination with the other troopers.

The enemy began tumbling from their saddles in twos and threes. Suddenly the Mexican bugler began sounding retreat. The attackers withdrew in a quick, orderly manner leaving dead sprawled around the front of the camp.

Once again the fighting eased down into a lull. The heavy smoke from the fierce firing drifted out into the desert, gently propelled by an easy but persistent west wind.

Sergeant Clooney wasted no time in scrambling from the pits and finding his commanding officer. "Sir, we took one hit and the squads outside took two. Three men total kilt in that last charge."

"Eight out of a total of twenty-four now," Grant said "That leaves us with a grand total of sixteen effectives."

"At this moment, sir," Clooney reminded him. "They'l keep whittling us away with more attacks 'til our detach ment is wiped out."

196

"That leaves us little time to plan an elaborate scheme to escape," Grant said. He smiled wryly. "But it does relieve any pressure on me for coming up with any grand tactics to turn the day in our favor. That makes a reasonable excuse for any blunders on my part."

"Remember what I said about miracles, Grant," Eruditus reminded him.

"I am more concerned with escape at the moment," Grant said. "If any miracles take place in the next couple of hours, then I shall be grateful to the Almighty for them. But we must leave this place. Even if we have plenty of water, we are simply hemmed in for the final slaughter."

"Begging your pardon, sir," Clooney said. "But we won't stand much more of a chance out there on that desert. In fact, it might be a hell of a lot worse for us."

"I agree," Grant said. "But I believe I've come up with our only solution."

"Thank God!" Eruditus exclaimed.

"A solution in this case, doesn't necessarily guarantee success," Grant admitted. "It is more accurate to describe it as an attempt."

"Then you don't think it'll work, sir?" Clooney asked.

"No," Grant answered in a frank tone. "But I'm all set to give it a try."

"Aerumna nos est," Eruditus said. "Woe is us!"

Clooney shrugged. "When I took up soldiering I never figgered to live forever anyhow." He stood up straighter and pulled his shoulders back. "Orders, sir?"

Chapter Eighteen

Preparing for the breakout had been one hell of an undertaking for the beleaguered dragoons.

The activity necessary to put Captain Grant Drummond's escape plan into effect was interrupted twice when the Mexican commander decided to launch attacks. These assaults were pressed to the limits, but the enemy had grown more cautious. Their conduct of the assaults showed a changed attitude in the fighting.

The Mexicans' present leader, unlike the one who had attacked Grant and Eruditus out on the desert, was not going to spill any more of his men's blood than necessary in this fight against an outnumbered enemy. He took more time between sending his men storming at the thin blue line of U.S. soldiers, and he pulled them out quicker. Yet his men did manage to kill two more dragoons in their latest assaults.

The dragoons' fighting spirit, buoyed by sheer desperation, was a fierceness not to be denied as their shallow line of defense blasted volley after volley at the attacker during the fierce latest attempts to overpower the camp. Weary and powder-grimed, the American soldiers well appreciated the fact that the battle had evolved into a slower pace. Particularly since their already sparse ranks had been thinned at a slow, but alarmingly steady rate.

In spite of this lessening of fighting, the threat of further assaults continued to cause anxious feelings in the dragoon camp as the noncommissioned officers made sure Captain Grant Drummond's instructions were carried out as quickly and efficiently as possible.

A small, but most important part of this effort was under the personal command of Corporal Charlie Rush. Following his frantic orders, a detail of men had retired to the horse picket lines to begin saddling as many mounts needed for the survivors of the dragoon detachment. When the job was done, Charlie, urging his men to hurry, led them in a rapid dash back to the defensive perimeter. He left them there and went to find Grant Drummond and Eruditus Fletcher where they had positioned themselves.

"The horses is ready, sir," Charlie Rush reported with a salute to the captain. "All saddled and bridled and waiting for riders."

"And in good time, Corporal," Grant said. "Well done. You may return to your places in the rifle pits. When you get there, tell Sergeant Clooney I wish to speak to him."

"Yes, sir," Charlie said.

Eruditus loaded his musket. "The barrel of this old blaster is growing fouled after so many shots, Grant."

"I'm sure my men are beginning to face that dilemma with their carbines," Grant said. "Another damned good reason for a move on our part, no matter how desperate. We cannot simply remain situated here and fire away until the bores of the weapons become so encrusted that ramrods can't be forced down them, much less musket balls."

"No matter the reason, it is a shame we'll all have to leave personal possessions behind," Eruditus said. "The Mexicans will enjoy the loot."

"As long as there is nothing to aid them in their fight, I'll not worry about that," Grant said. "All the powder and shot have been issued out."

"Yes," Eruditus said. "Along with some of that disgusting hardtack and saltpork." He forced a grin and a wink. "It will serve those blackguards right if they eat some of it."

Grant winked back. "Well, friend Eruditus, with luck, we'll not have to endure that diet long before we can add some fresh meat to it," Grant said.

"With bad luck, we'll not be consuming those victuals too many times either," Eruditus pointed out. "We'll be corpses spread around the desert."

Further conversation was interrupted when Clooney reported to his commanding officer. "It looks like the Mexicans is growing even more cautious, sir," he remarked. "They've galloped off out of sight. But that sure as hell don't mean they won't be back."

"They know we're pinned in and can't get out," Grant said. "At least that's what I'm counting on."

"The enemy'll keep pressing though, sir," Clooney said. "Them Mexicans can see that waterfall so they know they can't just wait us out to die o' thirst. If they try to starve us out, it could take weeks." He ruefully shook his head. "And I ain't sure how many more rounds we're gonna be blasting outta these dirty carbines."

"Mister Fletcher and I have discussed that problem," Grant said. "I'm sure it has occurred to the Mexican commander as well."

Eruditus slipped a cap in place on his musket. "Therefore, we can count on continuous attacks even if the Mexican commander wants to conserve his men's lives. Our only hope is that help will arrive from Santa Fe."

"We can't depend on that," Grant said. "So we'll put my plan into effect immediately."

"It might work, sir," Clooney said. Then he added, "Or we could end up buzzard bait out there."

"That's something else Mister Fletcher just brought up," Grant said. He looked at both of them. "You two are not the jolliest of companions, are you?"

Clooney missed the point. "This ain't exactly a funny situation, sir."

Eruditus again winked at Grant. "Let's see if something happens to lighten our moods."

"I'll issue orders right now," Grant said.

"We're all ready, sir," Clooney assured him.

"Have all the men equipped themselves with pistols and sabers?" Grant asked.

"Yes, sir," Clooney said. "They're ready to hop into the saddle for any horseback battling they may be called on to do."

"Very well," Grant said. "Now I want you to send one man back to the picket lines for every three horses. That means they'll ride one and lead two others up to the line. Counting Eruditus and me, gives us a need for a total of sixteen animals. Detail Trumpeter Lundari to ride with us. He can take care of our mounts."

"That means how many men, sir?" Clooney asked. "I ain't real fast with figures."

"Five horse handlers plus Lundari," Grant answered. "One of them will only have to take care of his own horse and only one other. Tell them to stay back there ready to mount up and lead the extra horses forward when I give the order. At that time the handlers are to come as fast as possible to the line, but under control. Everyone gets a horse and mounts up without further orders."

"I understand, sir," Clooney said.

"The horses that will have no riders will also be set free," Grant said. "They will follow us through habit and training."

Eruditus nodded. "The extra animals will help us out even if they don't mean to."

"Right," Grant said. "When the detachment is mounted, they are to follow me out into the desert."

"I've explained what's to happen once we've left the camp, sir," Clooney said. "Ever' manjack in the detachment understands."

"Excellent, Sergeant," Grant said. "Detail the men to the horses."

"Right away, sir," Clooney said.

Eruditus shaded his eyes and looked toward the enemy, studying the empty terrain. "No sign of the Mexicans."

"I wonder what they're up to," Grant said.

"I would say our antagonists are treating themselves to some refreshments before making another attempt to murder us," Eruditus answered.

"Then there is no better time like the present to try something risky but necessary," Grant said. He waved toward the horse picket line and yelled, "Horse handlers! Bring the mounts! Now! Move!"

The soldiers responded quickly, galloping toward the waiting troops. Those horses without riders, now loose, milled around a bit then immediately took off after the others in a loose formation of bareback animals.

Trumpeter Lundari, an Italian immigrant who had joined the U.S. Army less than a month after arriving in the country, rode up to Grant and Eruditus, leading their mounts.

"Here are your horses, sirs," he said.

Grant leaped into the saddle. "Very well. Are you ready for a wild and dangerous ride, Lundari?"

"Oh, yes, Captain," the trumpeter answered. "But I could use a long drink of grappa first."

"What is grappa?" Grant asked.

Eruditus interjected, "A wonderful distilled drink that is certainly called for on this perilous occasion."

"You have had it before, eh, Signor Fletcher?" Lundari asked.

"Molte volte," Eruditus said. "Many times when I was back East."

"At this moment I would be pleased to have anything to drink," Grant said. "But we'll talk about liquor later. It is time to do or die."

"An unfortunate choice of words, yet true," Eruditus said. He now sat in his own saddle, ready for the plan to be put into effect.

Grant shouted, "Follow me!" He kicked his horse into a run, heading for the dragoons who were now mounted and waiting for him.

"Hurrah the Captain!" someone shouted.

The tension in the ranks was high. The men responded with another, louder, "Hurrah!"

"Let's go, Dragoons!" Grant shouted.

The entire detachment led by Grant, Eruditus, and Trumpeter Lundari thundered out of the camp into the desert. The loose horses accompanied them, confused but eager to tag along in what appeared to be a strange game to them.

Grant hoped to find the Mexicans pulled back a good distance in order to give him and his men plenty of maneuvering room. Instead, the moment he'd chosen to break out was the exact time the Mexican cavalry had formed up for another charge. Instead of wide-open space, the dragoons had ridden straight into a well-prepared enemy force of great numerical superiority.

"I've killed us all with bad timing!" Grant shouted over to Eruditus. "Damn me to hell!"

Eruditus shouted the Latin phrase about miracles. "Evenunt posse miraculi!"

The Mexicans immediately took off after the dragoons. Their formation now included the dreaded lancers—lanceros—those elite horsemen riding at the head of their pursuit. The dragoons noting this, loosened their single-shot pistols in the leather holsters. They knew well that their sabers were far out-reached by the long stabbing weapons now bearing down on them.

The loose dragoon mounts caused some initial confusion among the Mexicans by galloping in an ignorant lack of fear straight at them. This allowed the Americans to add a bit of distance in their run for safety. But eventually, the riderless animals worked their way out of the group and the pursuers were left unmolested to continue the chase.

Now the two groups raced at converging angles, every turn of the dragoons matched by the Mexicans. Ten minutes of galloping showed that the collision between them was imminent. The American troops gritted their teeth at the flashes of sunlight reflected off the blades of the lances.

Two minutes later the two forces slammed together in a yelling, brawling mass with the wild neighing of horses blending in over the thunder of hooves beating on the desert terrain.

Grant Drummond raised his revolver and fired twice at a lancero closing in on him. The first bullet missed, but the second hit the man in the chest, sending him into a flailing, screaming fall to the dirt.

Pistol shots could now be heard as other dragoons, forced to wait until the last possible moment to avoid missing their living targets, fired their single-shot pistols into the determined, brave Mexican horsemen. Three dragoons weren't quite quick enough and had the blades of lances driven into their bodies before being lifted out of their saddles to crash to the desert floor.

Eruditus, being the oldest man in the one-sided battle, decided the best thing he could do was to concentrate on protecting Grant. Hand-to-hand fighting with a younger, more nimble Mexican trooper was out of the question. He held onto his flintlock pistol, fiercely determined to use it only to save his younger friend's life, even if it meant sacrificing his own. He kept his faithful horse Plutarch in close to Grant as the run for life continued.

Trumpeter Lundari followed closely behind them, his now-useless pistol stuck back in its holster. The young Italian kept a wary lookout lest some eager lancero skewer him like a wild boar.

By the time Grant emptied his first pistol and drew the second, two more lanceros had been shot from their saddles through his marksmanship. One Mexican lay still in death while the other writhed with a painful chest wound out of which pink bubbles of blood oozed.

Grant checked his location during the ride, noting that the particular area he had determined as his destination was still some distance away.

To the participants of the running battle, the entire world had evolved into a booming, exploding hell punctuated with enraged shouts of fighting men. Dust rose up in thick clouds to clog the nostrils of both men and animals. Sweat-drenched, infuriated riders hacked and shot at each other in the frenzied crowd of battle-crazed men.

Unlucky participants, caught by bullet or blade, tumbled to the ground to roll and bounce on the Sonoran

Desert. These unfortunates were left behind as bloody debris by the rolling tumult of fighting.

Grant Drummond fired the final shot of his second revolver directly into the face of a bellowing lancero. Now, with no firepower, he reholstered the spent weapon and drew his saber. No sooner was it free from its scabbard than another rider bearing a lance closed in. Eruditus, yanking on Plutarch's reins, pulled over and raised his pistol. He fired too soon, missing the Mexican who, sensing a kill, closed in on the captain and his shorter weapon.

Rather than go for the rider, Grant struck the lance, forcing it over to one side. Then, leaning dangerously out of his saddle, he used his saber for which it had been designed—slashing and hacking. He swung only once, but the effort was successful. The Mexican's lance, with his severed hand still clutching it, flew forward a few yards, its flight propelled by the momentum of the ride's speed, then stuck in the sand. The lancero, in shock, simply slowed down and rode away from the fight, too dazed to stem the flow of his life's blood that pumped from the ragged stump of his left arm.

Grant took a fleeting second to glance back at his men. They still followed, he could tell, but the dust hid their numbers. All he could hope was that most were still in the saddle, galloping after him in this wild scheme of escape he had dreamed up.

Now the surviving horses on both sides began showing signs of exhaustion. Their riders also felt fatigue closing in. Yet all were forced to continue the battle with all the physical fierceness possible. The dragoons hacked with sabers out of pure desperation. Outnumbered, they could only trust in Captain Drummond's plan to guarantee even the slightest chance of survival.

The Mexicans, on the other hand, felt that victory was at hand. Their sense of a sure triumph gave them strength and courage as they continued pressing in on the hard-riding American dragoons.

Sergeant William Clooney, Corporal Charlie Rush, and Private Tim Donegan had formed an impromptu team. All veterans of many battles, their three-man formation gave them all cover as they desperately protected each other with vicious swings of their sabers. They, like the others of the dragoon detachment, could not see the rest of their group. They could only follow along after their captain, trusting in his luck and skill.

Up ahead, a Mexican officer, his saber drawn, closed in on Grant Drummond. The American struck first, executing a vicious horizontal stroke that was skillfully parried.

"Ay, Gringo!" the Mexican yelled. "Tu mueres!"

He tried an overhead stroke. His blade barely missed Grant, going deep into the cantle of the American's saddle. It stuck fast in the thick leather.

"Chingado!" the Mexican cursed as he lost his grip on the saber.

Grant took immediate advantage of the situation, making a backhand slash that split the attacker open across his chest. The man grabbed at the long, deep wound before rolling over to the side and losing his seat to disappear into the dust.

"Grant! Grant!" Eruditus yelled. "We're here!"

Grant glanced over at the foothills of the Culebras. They had finally reached the destination he so desperately sought. "To me, Dragoons!" he yelled as he yanked the reins of his horse to ride straight at the mountains.

The sudden turn caught the Mexicans by surprise. Although it took them several moments to recover, they were not too worried. The Americans were heading directly for a spot where they would be pinned in again between the desert and the high country.

"Son estupidos!"

More than one grinning attacker said that to himself as he turned to close in on the dragoons. Being soldiers, they steadied themselves as shouted orders once again formed them into a cohesive fighting unit.

Then the Mexicans moved in for the kill.

Chapter Nineteen

Captain Grant Drummond still gripped his saber as he rode like hell toward the one spot he sought in the foothills. The location was easy enough to discern if one knew it was there, but it would never attract the attention of someone unfamiliar with the area. The dark, greenish area would seem but shadows at the bottom of the mountainside to any casual visitor to the Vano Basin.

But Grant knew what was there and, as he closed in on it, he made ready to dismount. One glance back showed his companions were close behind. At the right moment, the captain pulled on the reins and swung out of the saddle, hitting the ground so hard that he almost stumbled. But he regained his balance.

"Go! Go like hell!" he yelled at his men.

They whipped past him and hit their destination — the narrow trail leading up to the heights of the Culebras that was partially hidden in the mesquite and other vegetation.

Grant, in his excitement, called out the names of those who passed him. "Eruditus! Lundari! Clooney! Donegan!" he yelled. "Stop and load when you reach the summit!"

The last two men, with one determined Mexican close to them, galloped by.

"Schossmeyer! MacLaren!" Grant hollered. "Load your

carbines at the top!" The American captain waited for the Mexican who had not expected to see a dismounted dragoon. A furious swing of the saber bit deep into hard chest and shoulder muscles, and the rider shrieked in shocked pain with a nerve-severed, useless arm dangling at his side. His horse turned, blocking other riders trying to close in.

Taking advantage of their confusion, Grant leaped back into the saddle and turned to gallop furiously up the narrow, rocky trail whose narrow width had room for but one rider. After a few moments, he could hear other horses closing in behind him. A couple of shots whipped past his head, whistling through the air. It worried the hell out of the hard-riding captain, but there was nothing he could do but hope he'd make it to safety where his companions waited.

The vegetation thickened around the track, giving him more cover and concealment. Finally, as the air cooled noticeably, he peaked the trail. Sergeant William Clooney and Private Tim Donegan knelt on either side of the thin track, their carbines aimed past the captain. Two quick shots brought down one fanatically stubborn pursuer. Angry shouts in Spanish could be heard farther down the trail.

Donegan stood up for a better look. "They're going back now, the devils!" he yelled.

Grant halted and once again dismounted. He turned and glanced back at the narrow escape route. The Mexicans had turned back, knowing they stood no chance of safely ascending into the Culebras. All the dragoons would have to do would be to casually shoot them as they approached one at a time.

Suddenly it was quiet.

No hooves of horses pounded the ground, no men

shouted or bellowed, and no weapons fired. Feeling relief, the escapees glanced at each other.

"Silence alone is great," Eruditus finally said. "All else is feebleness." He smiled. "A French gentleman by the name of Alfred De Vigny wrote that."

"Well, he was absolutely correct," Grant said. "Particularly after a hard-fought battle." He glanced at his men and counted. "Let's take stock here. There're eight of us." He sighed. "Damn! That means we've lost eighteen killed or missing."

"You can put 'em on the death list, sir," Clooney said. "None would be allowed to live by that bunch."

"You're right," Grant said. "The last thing De La Nobleza wants is prisoners who might survive captivity and later tell what's been going on out here."

"More death will follow, Grant," Eruditus said. "The scalphunters can now track down scattered bands of Chirinatos out on the desert and murder them for their hair without having to worry about us."

"Right," Clooney agreed. "That'll be easy for 'em now that there's not enough U.S. dragoons to stop them."

"What are we to do then?" Eruditus asked. "Simply stay hidden up in this mountain forest until the scalphunters have killed all the Indians available and leave Arizona?"

Clooney had a suggestion. "We could wait and see if reinforcements from Santa Fe will be showing up soon, the sergeant said. "If the dispatch rider got through, they could be here in another three or four days."

"I suppose we should be thankful we escaped with our lives, Grant said.

"Sometimes even that is not enough to soothe one's soul, friend Grant," Eruditus said.

"You're right," Grant agreed. He fell into silence for a few moments. Then his eyes suddenly opened wide as a

211

thought leaped into his mind. "No! No, by God! We're far from licked yet!"

"We are?" Donegan asked in surprise.

"Shut yer yap, Donegan!" Clooney snapped.

Donegan's mess mates Schossmeyer and MacLaren grinned. Lundari, Charlie Rush, and Clooney felt an anxious curiosity about what their commanding officer might have to say. They didn't have long to wait.

Within moments, but without explaining anything, the captain was back in action. "Mount up!" Grant ordered.

"Where are we going, friend Grant?" Eruditus asked.

"We're going to war," Grant answered. "Then, to top it off, we're going to break just about every army regulation written down about operations out here. And, if that's not enough, we're also going to ignore every goddamned rule of international etiquette and diplomatic protocol known to civilized man." He shrugged. "Well, at least *I* am. After all I'm the one in command. So if anybody is charged with a multitude of crimes, it'll be me."

"What the hell've ye got on yer mind, sir?" Clooney asked with a worried look.

"I told you, Sergeant Clooney. This detachment is going to war," Grant replied.

"Damn!" Donegan said. "I thought we *was* at war."

"Shut yer yap, Donegan!" Clooney barked.

The captain forked his saddle. "Come ride with me, Eruditus and I'll explain what must be done."

"As you wish," Eruditus answered.

Impatient to hear what the captain was going to do, the small band rode through the woods, climbing higher into the Culebra Mountains. At the head of the thin column, Grant and Eruditus were locked in quiet but earnest conversation.

Only one stop was allowed. The horses were treated to

212

deep drinks of the cool, clear water from the creek that flowed through the area. The men refilled their canteens after slaking their own thirst.

"I'm thinking this water flows on down this mountain and finally plummets over the cliff into the pool at our bivouac," Donegan said.

"So what made that jump into yer mind then?" MacLaren asked.

"That's where them thieving scalphunters and Mexican soldiers is looting our personal possessions," Donegan said angrily.

Charlie Rush chuckled. "So what'ye got that's so damned expensive, Donegan? Ain't ever'thing you own give to you by the army?"

"Not ever'thing, "Donegan said in indignation. "I own a deck o' marked cards."

Schossmeyer, a German, snapped his head around to glare at him. "Zo! Dot is how you vin the poker, nicht wahr?"

"I only use 'em in town against civvies," Donegan said defensively. "I ain't never cheated another soldier."

"Clam up!" Clooney said. "If we get our things back, I want them cards turned in, Donegan. Sometime when it's a long spell between paydays you might get tempted to wring a dollar or two outta yer bunkies."

Grant interrupted the bantering with terse orders to mount up and start moving again.

They climbed back into their saddles to ride slowly upward into the growing numbers of trees, the horses now treading on thick grass. Birds flitted through the forest, scolding and chirping the travelers. A cool breeze shook the leaves above, sending some to float gently earthward.

"God! It's good to be offa that damn desert," Donegan said.

"Amen!" Charlie Rush agreed.

A half hour passed, then Grant ordered another halt. "Take off the saddles and give your horses a rest," the captain instructed them. "Sergeant Clooney, set up a one-man guard post and appoint the reliefs."

Grant stepped down to the ground and walked over to Eruditus who remained aboard Plutarch's back. Grant asked, "When do you think you'll be back?"

Eruditus shrugged. "Two to four hours, my friend. But I'll make it as fast as I can. Hasta luego."

"See you later," Grant said.

Eruditus rode off while everyone, with the exception of Trumpeter Lundari who had the first turn at guard, formed up in front of Sergeant Clooney.

"Afore I see one manjack o' yez dozing off, I want them carbine barrels cleaned out good," the noncommissioned officer instructed them. "Another three or four hours and that burnt power in there is gonna be like hardened tar."

The men, realizing the seriousness of the chore, turned to it with gusto. Their lives depended on the operating condition of their weapons. It took an hour before they managed to pass Clooney's inspection and turn to thoughts of relaxation.

As they lounged in the clearing, leaning against trees or spread out in the thick carpet of grass, the fatigue of the furious battle finally settled in. Long minutes passed as Donegan and Schossmeyer drifted off to sleep, the latter snoring softly.

Charlie Rush suddenly sat up. "Oh, my God!"

Donegan, disturbed, came awake. "What the hell?"

Charlie took a deep breath. "We lost a lot of messmates in these last hours, boys. Now that all the excitement of the fight has died away, that just popped into my head. Our detachment is short some good soldiers as of today."

"Yeah, by God, it sure is," Donegan said. He lay propped up on his elbows. "I've been soldiering with some of them fellers for as long as ten years."

"They're out there under the hot sun now," Clooney said. "Them that didn't die outright was sure to be did in by the Mexicans or scalphunters."

"The sons of bitches!" Donegan said.

MacLaren rubbed his powder-stained hands on his buckskin trousers. "I just hope we get a chance to even the score sometime. We can't let the fellers go without taking down some o' them bastards!"

"Them Mexican soldiers and scalphunters didn't have no right up here anyhow," Donegan said. "This here is the United States now."

Captain Grant Drummond looked over from where he sat under a large pine enjoying a quiet pipeful of tobacco. "Am I correct in assuming you men want vengeance?"

"Damn right, sir!" Donegan said.

"Then you just might get your chance very soon," Grant said. He relit his pipe and puffed for a few moments before speaking again. "I know we're outnumbered and outgunned right now. But there is a way to strike back."

"We figgered you had something on your mind, sir," Clooney said. "And it must be damn good if ye're willing to risk yer career on it."

"I most certainly am," Grant assured him. "We're going to fight back, and fight back hard."

"Let's do it as quick as we can, sir!" Clooney said.

"We shall," Grant said. "In the meantime, I suggest we all stay quiet and restful to replenish our strength."

"Yez heard the cap'n!" Clooney snapped. "At ease!"

The men settled down once again, napping without talking. The only disturbance was when the guard was changed from time to time.

The sun had begun to dip low and the forest was quickly darkening when Eruditus returned. Riding beside him was the old Apache Aguila. The soldiers, seeing this unexpected sight, all sat up to find out what was going on.

Aguila spoke some words to Grant which Eruditus translated as, "Greetings from Lobo Cano and the council."

"Thank you," Grant said.

"We are being given a great honor," Eruditus said to Grant and the dragoons. "We have been invited to stay at the Chirinato camp. It is several hours from here, so I suggest we leave first thing in the morning." He reached in his saddlebag and withdrew some skin pouches. "They send us food for tonight. Some dried venison and squash."

"We thank our Chirinato brothers," Grant said.

"Aguila will share our bivouac this night," Eruditus said. "He wishes to express his sorrow for the loss of our brothers in the battle on the desert."

"You told the Apaches about the fight?" Grant asked.

"Yes," Eruditus answered. "I also passed on the information that you desire to speak to the whole tribe. That can be done tomorrow in the evening."

"Excellent!" Grant said. "Now let's try some of that venison and squash. It sounds a lot better than hardtack and salt pork."

"Which we ain't got anyhow," Donegan was quick to point out.

Clooney exclaimed, "Donegan—"

"I know! I know!" the dragoon interrupted. "Shut my yap!"

"That's right," Clooney said. "Now let's form up for mess call."

The Apache food was gratefully accepted. The men built some small cookfires, roasting both the squash and the dried meat. With no coffee, they washed down the food with gulps of cold water from their canteens. By the time they finished the meal, the moon was up above the treetops, its yellow light coming through the leafy branches casting weak illumination through the forest's darkness.

The long night was quiet. Occasionally a horse whinnied and stomped its hoof or one of the dragoons grumbled sleepily when awakened to go on guard duty. But mostly, the only sound was the deep, even breathing of exhausted men lost in deep slumber after going through a day of fiery, galloping hell.

Dawn's pinkness found the dragoons damp with morning dew and shivering slightly. Most had been so deep in sleep they hadn't realized how chilly they were until Sergeant William Clooney ungently nudged them awake with the toe of his boot.

"Turn out there, Schossmeyer! Reveille! Wake up, Lundari!" the sergeant said.

MacLaren, on guard duty, leaned against a handy tree and watched the camp come to life. Corporal Charlie Rush sat up and reached over to shake Donegan.

"Let's go! Reveille!"

Donegan groaned and sat up, then folded his arms around himself. "God Almighty! Now it's cold, ain't it!" He stood up and walked around on stiff legs. "First we bake on the desert, now we freeze up here."

"It'll warm up directly when the sun's higher," Clooney said. "Now fall in."

"Fall in?" Donegan asked. "For what?"

"Ye been in the army fer fifteen years," Clooney snapped. "When didn't ye have roll call at reveille?"

217

The men dutifully lined up. Even MacLaren came over to join the small formation.

"Corp'ral Rush!"

"Here, Sergeant!"

"Trumpeter Lundari!"

"Here, Sergeant!"

Clooney called off Donegan, Schossmeyer, and MacLaren. Then he executed an about-face movement and waited for the captain to walk up.

Grant, who had watched the proceedings, immediately responded. He marched to the front of the group and took Clooney's salute.

The sergeant said, "Two noncommissioned officers, one trumpeter, and two privates present for duty, sir. Eighteen men dead or missing."

"Thank you, Sergeant," Grant said. "Have the detachment eat a quick breakfast, then break camp. We'll be journeying to the Chirinato village first thing this morning."

"Yes, sir!"

Grant took one more salute, then returned to where Eruditus and Aguila had lit a small fire. Eruditus grinned, saying, "Aguila wants to know if you all were making medicine with that ceremony."

Grant nodded. "In a way, I suppose we were. Holding reveille reminds us that we're still soldiers and belong to the United States Army. It's a way of showing ourselves we're still professionals, no matter what sort of circumstances we find ourselves in."

Eruditus explained it to Aguila by saying that the ritual was a sign of respect to the Big Chief of the Americans. Aguila, understanding the spiritual side of certain gestures, stated that the dragoons would be all the stronger for it.

It took but little time to consume the remainder of the venison and squash. With no utensils to wash, the men were in their saddles in less than a half hour from their reveille formation. Feeling refreshed, the column moved out to climb higher into the mountains.

The ride through the thick forest was a pleasant one. The density of the vegetation both above and around them deadened all sounds. Aguila led the way with the army horses — and faithful Plutarch — plodding along, playing an equine game of follow the leader. The dragoons dozed in the saddle, the slow motion of the ride lulling and soothing them. It was nice in the cool shadows out of the sun and blistering gusts of the desert.

After a ride of two hours, Aguila shouted loudly. The white men snapped wide awake as they went down a gently sloping hill and finally broke out of the trees to enter a long valley along whose length were scattered close to a hundred hogans.

Eruditus stood in his stirrups and shouted greetings in the Chirinato language to each side. The Indians who knew him, and they were numerous, returned the salutation with their own friendly yelling.

"Sure now and ye've come home, Mister Fletcher," Donegan said.

"In a way I have," Eruditus answered.

They continued through the entire village until Aguila brought them up before a place where a large hogan was situated. Here the rest of the Chirinato council stood. Lobo Cano, Zorro, and Terron raised their hands in greeting.

Chief Lobo Cano stepped forward and said a few words. Eruditus turned to the dragoons. "The chief bids you welcome and invites you to visit here for as long as you want."

Now Zorro spoke, gesturing excitedly, his voice high-pitched and intense.

"Zorro tells you that you are in your own village," Eruditus said. "He says you will find other brave fighting men here."

Terron only spoke a short sentence, then turned and went inside the hogan.

"Our friend Terron says he will eagerly await hearing Captain Drummond speak at the council tonight," Eruditus interpreted.

Lobo Cano and Zorro gave one more wave of greeting, then went to join Terron. Eruditus motioned the dragoons to follow him. He led them over to a spot where a freshly constructed lodge had been erected.

"This is home, lads," he announced climbing down from the saddle. "Settle in. You'll find a small corral in the back and blankets inside."

Clooney, being a natural-born sergeant, was the first to dismount. He went directly inside the hogan. A minute later he came out.

"It's clean as a pin, lads, and filled with fresh pine needles to give it a nice smell." Then the sergeant scowled, "Mind yez keep it that way!"

Corporal Charlie Rush saw to it that the other three dragoons turned to the corralling and unsaddling of the horses. He detailed Schossmeyer to take the captain's horse. Eruditus preferred to see to Plutarch by himself. When they finished the chore, a trio of young Chirinato women shyly approached bearing clay pots of cooked food.

"Now ain't you lovely," Donegan said to one with a wink.

The girl said something to the others who laughed. Eruditus said, "She told her friends the old crow must have something in his eye."

The other dragoons burst out laughing and Donegan grinned. "Maybe that's my Chirinato name, eh? Old Crow."

The girls left and the men turned to the food. Rabbit stew, boiled corn, and more squash made up the meal. There was plenty for all, and by the time they finished stuffing their bellies, the dragoons were more than ready to enjoy the blankets laid across a thick carpeting of pine needles.

Captain Grant Drummond and Eruditus Fletcher, on the other hand, had some important matters to discuss. They withdrew behind the corral and sat down in the shade of a pine grove to have a long conversation consisting of the best way to address the assembled Chirinatos that evening.

Inside the hogan, the men slept the day away. The unaccustomed inactivity was something any good soldier had the sense to take advantage of. Now and then, when hunger stirred one of them, he would get up and take a few more bites from one of the pots, then return inside the hogan to nap a bit longer.

By the time evening rolled by, the entire village had gone to the front of the council's hogan. The warrior Quintero was also there with his friends Chaparro, Bistozo, and Zalea. Like the others, the quartet settled down to wait whatever was going to happen. Presently, Aguila, Lobo Cano, Zorro, and Terron came out and took seats in the proper place.

A sudden shouting from Sergeant Clooney over at the soldier's lodge caused the Indians to turn around. They looked with amazement at the sight of the dragoons marching up in step, looking dignified, with Grant and Eruditus leading the way. When they reached the council they came to a foot-stomping halt. Trumpeter Lundari stepped out and put his bugle to his lips. He sounded *Assembly* three times.

The dragoons, including Grant, sat down. Now Eruditus was the center of attention. He turned to the Chirinatos and spoke in a loud, strong voice:

"My friends, we have fought another battle. This time even more of the enemy attacked us, forcing us to leave our camp. We fought our way into the desert, then got into a running battle on horseback. Many soldiers died until we reached the mountains and rode up into them. We are sad because we lost friends and we are sad because the scalphunters along with their brothers the Mexican soldiers now roam El Vano. They are more numerous than ever because of the treachery and lying to the soldier chief Drummond by the Mexican soldier chief. Right now the Big Chief of the Americans does not know what is going on. We cannot get a message to him. But when he finds out, he will send help. Until then, more Chirinatos will die because the sealphunters and the Mexican soldiers are very numerous and well-armed."

Lobo Cano's face bore a grim expression. "We are safe in the mountains, but several bands of our people are on the desert. They are few and include more women and children than warriors. All will die."

Eruditus spoke again. "That does not have to happen. Soldier Chief Drummond wants to speak to you." He motioned Grant to join him.

Grant left his place with the dragoons and stood beside his older friend. He began to speak, stopping periodically to allow Eruditus to translate his words:

"It is true the enemy is strong and numbers more than my soldiers and the Chirinato warriors put together. But there is a way to fight them that might give us victory. I

222

learned this method of fighting when I did battle against the Indians in Florida. We outnumbered them, but they fought us hard and caused us many deaths. Only after a long time did the Big Chief of the Americans win that war."

Quintero was anxious to do battle with the scalphunters, but wanted to win. "How is it those faraway Indians fought?"

"They used the forest and darkness as their allies," Grant said. "They struck when all was in their favor and withdrew when the odds went against them. They floated through the countryside like invisible birds, then fell on us as striking eagles."

"If that tribe lost their war, why would we win ours fighting the way they did?" Quintero asked in professional curiosity.

"They eventually lost because they could get no outside help," Grant said. "We will have other soldiers of the Big Chief of the Americans here sometime. But we cannot wait here for them or the Chirinatos on the desert will be killed."

Quintero was impressed. "Then rather than stay safe in this village, you and your soldiers are willing to go seek battle with the scalphunters to save lives in our tribe?"

"Yes," Grant answered. "My big chief would have it no other way."

Quintero's emotions gushed out, and he emitted a war cry. "I will follow you, Soldier Chief! I care not what the council says. If you will risk your life for us, then I am your warrior brother! I will follow you on the warpath and fight as you tell me to fight!"

"And I!" shouted Chaparro.

"And I!" others yelled out.

Within moments the entire village was hollering their

support for Grant. The women began singing war songs to encourage their men.

Once again Lobo Cano stood up. "It is thus! The Chirinatos will go to war with the Soldier Chief leading us in the style of fighting he knows will give us the best chance for victory."

Eruditus translated for Grant, adding, "You now have a small army to lead, Captain my friend."

"I only hope I will not lead them to death," Grant said.

"It would mean the extermination of this tribe," Eruditus said.

"Not to mention ourselves," Grant added.

Chapter Twenty

Sounds of laughter and shouting filled the dragoon bivouac as Mexican soldiers and scalphunters alike went through the tents, pulling out the former inhabitants' personal belongings to see what was worth taking.

It was a scene of wild plunder, with bits of uniforms, slashed remnants of tents, broken boxes, and other debris flung about the area to be trampled on by the raiders. Newspapers and letters were ripped apart and the pieces thrown to float about in the breeze. Anything deemed without value was destroyed in the orgy of searching for booty.

A short time previously, the same men now ripping apart the bivouac, had put single bullets in the heads of fallen dragoons found in the desert. This included a half dozen wounded. Roberto Weismann, following the explicit instructions of General De La Nobleza, personally made sure this crime was carried out. This was to ensure there would be no potential informers.

Upon arrival at the camp, the same thing was done to the fallen defenders found in and around the rifle pits. Captain Ricardo Perez had objected bitterly to the killings but could do nothing to stop the outrage.

Now the killers and mutilators of the dead rifled the personal effects of their soldier victims.

Roberto Weismann, Penrod Donaldson, and Captain Perez stood around a campfire sipping fresh coffee as they watched the combination celebration and looting.

Donaldson spat. "Christ! You'd think they'd found an unattended gold mine from the way they're acting."

"One couldn't expect much loot from a military camp," Weismann said.

"That is true," Perez noted. "Soldiers are always poor. What could one possibly possess besides some tobacco, a little liquor, or some valueless remembrance of former days?"

"I think they are enjoying this unique opportunity of unhindered plundering, no matter how small the loot," Weismann observed. He continued to watch the activity without emotion. "They seem to be fond of the American caps and uniforms. I suppose such things are novelties to them."

A good number of the looters found the martial clothing the dragoons wore only for formal occasions something to amuse themselves with. Several of the Mexican soldiers and scalphunters danced around and hollered while sporting the caps and yellow-piped jackets that had been left neatly folded in locker boxes in the tents.

Wild River Garvey left the fun and walked up to the fire, tossing away the U.S. Army cap he had found. "Hell! I couldn't get my meat-hooks on nothing more'n a few pair o' worned out socks and some handkerchiefs and that damn cap." He laughed. "I coulda used a good pair o' boots but there wasn't none. As far as that fancy uniform stuff, well I ain't got much use for none of it."

"Now you see why them soljer boys wear buckskin and wide-brimmed hats instead o' them military suits,"

Donaldson said. "That's the way I dressed during my short spells in the army on account them kind o' duds served better out here in the west."

"The Americans were smart enough to take the real valuables with them," Weismann said. "There was hardly any powder or ball left. All the horses have been run off."

"I was aware of that when riderless horses ran with the dragoons during their gallop out of here," Perez said. "The loose animals hindered our pursuit to no small degree."

"Well, I got to admit your boys didn't do too bad anyhow," Donaldson said. "Only about a half a dozen of them soljer boys got away. The rest was spread across the desert."

"Mostly dead, I would point out," Perez said.

"Well, now, Cap'n Perez, we sure as hell took care of them that wasn't," Garvey said. "One bullet in the head and they was headed for them pearly gates."

Perez did not like the way the American spoke of dispatching the wounded dragoons. "That was not the way I was trained to deal with the enemy."

Weismann quickly reminded him, "Those were General De La Nobleza's orders, Captain Perez."

"I am aware of that, Don Roberto," Perez said. "I would also like to point out that there are still a few surviving Americanos who will speak of this in the future."

"By then most or all of them Chirinatos is gonna be dead anyhow," Donaldson said. "Us scalphunters is gonna be back in Mexico with silver pesos jingling in our pockets."

"True," Perez agreed. "That is because right now there is not a sufficient number of Gringo soldiers to offer you scalphunters any threat. And, since we also intercepted and killed the dispatch rider going to Santa Fe for help, you may continue your activities without hindrance."

"I appreciate that, Captain Perez," Weismann said.

"It could be a month before more American troops come out here to find out why they've not heard from this camp," Perez said. "I suppose that by then so much time will have passed that no one will be able to give proper testimony about what happened here. It will be impossible to get any of us on this side of the border."

"Not unless they come down and hunt for us," Donaldson said.

"The Americans will have to rely on Mexican authorities for that," Perez said. "Such a thing will not happen."

"I'll not take any credit from you or your men," Weismann said. "Thanks to you, we shall have time to get most if not all the scalps of the Chirinato Apaches."

"At any rate," Donaldson said, "we sure could have used them loose horses that got away."

"They'se some saddles over yonder," Garvey reported. "And some crackers and salted meat."

"That horse furniture is wore out and needs replacing," Donaldson said. "I ain't surprised at that neither. The U.S. of A. government is right stingy with the army on the frontier."

"We don't need any of the food," Weismann said. "We're not stupid enough to stay out here any longer than necessary."

Perez agreed. "Under the circumstances you should be able to wipe out the Chirinatos and return to Mexico within a very short time."

"What's the rush?" Donaldson asked. "It's just like you said, Perez, them boys o' your'n got that U.S. Army dispatch rider with the message asking for help from Santa Fe, didn't they? So there ain't gonna be no troopers riding in here looking for us. I reckon we got no worries a'tall about soljer boys chasing after us."

Perez shrugged. "Nevertheless, it will probably be safe for no more than another month."

"We need only half that time," Weismann said.

"I still advise you to make haste," Perez advised him. "My soldiers are not happy that they will earn no silver pesos like you and your men. They do not wish to remain out here in the wilderness for any longer than necessary. You must also take into consideration that they have their women and comfortable quarters back at the General's hacienda."

"Do they want to scalp Apaches?" Weismann asked.

"They are soldiers," Perez said. "As military professionals, they fight honorably. As you saw only yesterday. If it wasn't for them taking on the dragoons, you would not be able to conduct your bounty hunts on the Chirinatos."

"You are not going to let me forget that, are you?" Weismann said irritated. "You keep bringing up that fact in this conversation."

"I am proud to have accomplished my mission," Perez said. "I simply want my general to know that its success was of my doing."

"I am not doing this for medals like a stupid soldier," Weismann said. "I kill for money."

"Look at it this way, Perez," Donaldson said with a laugh. "It's good for your personal safety too. I'd say it was a smart thing you and your soljers done a hell of a job. If'n you hadn't, you would've ended up against the wall like that other feller De La Nobleza had shot."

Wild River Garvey glanced outward into the desert. "Riders coming in. They look like your scouts, Boss."

Weismann looked in the direction indicated. "Yes. From the way they are waving, I presume they have found a vulnerable group of Apaches for us."

"Easy pickings," Donaldson said with a grin.

"Easy scalpings," Garvey added with a guffaw.

The scouting party, made up of the scalphunters Osito, Costuron, and the American called the Mississippi Kid arrived within a few moments.

The leader Costuron dismounted. "We found an Apache camp less than a half day from here, Don Roberto," he said. "It looks like it just got set up. They're twenty people there. I counted eight men and twelve women."

"How many children?" Weismann asked.

Donaldson interrupted, saying, "Who gives a shit? The little bastards ain't worth but twenty-five pesos a piece anyhow. With what he counted we can get —" He knelt down and scratched figures in the sand with his finger. "— lemme see. That comes to eight hunnerd pesos for the men —" He worked some more numbers. "— and six hunnerd for the women. Add it all up and we're gonna get us a grand total of a thousand and four hunnerd pesos, by God! And that ain't bad for about a four hour ride and fifteen minutes of killing."

Weismann looked at Costuron. "What are the Indians doing?"

"They're just sitting around and doing some ceremonial things, Don Roberto," Costuron said. "I think that is why they come out on the desert."

"I have heard this of the Chirinatos," Perez said. "To them parts of El Vano are sacred."

The Mississippi Kid added, "They don't seem worried about nothing. They wasn't no guards out or nothing."

"They think we have been told to stay out of Arizona," Weismann said. "They are undoubtedly unaware the American soldiers have been killed or driven away."

"Anyhow," the Mississippi Kid continued, "I'll bet there's more camps on down the way from there. Tomorrow could be a good day for earning them silver pesos."

"How'd them women look, Mississippi?" Garvey asked.

"Smaller'n the men," he answered.

"He don't mean their size, you dumb son of a bitch," Donaldson said. "He means was they pretty."

"We was out a ways, and they were wearing long dresses. But they'll do I reckon," the other American said with a leer.

"That's good," Garvey said. "I ain't had me a taste since we left Juntera. I'll just dip my ol' wick afore I take all that hair." He glanced at Donaldson. "Y'all do it that way sometimes, don't you?"

"If we got time," Donaldson said. He looked at Weismann. "What do you say, Roberto?"

"It will be good for the men," Weismann said. "Have them spare the women until they are used, then scalp them."

Donaldson laughed. "Now I'm real anxious to get this show on the road too. Let's get moving, Roberto."

"Very well," Weismann said. "Gather the men. We'll leave now and stay a few miles from that Chirinato camp. We can have the Apaches watched through the night, then hit them in the morning."

Donaldson let out a whistle so loud that it could be heard over the noise of the celebrating and looting. Everyone glanced his way as he signaled them to stop the fun and gather around.

"Trompetero!" Captain Perez shouted to his bugler. "Toca Asemblea!"

The soldier put his instrument to his lips and sounded the call. The soldiers immediately formed up under their sergeants and marched over to the spot to where the scalphunters now sauntered to see what their chief wanted.

231

Although the scalphunters' discipline was not as apparent as that of the soldiers, Weismann still maintained strong control over the conduct of his men. This submission was given him out of fear and respect. Those same feelings kept Penrod Donaldson in power. Not even the likes of Wild River Garvey would challenge either one of them.

Weismann quickly explained what was going on while Perez prepared his men to act as security while the planned butchering took place. The passing of information was efficient and brief. Within a quarter of an hour, the entire group had mounted up and were riding across the desert as Costuron and the Yaqui halfbreed Osito led the way.

The band traveled at a steady pace, pausing only long enough to send a couple of two-man teams out to scout the vicinity every three or four miles. Weismann had no desire for accidental encounters with large groups of Chirinatos. Although he had no fear of being able to defeat and slaughter them, he didn't want to take the chance of alarming any other groups that might be wandering around practicing their tribal religion.

Toward dusk the group reached a spot Weismann deemed proper for camping until the attack in the morning. At that point the scalphunter chief laid on hard noise and light discipline, making everyone stay quiet and not build fires. Since the soldiers would not be going on the raid in the morning, all guard duties fell to them.

Captain Perez, still seething inside about having to take orders from someone he regarded as not much better than a common murderer, made sure his sergeants properly supervised the camp security. With his force reduced to no more than a dozen men by the fierce resistance of the

American dragoons, the captain's soldiers would not get much sleep in the night as they took their turns at the sentry positions.

Weismann and his scalphunters slumbered peacefully in their blankets as if nothing special was to happen the next day. They were all cold-hearted murderers whose lives had been ones of untold cruelties and brutality. The idea of killing and mutilating men, women, and children the next day did nothing to interfere with their rest. They slept like altar boys.

Instinct brought Weismann awake in the predawn inky blackness of the desert night. He reached over and shook Donaldson who immediately woke up. That began a series of nudges and kicks that brought the scalphunting gang from their sleep. Knowing that any slowness on their part would bring swift and painful punishment, the killers quickly rolled out of their blankets to begin preparing for the short trip. Gear was packed away, horses were saddled, and weapons checked in silence. When all was ready, Weismann pulled himself into the saddle and rode out of camp, his men following behind.

Captain Perez watched them leave. "Sera asesinato," he said to himself. "Murder will be done."

Osito, the Yaqui breed, went a bit ahead of the scalphunters as scout and guide. He and Weismann were followed by Penrod Donaldson, scar-faced Costuron, the Americans Wild River Garvey and the Mississippi Kid, and the African called Mjeledi. The Mexicans Martinez, Garcia, Toledo, Jacumba, and Bendito brought up the rear of the murderous column.

In less than an hour the eastern horizon to their backs had begun to lighten with the day's coming sun. Osito signaled a halt and waited for Weismann to join him. When the scalphunter chief rode up, the Yaqui pointed to a spot that nestled into the foothills of the Culebra Mountains.

Weismann peered through the gloom and could see a couple of small fires in front of a group of very primitive hogans. "They do not even have a guard out," he said.

"It was the same yesterday, mi jefe," Osito said. "They are not expecting trouble."

They returned to the main group where Weismann formed them up in a single rank. "I will ride in the middle. Keep your eyes on me and match my speed," he instructed his men in a soft voice. "When I break into a gallop, you do so too and be prepared to shoot any Apache who shows himself."

"Mind the women, boys," Donaldson reminded them. "If'n you kill 'em all right off the bat we ain't gonna have no fun time this morning. Either that or we'll have to take turns with just a couple of 'em."

"It's messy, but not so bad," Wild River Garvey said with a grin.

When Weismann judged everyone was ready, he urged his horse forward in a walk. The scalphunters, three to five yards apart, maintained the formation as they eyed the Apache camp, ready to shoot down anything that moved.

Weismann moved his horse into a canter, riding easily in the saddle. He glanced right and left, glad to see his men keeping up with him. A coordinated attack was always more effective than a strung-out run at the enemy.

Another fifty yards was traveled before the scalphunter chief broke into an all-out gallop. The group swept toward their destination at full speed, their weapons ready to fire. When they hit the outskirts of the camp, they broke into wild yelling and whooping.

The unexpected volley of fire exploded from the vegetation in the foothills, the flying musket balls cutting into the scalphunters. Martinez, Toledo, and Jacumba flew out of their saddles, their flesh ripped by the incoming fire.

Weismann whipped his head around. "Dragoons!" he yelled, sighting more firing coming from an unexpected position to the south of the camp. "Por Dios. Those are American Dragoons!"

Garcia damned whatever was going on. He continued straight into the camp. He saw a woman run out toward the desert. He turned toward her, ready to reach down and carry her off. But suddenly her dress dropped off and the figure turned to show it was an Apache warrior in disguise. The Indian waited until the last minute to loose the arrow.

Garcia took the shaft in his chest. He grabbed at it and yelped at the pain he caused himself. His horse continued to run as its rider started to slide to one side in the saddle. The scalphunter's vision blurred as death took him and when he hit the ground he was dead before he stopped rolling.

Osito and Bendito were also surprised to find that the women they chased were in actuality armed warriors in feminine dress. They, like Garcia, paid for their mistake with their lives when arrows slapped into their bodies. Osito took three before his strength gave way and he joined the others in death.

Weismann damned himself for riding into the trap. Who would have considered the possibility of the dragoons and Apaches combining forces? This was particularly bad since the scalphunters and Mexican soldiers had split their group.

The scalphunter scarcely noticed the quick loss of six of his men. Instead, the sight of dragoons and Chirinatos pursuing him, kept his attention. His only chance was to get back to the camp where Perez and the soldiers waited for him.

Penrod Donaldson also knew what must be done. He rode in close to his chief while Wild River Garvey and the Mississippi Kid followed in the middle. Mjeledi and Costuron brought up the rear, but made sure they kept in tight with their fleeing comrades. With moments a shower of arrows flew around them.

Back behind the scalphunters, going like hell, Captain Grant Drummond and the Chirinato warrior Quintero, swung out with their force of almost two dozen riders behind them. With fresh horses full of energy, they easily cut off the scalphunters' attempt to turn back. Although the dragoons made no attempt to fire their carbines, the Apaches fired arrows from the backs of their running horses. Exact accuracy was impossible but the missiles served to keep the scalphunters nervous.

Now Weismann and his men were turned back in toward the foothills. After a few more minutes, he made another attempt to out ride the avengers who now herded him and his surviving scalphunters like they were running buffalo. Ten minutes of desperate maneuvering, with arrows whipping among them, accomplished nothing except to move the scalphunters farther away from the rescue offered by Perez and his men. With no other choice, Weismann turned in toward the foothills. He realized the only available sanctuary was among the trees on the higher ground.

The scalphunting group whipped inward, galloping madly toward the mountains. They endured another rain of arrows with no hits among themselves before riding up a slight rise and crashing into the waist-high mesquite of the foothills. Although this slowed them down considerably, they were finally able to get inside the tree line where more cover was available.

Costuron's horse stumbled, then fell. The scar-faced Mexican flew forward and hit the ground. Uninjured he leaped to his feet and held out his hands for one of his comrades to grab to swing him up on their saddles. But they passed Costuron by, leaving him alone as the combined force of dragoons and Apaches charged in.

Quintero spotted the man on foot before anybody else. Turning toward him, he waited until the time was right. Then he dove from his horse and hit Costuron, the both of them rolling in the underbrush. The Mexican clawed the ground in desperation to get away from the warrior, but before he knew it he was surrounded by three more.

Quintero yelled his sacred war cry and slit Costuron with his knife. The scalphunter turned in desperation only to receive another deep gash from Chaparro. As he spun around and around in a wild effort to find a way out of the circle of death, Bistozo and Zalea used their knives on him. Within moments, the Mexican was a mass of long, deep wounds as blood soaked his slashed clothing. When the Chirinato warriors were convinced he was cut too much to escape and not enough to die right away, they left him lying where he had finally fallen.

Wild River Garvey, the Mississippi Kid, and Mjeledi finally reached a spot in the trees where it was impossible to continue riding. They swung from their saddles and formed a fearful, desperate defensive formation. Frightened almost witless, they looked around in head-jerking, wide-eyes stares.

Sergeant William Clooney and the five dragoons discovered the trio. Clooney ordered his men to dismount. Then, with their carbines at the ready, they took cover with the scalphunters in their weapons' sights.

"Throw down yer arms and raise yer hands!" Clooney commanded.

237

The answer came from Mjeledi who fired without thinking in the direction of Clooney's voice.

Wild River Garvey had only time to express his regret at the rash action by saying, "Oh, shit!"

A half dozen carbines belched fire, smoke, and six .54 caliber balls that punched the scalphunters into spasmatic, bloody deaths.

Up ahead, and a bit to the left, Captain Grant Drummond, Eruditus Fletcher, and Aguila rode together. They could hear horses that were obviously those of the scalphunters deeper in the woods. Also, very audible, were the shouts of Chirinato warriors farther over.

"We're hemming them in," Grant said slowing down.

"It won't be long," Eruditus said. "Listen!"

The thrashing and crashing of animals through the woods stopped. This was immediately followed by the triumphant shouts of warriors echoing among the trees.

Aguila leaped from his horse and joined in the whoops, then rushed into the forest. Grant and Eruditus followed at a run, dodging through the vegetation. Finally they reached a spot where two scalphunters stood in the dubious cover of a grove of thin trees. They were completely surrounded by Chirinatos, but keeping them at bay with threatening motions of their weapons.

Grant looked at Eruditus. "Can we guarantee them safety?"

Eruditus shook his head. "I'm afraid not, my friend. No power on this earth can change the fate of those miserable sinners."

Penrod Donaldson, his voice almost shrieking with fear and fury, screeched, "I'll kill you, goddamn you! Get away or I'll kill you!"

An arrow hit his neck and he dropped his pistol, choking and coughing as he tried to pull it out. A small boy's voice now sounded loudly in the Chirinato tongue.

Eruditus explained, saying, "That was Nitchito, the son of the murdered medicine man. He shot that arrow and shouted that he had avenged his grandfather."

Donaldson didn't last long as his life's blood emptied out his jugular vein.

Roberto Weismann, calm and cool, ignored his companion's fate. He caught sight of Eruditus Fletcher, recognizing him. He smiled slightly and nodded in a strangely polite manner. Then he stuck his revolver in his mouth and pulled the trigger. The back of his head exploded outward and he went down as the warriors rushed in to cut the scalphunter into bits.

Knives and hatchets slashed into Weismann's body, rendering him into unrecognizable hunks of bloody flesh and meat.

Grant and Eruditus turned away from the sight, walking back toward their horses. "Pardon the cliche," the older man said. "But all's well that ends well."

"It isn't over yet," Grant said.

"What do you mean?" Eruditus asked.

"If we stop here and simply file a report, the investigation could take years to complete," Grant said. "It might even be forgotten."

"You're right, of course," Eruditus said. "That means a probability of the guilty getting away free."

"I know a way to speed the process," Grant said.

Chapter Twenty-one

The sergeant of the guard was a corpulent fellow named Calderon who was just approaching his middle years. His job, unlike in most military units, was not a temporary position based on a roster that rotated the chore among other sergeants. Calderon had volunteered to take the responsibility on a permanent basis, even though it meant working seven days a week at something that was repetitious routine.

The fat sergeant's reason for seeking the post was not out of an unusual dedication to the security of his commanding officer General Antonio De La Noblesa. Rather, he sought the safety and security of remaining in the fortified hacienda where it was always safe and secure, with plenty of good food and drink, and his plump wife available. That was much better than going out on patrols and raids where a bullet or arrow was always waiting for the unwary and unlucky.

Being a permanent sergeant of the guard meant he could spend all his days within the walls and never, never have to face Apaches, bandidos, or other enemies such as American dragoons who were decidedly dangerous and aggressive.

That was what had happened to Captain Perez and the three frightened, miserable soldiers who had returned to the hacienda the day before. They had gone out a hundred-and-fifty strong to accompany Don Roberto Weismann the scalphunter chief on an Indian-hunting mission in Arizona. But, in less than a week, the detachment had been practically wiped out. Although Calderon didn't know the full story, he had heard that a combined group of American soldiers and Chirinato Apaches had fallen on Perez's camp in a most unexpected and fierce manner, killing nearly everyone. Those that escaped had barely made it to the safety of the Mexican side of the border before those pursuing them finally broke off the chase.

It was well-known that Perez had pleaded for his life, telling how hundreds of soldiers and Indians had appeared from nowhere and slaughtered his brave soldiers. He was so convincing that De La Nobleza did not have him shot.

No one knew the fate of the scalphunters, but it didn't look good for them. Not one, including Roberto Weismann or the Gringo called Donaldson, had wandered up to seek admittance to General De La Nobleza's sanctuary.

The sergeant pulled his watch from the waistband that stretched across his enormous belly. It was three o'clock in the morning, the proper time to check the posts to make sure none of the guards had decided to catnap during their tours of duty. Calderon would start with the front gate as was his custom. Finishing the last of his burrito and washing it down with a gulp of coffee, Calderon stood up and put his plumed cap on his head. Then he walked from the guard house in his ponderous way, to inspect the sentry. Although it was very dark, he knew every inch of the hacienda's yard.

He reached the heavy door and pulled out the large key necessary to unlock it.

"Chavez!" he called out.

No answer came from the sentry box.

241

Calderon cursed under his breath. "Contestame, Soldado Chavez! Answer me!"

If that hijo de la chingada was sleeping, he'd see to it that the lazy bastard was given a most severe punishment. A couple of dozen lashes across his bare back with a buggy whip would put the errant trooper back on the straight and narrow damned quick.

The sergeant stepped through the door and could see the sentry slumped on the seat inside the box. He angrily waddled up and slammed a fat hand against the wooden sides as hard as he could.

"Despiertate!" Calderon said angrily. "Wake up!"

The shadow came around the small structure, moving in silent swiftness. Calderon had only time to note it was the face of an American before Grant Drummond shoved his knife into the fat body. The blade slipped in just under the ribs. Then the captain ripped upward into the lungs, his hand clasped tight over the dying man's mouth. Calderon struggled a bit, not realizing that someone else had come up behind and was holding him. He defecated and urinated in his pants as his sphincter muscle relaxed in death.

Sergeant William Clooney had slipped behind the Mexican and now gently lowered him to the ground. "He smells like that scalphunter in the woods," he said under his breath. "Whew!"

"Take his cap, Eruditus," Grant instructed. "Clooney, you get the other fellow's. In the gloom you can pass as Mexicans."

The pair rolled up their wide-brimmed hats and shoved them inside their jackets, donning the Mexican headgear.

Eruditus Fletcher moved up to the door and peered into the interior of the hacienda. He signaled all was clear, then stepped inside with Grant and Clooney following.

242

They quietly eased the heavy portal shut, then moved in the deeper shadows along the walls.

"Do you remember the way?" Grant whispered to Eruditus.

"Yes," he answered. "I've been here twice, remember?"

The trio of intruders moved down the bulwark to a spot opposite the large well that was located in the middle of a courtyard. After making sure no one stirred, they quickly and silently crossed the open space and entered the house passing the same table where, a few weeks ago, Grant and Eruditus had enjoyed refreshments.

Going through a door, they continued down a hallway. A tiled floor caused them to step lightly to keep the sound of footsteps down. Eruditus, in the lead, came to a spot where the hall turned sharply to the left. He suddenly signaled a halt, gesturing Grant to join him.

The sound of someone approaching could easily be heard. Grant drew his knife and chanced a look around the corner. He could see a light bouncing off the walls as it drew closer. Then the form of a candle-carrying soldier, walking his beat came into view.

Grant whispered to his companions, "Interior sentry." Then leaned back and waited.

The guard moved slowly, obviously bored and sleepy. The sound of his walking showed he was wearing sandals as was the custom of the Mexican army in informal situations. When he passed in front of Grant, the captain grabbed him and pulled hard.

"Que es esto?" the man grumbled, not comprehending exactly who had grasped him. "Sargento Calderon?"

Grant's knife struck again in the same fashion. Eruditus grabbed the candle from the dying man's hand to keep it from falling to the floor while Clooney made sure the sentry did not make any noise falling.

"Another cap," Grant said. "It should do me just fine."

They moved on with Eruditus again going first. They made one more turn and went to a door at the end of a long corridor.

"Here is where His Excellency sleeps," Eruditus said.

"Then let us visit him post haste," Grant said.

The door was eased open and the three Americans stepped through to the interior. They found a small sitting room. After crossing it, they went through a curtained entry to find themselves in a bedroom. A small candle burned on a nearby table. They could see General De La Nobleza peacefully sleeping in its light.

Eruditus smiled. "He's afraid of the dark."

"He'll soon have more than that to fear," Grant said. He took a careful look. "Thank God he doesn't have a woman with him. We'd have to take her with us." He went to the bed and gently shook the sleeping officer.

De La Nobleza stirred. "Eh? Que paso?"

Eruditus leaned forward. "Levantase, Excelencia."

"Eres tu, Luis?" De La Nobleza asked thinking it was his servant. He rose up on his elbows and immediately came awake as he saw Grant and Eruditus.

"Tell him what to do, Eruditus," Grant said.

Eruditus spoke rapidly in Spanish, instructing De La Nobleza to get up and dress as quickly as possible. The general uttered a few words, then shut up as he was pulled from bed and a knife pressed to his throat.

"What's his problem?" Grant asked grinning.

"He says we'll not get away with this," Eruditus said.

"Tell him, he dies either way," Grant said. "At the first instant we lose our advantage, all three of us will shoot him before we do anything else."

Eruditus passed the information on, then looked back at Grant. "He believes you."

A few nudges and punches hurried the general along as he dressed. Then, with the three Americans, he walked out of the room. Eruditus led the way with Grant and Clooney on either side of their prisoner.

De La Nobleza gasped when they reached the dead sentry in the hallway. If he had any doubts about the seriousness of the Americans' intentions, they were swept away.

The four men continued down the hall and stepped out into the dark courtyard. No attempt was made to be quiet, since Grant wanted them to appear normal and perfectly proper in the gloom.

"Alto!" a voice commanded. "Quien es?"

Eruditus spun around and looked straight into the general's eyes. Grant had never seen such a fierce expression on the older man's face. Eruditus spoke under his breath in terse tones.

De La Nobleza took a deep breath and said, "Soy yo el general con mi escolta."

"Pase usted, mi general!" the sentry said. They could hear him click his heels and knew he had assumed a sharp position of present arms to properly salute his commanding officer.

The group continued on past the well. Once more they utilized the darkness next to the walls to keep under cover. They moved more rapidly then they had previously. Everyone stayed in step so that if any sound came from them it would appear to be from a squad of soldiers marching to some nocturnal duty to which they had been called.

Suddenly a flash of lantern light hit them square as a door was thrown open. Grant grabbed Eruditus and pulled him back out of the light while pushing De La Nobleza forward.

A garrison prisoner under sentence for some minor offense, was sweeping out the guardhouse. He peered into the pale, yellow light. When he recognized the general, he snapped to attention holding the broom beside him like a musket. Then, as an afterthought, he presented arms with it.

"Tell the general to return the salute and step back into the shadows," Grant said to Eruditus. He couldn't help but grin at the sight.

De La Nobleza did as he was told, then was pulled back into the darkness near the wall. Grant pushed him along, murmuring warnings in English knowing that if the general didn't understand the words, he certainly could comprehend the threat behind them.

They reached the front gate, and went through without hesitating. Once more De La Nobleza gasped. This time at the sight of the bloated cadavers of Sergeant Calderon and the sentry. A dragoon stepped from the sentry box.

"Corp'ral Rush and the others is waiting over that way with the other'n," Donegan said.

Now the group hurried. De La Nobleza was roughly pushed and pulled along as they trotted across the sand to where a grove of barrel cactus stood. When they reached it, there were several men and horses waiting. For the third time that night, De La Noblesa had to gasp in shocked and fearful surprise.

Captain Ricardo Perez, his hands tied behind his back, sat in the saddle of one of the animals.

De La Nobleza was grabbed and similarly trussed up before being lifted aboard another mount. Then, at Grant Drummond's whispered command, the group rode from the grove and turned north toward Arizona.

After an hour of riding, De La Nobleza finally found the courage to speak up. "What are you going to do with us?" he asked through Eruditus.

"I would like to blow your goddamned heads off," Grant replied. "Or, better yet, I would love to turn you over to the tender mercies of the Chirinato Apaches."

De La Nobleza spoke rapidly and fearfully, which Eruditus translated as, "We are all officers and gentlemen. Such conduct would not be appropriate for our social or military class."

"You are both butchering sons of a bitches as far as I'm concerned," Grant said.

Perez, understanding English, immediately objected. "I protest! I have killed no Indian women and children! Nor have I been paid any bounty money on them."

"But you did come into the United States of America, leading an invasion," Grant said.

"I was obeying orders!" Perez said.

"I don't know about that," Grant said. "But you both are going to be turned over to the American authorities. I have sent a message to my headquarters in Santa Fe. By the time we return to our camp, the departmental commander and provost marshal should be there with an escort of dragoons to take you to trial."

De La Nobleza said nothing, fully realizing that he faced severe punishment for conducting an unauthorized war and even murder. His own government would not be happy with him. The Mexican law called Proyecto de Guerra that paid for Apache scalps would have no application in Arizona Territory.

The sun rose, casting a glow over the desert as the group continued on into Arizona. Grant looked over at Eruditus and said, "You can say it now."

"What is that, my young friend?" Eruditus asked.

"All's well that ends well," Grant said.

"I can think of something more appropriate," Eruditus said looking at their forlorn prisoners. "It was said by

William Watson the English priest executed for his part in a plot against King James I."

"And what did the condemned man say?" Grant asked.

"Fiat justitia et ruan coeli," Eruditus said. "Let justice be done though the heavens fall."

Grant smiled. "Amen!"

Epilogue

A hawk, using the instinctive skills bred for eons into its species, soared on the thermals lifted off the floor of the Vano Basin. The bird of prey's keen vision scoured the terrain a thousand feet below in an eager search for food. A slight wiggle in the sand far below caught the sky hunter's alert eye. Folding in his wings and nosing over, the hawk began a rapid, steep dive toward the target.

Sitting on the edge of a cliff, almost at the same altitude as the bird, Eruditus Fletcher and his old boyhood chum Aguila watched it go for its prey.

"That hawk is a friend of mine," Eruditus said. "I have watched him hunt before." He reached for the jug of tiswin corn beer that sat between them. Three more cooled in the waters of the creek flowing past their resting spot.

"You are more alert to such things than most white men," Aguila said in an approving tone. He took a drink and belched with pleasure.

The pair, contentedly drunk, could look down at the newly established garrison of Fort Vano that had been set up where the original dragoon detachment had bivouacked at the Pool-Beneath-the-Cliff.

"Have you finished your work with the soldiers?" Aguila asked his friend.

"Yes," Eruditus answered. "Since Grant was made to return to Washington, I no longer have any desire to act as their interpreter and scout."

"You miss your young companion, hey, Erudito?" Aguila asked. "His leaving made you feel sad."

"I am also disgusted with the way things went after the big council meeting between the Americans and the Mexicans," Eruditus said.

Aguila shook his head. "It is hard to figure the White-Eyes and Mexicans sometimes. They take something simple and turn it into a confusion that would outdo trying to track a coyote on the desert. It would seem quite sensible to kill De La Nobleza and his man Perez."

"The so-called civilized tribes could learn much from the Chirinatos," Eruditus said. "Give me some more of that tiswin, my friend."

"Yes, amigo," Aguila responded. "You need it."

After bringing General De La Nobleza and Captain Perez back into Arizona, Captain Grant Drummond had sent word to headquarters in Santa Fe about what had gone on. He expected the departmental commanding general to come out and convene a court-martial that would lead to the execution of the general and a long prison sentence for the captain. Instead, a bevy of diplomatic and political hacks came out with the American commander and a great hullabaloo started as soon as a delegation from Mexico arrived.

The big conference had taken place on the boundary between Arizona Territory and the Mexican state of Sonora. Dozens of politicians and diplomats from both countries had shown up presumably to straighten out the slightly tangled affair of the intrusion by scalphunters and soldiers from south of the border into American sovereignty.

By the time those international worthies had finished, the situation was a complicated, confused, and completely enigmatic affair that defied logic.

The Mexican government strongly protested the fact that Grant had led some men down into their country to kidnap De La Nobleza and Perez. The representatives from south of the border didn't give a damn whether illegal scalphunting had taken place in Arizona or not. After all, the two hadn't been acting on orders from Mexico City. Therefore, the Mexicans argued, it was up to them to punish De La Nobleza and Perez not the Americans. Therefore, they wanted their two army officers returned pronto.

The Americans countered with their own charges of sovereign infringement, demanding apologies for the attack on an American army post which resulted in the deaths of several dragoons. There was also the matter of the murder and mutilation of Chirinato Apaches who dwelt within the border of the United States of America.

After a full week of testimony, declarations, disclosures, allegations combined with a myriad of affirmations and denials an agreement was finally hammered out:

Neither side would have to apologize to the other.

General De La Nobleza would be immediately struck from the roles of the Mexican army. Captain Perez was to be pardoned since he only obeyed the orders of his commanding officer. However, he would be reduced to lieutenant and transferred to the Yucatan Peninsula as assistant commander of a military jail.

The Mexican government agreed to pay a total of twenty-five thousand pesos to the Chirinato Apaches.

Captain Grant Drummond had to be permanently removed from serving on the American-Mexican border for the rest of his career in the United States Army or any other government position he might occupy at a later date.

The participants in the conference quickly signed the agreement and everyone went home to put the stipulations into effect.

Now Eruditus thought about it and became more despondent. "Give me some more of that tiswin." He took the jug and drained it. "I wish this was mescal."

"Me too," Aguila said. "Then you would forget how bad you feel."

"The Soldier Chief Grant feels bad too," Eruditus said.

"He was angry about his soldiers, was he not?" Aguila asked. "He did not like what happened to them."

"Of course he was upset," Eruditus answered. "That was another damned good reason for me to resign my position as an army scout. Clooney, Charlie Rush, Donegan and the rest were sent to Fort Leavenworth in Kansas Territory."

"Maybe they will like it," Aguila suggested. "Did you not tell me the weather is cooler there?"

"Since they were sent to a new regiment, Clooney and Rush lost their ranks," Eruditus said angrily. "They became privates."

"I do not understand what that means," Aguila said.

"It is like they were denied war honors they had earned," Eruditus explained.

"I see," Aguila said. "That is not fair."

"Then the Soldier Chief Grant was sent to the place where the Big Chief of the Americans lives," Eruditus said. "It is a long way from here."

Captain Grant Drummond had been given a severe dressing down for several reasons. Only the fear of public opinion saved him from formal charges and a court martial. Kidnapping De La Nobleza and Perez, however, was not considered his worst transgression.

The first and foremost sin he committed, as far as the bigwigs in the army were concerned, was his unapproved action of bringing the Chirinatos into the fighting with his dragoons. Even the commanding general of the army could not do such a thing without an authorization that had to come from an act of the U.S. Congress.

Aguila swallowed some more tiswin. "The Soldier Chief Grant will not like going to where the Big Chief of the Americans lives," the Apache said. "You said it was not a place where he could fight."

"Oh, he'll fight again, don't worry about that," Eruditus said. "The way the northern states and southern states of this country are arguing and threatening, they will be in a war someday. Grant will be a general then, and can lead many more troops than he ever imagined. And to more glory!"

"Do you mean the White-Eyes will fight each other?" Aguila asked.

"Yes," Eruditus answered. "I know it will be a long and bloody war between them."

Aguila shrugged and reached for one of the jugs in the creek. "I don't fully understand what you said, but I will believe you just the same."

"But now I worry about the Chirinatos," Eruditus said.

"Why?" Aguila asked. "We have avenged our dead have we not?"

"Oh, that you did!" Eruditus agreed.

After Antonio Eduardo San Andres de la Nobleza was kicked from the Mexican army, he settled in the town of Juntera where he took the paltry amount of money he could save from his treasury to open a small cantina. But a Chirinato raid on the town, led by Quintero and his friends, resulted in yet another kidnapping of the former general.

The Apaches carried him out onto the Vano Basin where they spent a day and a half killing him. Some say his shrieks still echo along the foothills of the Culebra Mountains.

"At least my tribe is at peace thanks to the soldier chief Grant Drummond," Aguila said. "No matter what others think, he acted with courage and honor."

"I am sure that consoles him," Eruditus said.

"Yes," Aguila agreed. "He knows we Chirinatos can go out on the desert and make our medicine for Spirit Woman without being murdered by Mexicans and scalphunters."

"I am still filled with worry about your tribe," Eruditus said.

"But why are you troubled for your Indian friends?" Aguila asked.

Eruditus pointed down at the Pool-Beneath-the-Cliff. "See the army fort there? That is just the first permanent intrusion of the White-Eyes. Soon there will be more and more of them. Many will want to live here. Especially in the Culebra Mountains. I realize that now."

"What will happen to us?" Aguila asked.

"They will put you on a reservation or make you move to some other place," Eruditus sadly explained. He took the jug and treated himself to several deep swallows.

"Let us not worry about things yet to happen," Aguila suggested. "We are old men, Erudito. Let us spend our last years together up here in the comfort of the Culebra Mountains and get drunk every day until we die."

"That is my intention, Aguila," Eruditus said. "You will forgive me if I become sad sometimes, will you not?"

"Of course," Aguila said.

The hawk rose back into the air. A small rodent was grasped in its cruel talons as it flew toward a nest high in the Culebra Mountains. The two old men watching it continued to get drunk.

The Vano Basin, as it always had, lay beneath the Arizona sun in patience and dignity, waiting for whatever fate the slow whirl of passing years would bring to it and those who lived there.